THE CRY OF THE RED KITE

The Cry of the Red Kite

by Jane Burnard

Gwasg Carreg Gwalch

Published in 2022
© Jane Burnard/Carreg Gwalch. 2022

ISBN: 978-1-84527-885-4

ebook ISBN: 978-1-84524-504-7

CYNGOR LLYFRAU CYMRU
BOOKS COUNCIL of WALES

Published with the financial support of the Books Council of Wales

Cover design: Eleri Owen

Inside illustrations: Elin Manon

Published by Gwasg Carreg Gwalch,
12 Iard yr Orsaf, Llanrwst, Wales LL26 0EH.
tel: 01492 642031
email: books@carreg-gwalch.cymru
website: www.carreg-gwalch.cymru

Printed and published in Wales

To Mum and Dad,

with love.

Thanks

Diolch o galon i:

Myrddin and everyone at Gwasg Carreg Gwalch.
Elin, for her beautiful artwork.
The Books Council of Wales, for their support.
Gareth, for everything.

Annwyl Frawd – Dear Brother

OK – I know you're not my real brother. But who cares? That's what you are to me, anyway.

I've written another story. This one's called The Cry of the Red Kite, and it's about what happened over Christmas and the New Year. And now that you've read The Thirty-Third Owl, it'll tell you what happened next. Of course, you were part of the story too – but not all the time. So this should fill in the gaps for you. I hope you like it, anyway.

Love always, Rose

PS Like I did in The Thirty-Third Owl, I've put some Welsh in here and there, to show when people were speaking it.

Chapter 1

It was Christmas Eve, and early evening time. A small train, only one carriage long, was trundling through a Welsh valley – black hills looming either side, the illumination of the moon and stars extinguished by dark clouds, hanging heavy with snow. The only visible lights were tiny, amber squares that came from the windows of distant, far flung farmhouses. But inside the train, it was as full and as bright, as warm and as lively as a front room during a raucous family get-together. A happy mixture of voices – Welsh, English and a combination of the two – rang through the carriage. At one end a large group of ladies in Santa hats was having a Christmas sing-song. At the other, two old farmers in cloth caps were nodding off after an afternoon in the pub, the train rocking them home like babies, and a group of boys were shouting encouragement as two of them wrestled and squealed in the aisle. The conductor was nowhere to be seen – safely holed up in the cab with the driver.

At a table in the middle of the train, a thirteen-year-old girl called Rose sat next to her mother. Opposite them was a large lady with half-moon glasses who was reading a magazine and had three large bags, brimming with wrapped presents, at her side. She was wearing a jumper with a picture of a wolf knitted into it – majestic amber eyes, shining grey and white fur – and Rose thought how beautiful it was. And, of course, it reminded her of Bleddyn, and the adventures she and Ianto had had last summer. The lady caught her eye and smiled warmly at her, over her glasses. Rose felt herself blush and she smiled back, before cupping her hands to look out of the window, trying to see beyond the reflections and into the night. The train hooted, abruptly, as it rattled over a level crossing, and Rose saw two stationary cars, their headlights cutting through the dark – illuminating a sudden swirl of snowflakes. As the carriage pushed on into darkness, Rose realised that the snow was falling thick and fast now, flurrying past the windows, gathering in the corners of the window frames. She nudged her mother.

'It's snowing!' she said, turning to her, filled with the sudden excitement that new snow always brings.

'Hmm?' said Mum, looking up from her mobile. 'Oh, yes!' She screwed up her eyes to look through the window and smiled as the snow worked its magic on her, too. Then her brow creased a little. 'They didn't forecast snow. Hope that doesn't mean we have trouble getting back . . .' Abruptly, she changed tack, her face lighting up and her cheeks flushing pink. 'Rosie, how do you say "I'd be delighted to" in Welsh?'

'*Baswn i wrth fy modd*,' Rose replied immediately, turning away and cupping her hands again to look out at the snow. Then she felt a pang of anxiety. She whipped her head back to look at Mum. 'Why?'

'Why what?' Mum was blushing more brightly now.

'Why d'you want to say "I'd be delighted to" in Welsh?'

'Oh!' Mum gave a little laugh. 'Well, I . . .' Then she

glanced at the lady opposite, who was looking down again, apparently engrossed in her magazine.

'I've, er,' she said, dropping her voice so Rose could only just hear her, over the chorus of '*Ar Hyd y Nos*', the snoring of the farmers and the yells of the boys. 'I've met someone, Rosie.'

Then she went rushing on, brightly, as if to stop Rose interrupting her. Rose listened, her heart beginning to beat very fast. This couldn't be happening. 'He came into the bakery today. He was hungry and he wanted something to eat. He had dark, dark eyes, and there was just something about him . . . And, do you know, he only spoke Welsh – he can't speak English! Not a word. But I was very pleased with myself – I managed, with Delyth's help, to reply to him in Welsh, and I sold him a loaf of bread. Actually, I didn't sell him it – I ended up giving him it for free.'

Delyth was the lady that worked for Mum in the bakery, and she was a Welsh speaker. Now Rose was interested, despite herself. 'He only spoke Welsh?' she asked in surprise. Some of the older people in the village struggled a little with some English words, but Rose had never heard of a Welsh person these days who didn't speak English at all. 'How old is this guy?' she asked, suspiciously.

'Oh . . .' Mum looked dreamy, as if she was picturing him in her mind's eye. 'About my age, I'd say. Yes, about my age.'

Thirty-nine, then. Pretty old, but not old enough not to speak English. Maybe he just didn't want to speak English. Maybe that was it. Fair enough, thought Rose. But she still didn't like the sound of this.

'Mum, some random comes into the bakery, you give him

a loaf of bread, he walks out without paying, and suddenly, suddenly you've *met* someone! I don't get it. I mean, did you talk to him at all, apart from giving him the free bread?' Rose heard her voice rise, heard how mean she sounded. She glanced at the lady opposite, who was no longer pretending to read her magazine but was flicking her gaze from Rose to her mother, openly intrigued.

Mum was now as red as a beetroot. 'I – we – didn't talk very much – it was difficult, in the shop. And with me not speaking much Welsh – yet. But, when I looked into his eyes – I knew – I just knew. It's hard to explain, Rose . . . And, oh, he had a great sense of humour too!' Now Mum was smiling to herself, as if at a happy memory.

'How?'

'He was wearing antlers!'

'*What?*'

'Antlers. You know, pretend reindeer antlers, like people do at Christmas. Actually, they kind of suited him. He wore them well!' Mum was beaming now, pink-cheeked, defiant.

Rose felt stunned. Had Mum finally, completely, lost the plot? But underneath the outrage, she felt as if the ground had shifted beneath her feet. In this noisy, rocking train, she felt suddenly, terribly alone – alone and panicking, as if gasping for air.

'Mum!' she blurted. 'You can't have met someone. You can't . . .'

Mum looked down at her hands. Then she looked up, and her eyes held Rose's – direct and strong. 'Why can't I?' she said, her voice shaking a little.

'Because . . . because of . . .' Rose stumbled. She bit back the word 'me' and said instead – knowing that this was underhand, that it would hurt Mum, that it wasn't even true – 'Because of Dad.'

Mum's face crumpled before her eyes.

Rose wanted to hug her immediately, to say sorry, say she didn't mean it. But something inside held her back. Something nasty inside wanted to punish Mum, for daring to look beyond the two of them.

Now they were pulling in to a station, and the lights and sights of the outskirts of an industrial town – old brick warehouses with roofs coated white in snow, the huge sprawl of a steelworks; long chimneys puffing white smoke up into falling-down snow, the dark, untidy backs of houses – invaded the closed atmosphere of the train. The conductor appeared, as if by magic, opening a box next to the door with a long key and shouting out the name of the town. Suddenly the little community in the train broke up. The large lady opposite busied about, lifting her three bulging bags and shifting along the seat so she could get out. Then she stopped and did something unexpected. She grabbed Mum's hand across the table and squeezed it tightly.

She said, strongly, holding Mum's gaze, 'If you can't give a hungry stranger a loaf of bread on Christmas Eve . . . Well.' She did not look at Rose. Her hand on Mum's seemed to grip even harder as she went on, 'Gather ye rosebuds while ye may, darling, gather ye rosebuds while ye may.'

Then she shifted off the seat, hefted her bags in both hands and bustled off down the aisle to the doors, accidentally knocking one of the boys on the head as she passed.

Mum and Rose sat silently for a second or two. Rose felt heavy inside, deeply ashamed, and could not look at Mum.

Then Mum sprang up, as if out of a daze. 'This is us! Come on, Rosie, grab your things.'

Chapter 2

'Here we are,' said Mum and, a little hesitantly, she and Rose opened a small gate and crunched through snow that lay thickly in the front yard of a terraced house on a long, deserted street. The wind was tossing snowflakes around them, dizzyingly. A light was on in the front room, but the curtains were drawn.

Rose wasn't sure she was prepared for this. They seemed to've got here so easily – too easily. They had come to Dad's home town, for the very first time. His cousin, Sal, had grown up in this house and, when her mam had died, she'd carried on living here. They were about to meet her – for the very first time.

But more than that – and this fact made Rose's heart beat very fast – Dad had grown up in the house next door to Sal's. When his parents had died, it'd been sold. Rose looked at Dad's house now, over the little wall that separated the two front yards. The curtains were open in the bay window and a Christmas tree, full of flickering lights, filled the space there – making it look very cosy. She glanced up and saw a darkened window upstairs. Perhaps that had been his bedroom? She wanted to go inside, go from room to room, imagining Dad as a little boy, Dad growing up – tearing up and down the stairs, playing in the back garden – perhaps playing with Sal. Sal would be able to tell them all about him, about how he'd been as a child . . .

Mum pressed the button next to the front door and a chime sounded, muted, inside the house.

They heard footsteps from within, the door swung inwards a little, and there was Sal.

She stood holding the half-open door, lit harshly by a strip light in the narrow, dark-walled hall. Sal was taller, bigger-looking and older than Rose had expected. Her face looked lined and tired, deep lines between her brows, and she wore a restless, questioning expression.

'Yes?' she said.

Mum stepped forward, smiling brightly, but Sal didn't move to let her in. 'Sal? Sal! Lovely to meet you! It's us – Cath and Rose.'

Sal's wary expression didn't change. 'Yes?' she repeated.

Mum stumbled on, 'Cath and Rose . . . you know – Tony's family. You remember, we spoke on the phone . . . last week . . .'

'What are you doing here?' said Sal, in a brittle voice.

'I . . . we . . . we wanted to meet you – remember? We did talk on the phone, Sal. We've come to say Happy Christmas – maybe have a cup of tea. We'll only stay for a bit, won't we, Rosie?' Mum turned to Rose, asking for support.

Rose couldn't think of a thing to say. She caught Sal's unsettling hazel eyes and looked away, over the wall to Dad's house, where the Christmas tree flickered. All she wanted to do now was run away, run back through the snow to the station to catch the very next train home.

Sal was looking beyond them, out into the billowing snow, scanning up and down the street. She came to a decision, stepping back. 'Come in, then,' she said, opening the door enough for them to squeeze through, then quickly locking it behind them. As Mum and Rose stamped their feet and shrugged off their coats, Sal turned through a door on her left. She seemed too big for this tiny house.

Rose followed Mum into the living room, where Sal was now standing before an empty fireplace. She was clutching her hands in front of her, as if she didn't know what to do with them. Mum and Rose perched on the edge of a sofa, facing her.

'Did you drive here?' asked Sal.

'Drive?' said Mum, and she gave a little laugh. 'I wish! Well. There's a story! It seems the poor old car has finally given up the ghost. It failed its MOT on Tuesday and, what with being so busy and everything, coming up to Christmas, I just haven't got round to—'

'You came on the *train*? You'll never get a train back tonight. Not in this weather.'

Rose's heart sank. Sal was right. The train service – and many other things besides – ground to a halt in really snowy weather. They'd planned to get the last train back – leaving here at eight. It was now just after six, she saw, glancing at the big clock on Sal's wall, above the TV. She realised that, apart from the sofa and the curtains, these were the only objects in the room.

Then she pulled out her phone and her heart sank even further. All train services had been cancelled due to snow and there were none tomorrow, either, or the day after – because they were Christmas Day and Boxing Day. 'Mum,' said Rose, in a low voice. Wordlessly, she displayed the screen.

Watching them, Sal spoke again.

'You can't stay here. I'm going out.'

Silence. Even Mum seemed stumped for words. Then she rallied. 'That's nice, Sal! With friends?'

'No. For work.'

'Work – on Christmas Eve? Oh, what a shame, Sal. Do you really have to?'

'Christmas Eve, is it?' said Sal.

More silence. Mum seemed to have run out of ideas. Rose wondered if she should say something. She lacked Mum's skill at talking, at being friendly. Perhaps she was a bit like Sal herself, she thought. Both of them seemed unable to make small talk. Then she realised, surprised, *Sal is my aunty.* Watching her – her large form almost obscuring the empty fireplace, anxiously clutching at her own hands – Rose felt a sudden pang of love for this strange lady.

She cleared her throat. 'Um,' she said. Her voice sounded creaky, but she persisted, into the silence, 'Can you tell us anything about Dad, about when he was a child?'

The hard surface of Sal's face broke. She smiled, shrugging off the anxious lines.

'Mam used to say that Tony was my little doll – I was always playing with him, dressing him up, taking him out in his pram. I loved him to bits. But he was always just the baby to me and Eddie – we were nine years older, weren't we.'

'Who's Eddie?' asked Rose, smiling back at Sal and

drinking in the idea of Dad as a lovely little baby.

To her horror, Sal's smile disappeared. What had she said?

Sal lowered her hands, swallowed and shook her head, as if to clear it. Then she said, 'Didn't you know? Eddie was Tony's brother.'

Tony's *brother*? Rose felt stunned. Dad had never, ever mentioned a brother.

Next to her, Mum gasped then began to cough. Rose sat motionless, her mind whirling in confusion.

Finally, Mum stopped coughing. She spoke, in a husky voice. 'Sorry, Sal. It's just . . . Well, that's a bit of a shock. We didn't know Tony had a brother, you see, and – it's a bit of a thing to take in. What happened to him – to Eddie? Is he still . . .?'

'Didn't you know?' repeated Sal. She unclasped her hands and stepped forward abruptly, looming over them. Rose and Mum shrank back in alarm. Then Sal's eyes widened. 'Of course – you didn't know. Well, you do now. He disappeared,' she said loudly, almost wailing. 'And he was never found. When he was thirteen. When *I* was thirteen. It was in all the papers. I looked for him. I looked for him everywhere. I've never stopped looking for him. And— listen, you two. I told you – you can't stay here. You've got to get out of this house.'

Chapter 3

We're like two helpless captives, thought Rose, as Sal's car skidded and roared on a steeply climbing, snow-covered road out of town. They'd left the streetlights far behind and were heading into darkness now, snow still falling thickly. Sal had told them they could spend the night in her grandmother's old house, up in the hills. 'You'll be safer there,' she'd added, ominously.

Incredibly, Mum was still trying to make normal conversation. 'How lovely that you've kept the old family home,' she said, from the front passenger seat. 'You must love it very much.'

'Not at all,' replied Sal grimly, spinning the steering wheel expertly as the car's back wheels spun to the left, leaning forward to peer through the windscreen into darkness and falling snow. 'I hate coming up here,' she went on, as the car righted itself and ploughed on through the drifts. 'Just haven't got round to selling it. Nothing sells round here anyway.'

Then Rose remembered something. She spoke up loudly from the back seat, over the roar of the struggling engine. 'Is this the grandmother that spoke Welsh?'

Sal met her eyes in the rear-view mirror, briefly, before concentrating on the road once more. In that moment Rose saw her gaze soften, as it had at the mention of her dad as a baby.

'Yes. It was Mamgu lived here. Only ever spoke to us in Welsh, she did.'

'Do you speak Welsh?' asked Rose.

'No. Not any more. I understand it well enough, though.'

So. Sal was like Dad. She understood Welsh, but couldn't – or wouldn't – speak it. Interesting. Then Rose remembered the englyn on the little piece of vellum – the special poem entitled 'Y *Drydedd Dylluan ar Ddeg ar Hugain*' – 'The Thirty-Third Owl'.

'Do you know anything about an englyn, a poem in Welsh, that your mamgu gave to Dad before she died? Like, where it came from or anything?' she asked. But as she spoke, she knew she was pushing it. Sal had opened up a little bit, but she'd closed down again now. She'd had enough of them.

Sure enough, Sal didn't answer, didn't meet her eyes in the rear-view mirror, but changed gear, put her foot down and doggedly dragged the car up the road, as if by her own, desperate will.

Now they were pulling in, and the car's headlights lit up the solid bulk of a solitary house through the driving snow. Rose realised she had no idea where they were, where this looming house was.

The car stopped. Sal switched off the engine so all they could hear was the howl of the wind and the swish of the snow as it struck and stuck to the car. Rose had the sudden thought that anything out there that didn't move would be swamped, buried in snow. It seemed that Sal felt the same, because when Rose and Mum didn't move but stared, numbly, through the windscreen, she said, 'Key's under the doormat. You'll find everything you need in there – place is full of old junk. You see anything you want – just take it. Save me some trouble.'

'Oh, Sal, this is all very kind of you . . .' Mum began, turning to Sal, who was staring straight ahead, and then she trailed off. Accepting the inevitable, she pulled at the door handle. So did Rose. As soon as they'd left the shelter of the car and shut the doors behind them, Sal shifted into reverse and backed at speed down the drive so that headlights blinded their vision. Then she straightened up and roared off down the hill, leaving them in snow-filled darkness.

Wordlessly, Rose and Mum turned to the house. It seemed to tower above them through the blizzard – and it was the kind of house that looked out of place in the country, thought Rose, looking up: big and tall, with fancy stonework, long windows and an arched door – as if it had been transplanted from a town and stuck randomly in a deserted field.

Mum was scrabbling at the snow to find the doormat. She emerged clasping a large, old-fashioned key, which she fitted into the front door. Rose's face stung already where the driving snowflakes struck, and her teeth were beginning to chatter with cold. The door opened and the two of them bundled into the darkness of a hallway.

'Lights, lights – where are the lights,' murmured Mum, feeling the wall for switches. Rose could just make out stairs climbing upwards into deeper darkness, and doors to either side. She turned the round knob to open the left hand one, then felt around for switches herself. Her fingers connected with something cold and smooth and she pressed down on the protruding bit in the middle. It clicked. Nothing happened.

'They're not working!' Mum and Rose chimed together in low voices, Mum bumping into Rose in the darkness. 'The electricity must be off,' Mum whispered. 'Of course, you wouldn't keep it on, would you – the place standing empty.'

Rose fumbled for her phone and switched on the torch. That was better. A shiny, tiled fireplace glinted in its light, an upright piano made of dark wood, an old-fashioned sofa and two armchairs. She scanned the beam across pictures, hanging on walls – landscapes, mountains. A framed piece of embroidery. She stepped closer to examine it. It was the Welsh alphabet, together with a beautiful, delicately made picture of a red dragon, a leek and a daffodil. Below all this were the words:

Cenedl heb iaith –
Cenedl heb galon.
A nation without language is a nation without heart.

And beneath this, more writing – *Betty Morgan, 1926*. Betty Morgan – surely that was Dad and Sal's mamgu. *And Eddie's* . . . thought Rose, shivering, unexpectedly. My *hen famgu* – my great grandmother. She must have done this embroidery when she was a girl. 1926 – so very long ago –

almost a hundred years ago! How clever, and how beautiful.

Meanwhile, Mum had found the torch on her own phone and was pushing open another door. Rose followed, and they entered a second room, the torchlights revealing a huge, dark seld, or Welsh dresser, reflecting the glint and gleam of hundreds of pieces of neatly-arranged pottery and porcelain. A table and chairs, again made of dark wood, stood beneath a window, and an old, black, cast-iron range with a little grate and an oven to its side was set into the far wall. Behind this room was an open door that led into a tiny kitchen with a large, white sink, a little window, a back door and not much else. It was bitterly cold in there.

Rose stepped back into the room with the seld.

'Now then,' Mum was saying, crouching before the range. 'I can do something with this . . . Rosie – go outside and look for a coal bunker – there's bound to be one.' She grabbed a metal coal scuttle from the hearth. 'Fill this with coal.'

If there is any, thought Rose, shivering. It felt just as cold inside as it did outside. She took the scuttle and was about to head to the front door when she remembered the door in the kitchen. The coal bunker would be at the back of the house. There was a key in the lock. She turned it to open the door and was hit at once by driving snow. Snow-covered steps led down from the back door and there, close to the back wall of the house, was a low, brick bunker. Sure enough, when she'd scrabbled away the snow at its base, she found a little slotted wooden door that slid upwards. And inside – hooray! – the magical glint of nuggets of anthracite coal, sparkling like large, black diamonds in her torchlight. There was not much here – but there was certainly enough to fill this scuttle. And even better, just inside the bunker was a little metal hand shovel, which Rose used to scoop it up.

Then she rushed indoors with the heavy, full scuttle and the snow came with her, gusting through the door and lying, unmelting, on the cracked old lino of the floor.

Mum was rummaging through a drawer in the seld. She snatched at something and turned round. 'Well, I haven't seen one of these for years, but it'll do – if it works,' she said. She was holding a small, silver, rectangular object. She flicked open its top with a click and struck down with her thumb at the same time and, miraculously, a flame appeared, dancing strongly off the tip of a wick.

'Yay!' Mum and Rose celebrated spontaneously, jigging about hysterically while Mum held the precious flame aloft.

Then Mum said, 'Rosie – head upstairs and find us some bedding. We'll sleep down here next to the fire.'

Rose hesitated, the momentary fun forgotten. She really, really didn't fancy going upstairs, on her own. In the dark. But then she remembered everything that'd happened with Ianto and Mr Williams this summer, and thought – *Am I going soft or something*? She'd been in far scarier situations than this. Holding that thought she strode through the living room, into the hall and up the flight of stairs, her torchlight leading the way.

At the top of the stairs she stepped on to a little landing and found five closed doors. Her heart was beating faster, despite herself. Taking a deep breath, she turned the cold, round handle of the door right in front of her.

Chapter 4

And found herself in a small bedroom. Rose shone her torch
around. Her heart was still beating rapidly, but it began to
slow as the room's ordinary contents revealed themselves.
Up against the far wall was a set of bunk beds. Against the
opposite wall, a desk and a chair. A dusty guitar, standing in a
corner. And Rose realised, from its battered, unhomely look,
that this was a boys' room.

A window, with open curtains. The wind was hurling
snow at the window pane, and it rattled in response, loose in
its wooden frame. It was icy cold in here.

Her torch began to pick up details. There was a poster
pinned to the wall, above the top bunk. She moved closer to
look at it. Torn from the middle of a magazine, it was a pop
group – Slade. She'd never heard of them. She looked at the
picture, and she had to smile. She wished Ianto was here to
share it with her – he'd love this. Four guys in seventies
outfits with long hair and funny expressions were staring
meaningfully at the camera. One looked like a spaceman in a
gold suit, which said 'Super Yob' on it, and another wore a top
hat covered in badges.

She turned from the poster to the desk. On it was a worn
rugby ball. She picked it up, tentatively, feeling like a burglar.
It was surprisingly heavy. There was a little bit of dried mud

on it, which flaked off on to the floor. How old was that mud? Had Dad got the mud on it? Had he been kicking it about outside, when he was a kid, or a teenager – when he'd stayed in this room? Or was it Eddie's – this missing, older brother, that she was going to have to get her head round? Whichever brother it was – the mud had to be at least thirty years old. The thought made her feel a little dizzy, and she put the ball down.

Then she picked up the guitar and held it awkwardly on her knee, giving its strings an experimental strum. It let out a discordant, vibrating noise, which shocked her, and she put the instrument down. Then she shook herself. She was supposed to be finding bedding up here, not messing around looking at things. The mattresses on the bunk beds were narrow and thin, light-looking, each with a tightly tucked-in blanket and sheet. *Might as well take the whole thing – mattresses and all.* She grabbed the top mattress, together with its bedding, and pulled it down to the floor.

Then she saw something right in the middle of the bunk's slatted base, where it wouldn't be disturbed by the tucking in of sheets and blankets. Something rectangular, thin. She grabbed the torch and shone it at it.

It was an old school exercise book, with a dusky blue cover. It said, in handwritten letters on the front:

Eddie Morris
Form 2B
Maths Homework

And in a flash, the fear came back. She was desperate, suddenly, to get out of this room, to get downstairs and be with Mum. Pulling off the other mattress and piling it on to the first, she shoved them quickly out of the door with her feet, shivering involuntarily. Then she turned and, hesitantly – part of her didn't want to touch it – grabbed the exercise book. She couldn't just leave it there. She had to look inside it.

Then she was out on the landing again, surrounded by the five doors – one standing open now, revealing darkness. She turned, hurriedly pushing the mattresses before her then tipping them down the stairs, where they slid easily to the bottom on the worn wooden treads. As she did, her back twitched convulsively with the unknown contents of those rooms behind her. She raced down the stairs in terror, torchlight bouncing all over, her heel scuffing past a wooden step and missing it, then she was falling, headlong, breathless, banging her elbow and knees to land on the musty-smelling mattresses on the hall floor.

She lay for a moment, bearing the sharp pain in her elbow, then she sprang up, fearfully, grabbing the phone and the exercise book, which had fallen down the stairs with her. The darkness up there seemed to pursue her as she kicked and dragged the mattresses and their unravelling bedding through the living room and into the room beyond.

Only then did her heart begin to slow again and the awful, sudden terror to feel a bit silly. In the time she'd been upstairs, Mum had transformed the room. Lit candles glowed from the seld, banishing the shadows to the very corners of the room, and a good fire was burning strongly in the hearth.

A large black kettle hung over the fire, orange and blue flames licking its base. The heat of the fire was already beginning to warm the room.

'Oh, well done,' said Mum, turning round. 'Mattresses – as well as blankets!'

But when she'd helped pull them apart and looked at the bedding, she said, 'We're going to need more blankets than this, Rosie.'

Rose's heart fell. There was absolutely no way – *no way* – she was going back up those stairs. Thankfully, Mum said, 'My turn to explore. You stay down here and get yourself warmed up.' Then she headed out of the room, her own torch lighting her way.

Numbly, Rose pulled a mattress towards the hearth and settled on it cross-legged, staring into the fire and extending her hands, gratefully, to its heat. She was still wearing her coat, woolly hat and shoes – it was too cold to take them off. A wooden box in front of her was full of old newspapers and kindling. Mum must have used these to make the fire. She pulled out an edition of *The Western Mail*, dated 19 September 1993. Was that when Dad's mamgu had died? It seemed likely. Wow. That meant the house had stood empty for . . . twenty-nine years. Was that possible? Looking about at the place, remembering the room upstairs, Rose thought it was possible. The house was like a time capsule.

Then she took a deep breath and opened the blue exercise book at the first page. In the light of the flickering flames of the anthracite fire, she began to read.

Autumn Term, 1972. Maths – Mr Armitage. 15 September.

Eddie's writing seemed unable to make up its mind which way it wanted to go, slanting first left and then right, then somewhere in the middle.

There followed a very tedious-looking list of sums, written out in pencil with many rubbings and crossings outs. And the teacher – Mr Armitage – had been all over it with a red pen, drawing lines through numbers, making corrections in tiny numerals, then ending almost every sum with a cross. Only two ticks. At the bottom of the page the same red pen said, in neat little letters, 2/10. *Not the best of starts, Eddie. But keep working – you'll get there in the end! FWA.*

Rose was a little disappointed. Could this exercise book really be just that – a maths homework book? But then why was it hidden so carefully under the mattress?

Turning the pages, she moved through the autumn, spring and summer terms with Eddie and Mr Armitage, witnessing their increasingly strained relationship. Rose felt some sympathy for Eddie – she was rubbish at maths too. *Perhaps it runs in the family?* And these sums looked really hard – much harder than what they had to do.

It soon became obvious that Eddie wasn't getting any better and that Mr Armitage was losing patience. Remarks like *You must listen more carefully in class* and *Please do these again* turned into *This makes no sense at all* and *A five-year-old could do better!* Finally, on a page somewhere in the middle of the book, dated 17 May 1973, Eddie ran out of steam. There were no pencilled sums on the paper at all. Nothing but a little red *??? See me after school. FWA.*

Rose turned the page, then she sat up very straight. Because the maths exercise book had turned into something else altogether. She was holding Eddie Morris – the missing brother's – diary in her hands.

Chapter 5

Friday 18 May, 1973

Got myself expelled today, din' I.

I'm lying on my bed, looking out the window and watching Dad mow the grass in the back garden – he's shoving at the mower and it's getting stuck in the long grass and he's getting angry and shouting at it and banging it about. He's even angrier than he was at teatime, when he came in from work and I told him, 'Got myself expelled today,' and he gave me the biggest telling-off ever.

It was going to happen some time – but I wasn't expecting it today, all the same. When I went to see old Armitage after school yesterday, he sat me down in the empty classroom and banged on and on about me not listening in class, not working, not concentrating, messing about – bla bla bla. The usual. Then he asked if he could help me at all, with my maths – if I needed him to explain things better – if I wanted to ask him any questions.

I just sat there. Why was he trying to help? He's just another teacher – they don't care, do they? So I said nothing. Just sat there. In the end he sighed, looked at me sadly and let me go.

I grabbed my stuff and ran from the maths room, kept

running till I was out the gates. Then I saw Tomo. He'd been in detention.

'What you doing here?' asked Tomo.

I told him about seeing old Armitage.

Then Tomo said, 'Dare you to scratch *Slade* on his car.'

Armitage's car, a maroon Daf 66, was sitting on the kerb just outside the gates. I looked back at the school and I couldn't see him – he walks with a limp and it takes him ages to get anywhere – so I took out a 2p-piece and scratched *Slade* in big letters in the middle of the door panel. It looked pretty good, actually.

Then we ran off, laughing.

This morning, at the end of assembly, the Head said, 'Edward Morris – come directly to my study after assembly.'

Now I knew I was for it. They knew it was me that done the car. Next thing I knew I was in his study, standing in front of his desk. His face was all red, as usual, and old Armitage was sitting at his side, looking sad again.

First thing the Head said was, 'You know what you are, Morris?'

I said, 'Dunno, do I.'

'You're a yob. A disgrace. A vandal. Someone with no regard for either property or authority. Now tell me what you are.'

He glared at me. I could almost see the steam coming out his ears, like it does in cartoons.

I said, 'Dunno, do I.'

'You don't know. *Don't know*. Don't know much, do you? Look at your marks – appalling.' He grabbed at a piece of paper in front of him then spat, 'E in maths. E in geography. E in English—'

'That's cos I'm not English. I'm Welsh,' I said.

He exploded then. 'You,' he sprang to his feet and pointed his finger, furiously, 'you, yobbo – will keep your insolent remarks to yourself!'

Then he calmed down a bit and sat down again, straightening his tie. 'Now,' he said. 'Give me one reason why we should keep you at our fine school.'

I said nothing.

'I'm waiting. One reason, boy.'

I said nothing again. Then, after about half a minute, while he stewed away and got redder and redder, 'Keeping my insolent remarks to myself, aren't I,' I said.

Rose lowered the exercise book and stared into the fire. She needed to take a breath. She was deeply shocked. That a teacher – a *head* teacher – would speak like that to a pupil! Be so nasty, so abusive, so, so – what was the word? Petty. That was it. Her own teachers were all so kind. She thought of lovely Miss Evans, her form teacher, and how she'd helped her save the wood, in the summer. But she was frustrated with Eddie too. It was like he *wanted* to get excluded, like he was proud of it. What an idiot, to scratch old Armitage's car – especially when he'd only been trying to help him.

It was as if, she thought, there was a kind of war between

the grownups and the young people – and neither side would listen to a word the other said. Could things really have been so different, in those days?

She shrugged her shoulders, releasing tension. The fire burned brightly, and at last she felt she was thawing out. Exhaling, she lifted the book and began to read again.

I thought he was going to hit me then. He stood up and leapt round the side of the desk, hand raised. Old Armitage sprang to his feet as if to stop him.

He didn't hit me. He came to his senses, dropped his hand and said, between gritted teeth, 'You will go to your locker. You will collect your belongings. You will walk out of the school gates, and you will never come back through them again. You're expelled, boy. Now get out of my sight.'

So I did what he told me and went to collect my stuff. Everyone crowded round me at the lockers, wanting to know what'd happened, what I'd done, what the Head had said.

I kept quiet. I was pretty cool. All I said was 'Got myself expelled, din' I?' and I walked out the gates.

And so here I am, lying on my bed. It's been a big day, so I'm going to hit the sack now. Good night! *Nos da!*

Rose was about to turn the page when Mum came into the room, mounds of blankets and quilts in her arms. She quickly rolled the book up and stuck it in her coat pocket. For some reason, she didn't want to share her discovery with Mum. There was one person she wanted to share it with –

in fact, she couldn't *wait* to share it with – and that was Ianto.

'Sorry I took so long, love,' Mum said, dumping the bedding on the mattresses. 'Got distracted up there, nosing about. I felt a bit guilty at first, like I was a trespasser – then I thought, *Hey, we're family too!* and I went for it!'

Mum plonked herself on the mattress next to Rose and pulled a quilt around the two of them, slipping her arm around Rose's waist. Rose leant into her side and let out a breath, briefly closing her eyes.

Then Mum said, 'Oh, I forgot! I found this upstairs.' She reached into her coat pocket and when she pulled it out a folded newspaper cutting fell on to the mattress. It was about the opening of the Canolfan y Gromlech – the Cromlech Visitors' Centre – which had been built to house the ancient sword, helmet and staff that Rose, Ianto and Mr Williams had discovered during their adventures in the summer.

Rose was puzzled. 'You found this upstairs?' she asked.

Mum glanced at the cutting in her hands. 'No, sorry, love – I brought that along to show Sal – thought she'd be interested to hear about our adventures.' She handed Rose a black and white photo and said, '*This* is what I found. It was sitting on the dressing table in what must have been Mamgu Morris's bedroom.'

A very pleasant-looking old lady, wearing an old-fashioned dress and those glasses that end in little wings, was sitting on a low stone on what looked like a hilltop. Next to her was another stone, which stood higher. The photo had been taken on a beautiful, sunny day, and the breeze was blowing her short, curly grey hair to the side.

With her were three children. A girl, aged twelve or thirteen, was standing apart, outlined by the larger stone – big and strong-looking, awkward in a short dress, long socks and sandals, frowning at the camera. On the old lady's broad lap sat an angelic-looking little boy who wasn't looking at the camera but was gazing up, in obvious adoration, at another boy, who looked about the same age as the girl and had shoulder-length, shaggy dark hair. He was grinning cheekily, affectionately hugging the old lady's shoulders with his lanky arms.

Mamgu Morris, Sal, Dad . . . and Eddie.

Chapter 6

Rose had never seen a photo of Dad as a little boy – a toddler. Now she understood why Sal had loved him so much. And surely Eddie had too. Who could not? Dark, curly hair, a wide, innocent grin that pushed up his chubby cheeks so that his eyes were little more than tiny half moons, small, chubby arms and legs that you longed to *cwtsh* – to cuddle: he was gorgeous. Rose tilted the photo towards the fire to see him better in its light, to drink him in. This small image, which captured a fleeting moment of her father's childhood, was not enough for her, not nearly enough. And a huge, heavy pang of grief hit her. A loud sob bubbled up from deep within, and she turned and buried her head in Mum's shoulder. Mum was sobbing, suddenly, too, and for a while they held each other tightly, overwhelmed.

Eventually they ran out of tears, let each other go and stared into the glowing, everchanging colours – oranges, reds and blues – of the coals on the fire.

'Well,' said Mum, turning from the fire to look at Rose. 'This is a Christmas Eve we're never likely to forget, eh?'

Rose hiccupped with laughter. That was for sure!

'Hey, Mum – what's a yob?' she asked, suddenly.

'A yob?' Mum chuckled. 'Now that's a word I haven't heard in a long time. It means hooligan – or, like, bad boy. It's *boy* backwards, see?'

'Oh, yeah,' said Rose. So it was.

'Why d'you want to know?'

'Oh. There's a poster upstairs, in one of the rooms. Of a band called Slade. And one of them is wearing like a space suit with *Super Yob* written on it.' She didn't mention that Eddie's headteacher had also used the word in his rant against him.

'Slade!' Mum shuffled beside her. 'Now I know one of their songs – I know I do. Which one is it . . .' She began humming to herself, trying to summon it.

Then, 'Got it!' she said, launching into, *'So here it is, Merry Christmas, everybody's having fun . . .'*

Rose knew this one too, somehow, so she raised her own voice and joined in, laughing, *'Look to the future now, we've only just beguuu-uuu-uuun!'*

And that was it – neither of them could remember any more words. When they realised this, they looked at each other and laughed some more.

'Very appropriate,' said Mum. 'This being Christmas Eve.' Then, 'Aha! Here we are.' She stood up and pulled a white card box from her bag, placing it on the hearth in front of them. Then she stepped over to the seld, carefully took two plates and two dainty cups from the display and dusted them on her sleeve. A rummage in a drawer produced a knife and a teaspoon.

Rose realised, suddenly, that she was very, very hungry.

'Has that kettle boiled yet?' asked Mum. It had. Steam was shooting from its spout. 'Cut the cake, Rosie, while I make hot chocolate.'

Rose opened the flaps on the box to reveal a beautiful,

iced Christmas cake with *Nadolig Llawen* written across it in raised letters – Happy Christmas.

'It's lovely, Mum!' exclaimed Rose. It seemed a shame to pierce its perfectly smooth surface but she plunged the knife into it, cutting through the crust of icing into deep, soft, fruity darkness, taking out two large, crumbling slices and putting them on plates.

'I brought the cake to share with Sal,' said Mum, a little sadly, as she poured hot water into the mugs and stirred it. 'And this chocolate. But now, it's all going to make us a half-decent Christmas-Eve feast!'

She passed Rose a cup and Rose took a sip of melted dark chocolate mixed with water. It wasn't quite hot chocolate, but it was warm and sweet, and the cake was just delicious. Mum's cakes were always wonderful – but when you were really, really hungry, well, they were sublime.

When they'd eaten two large slices and drank three teacups of hot chocolate each, they lay back on the mattresses and arranged the bedding over them.

Then Rose turned from the fire to look at Mum. 'D'you think Sal is OK?' she asked.

Mum sighed. 'I don't know,' she said. 'It's confusing – she sounded fine on the phone last week. A bit abrupt, perhaps, but that's just her way, isn't it? No, she was OK then, I'm sure. And she said she was looking forward to seeing us and to catching up, and everything. But when we got there tonight . . . well.'

'Maybe something happened between the phone call and us going there,' said Rose.

'Maybe,' said Mum, sighing again. 'I hope she's all right.

And I hope we can all be friends – I know it might take time, but, well, I feel that we all need each other – there're not many of us Morrises left, after all.'

'Now we know of another one that's not left,' said Rose. 'Eddie.' She glanced over at the photo, which they'd placed, together with the newspaper cutting, propped up on the seld. She saw his cheeky grin, his shaggy hair. And she felt a bit deceitful. Because, of course, she now knew a lot more about him than Mum did.

'Well. That was a complete bombshell,' said Mum. 'When Sal told us about him I thought I might faint, Rosie. Really. Dad never mentioned him! Never! I don't understand that, I really don't.' Mum paused, then she said, suddenly, 'Do you think Sal might have made him up?'

'No,' said Rose immediately, turning over to stare at the glowing coals. 'I'm sure he really existed – that's got to be him in the photo, hasn't it?' She went on, 'And you never know, Mum, he may turn up again – sometimes people do, after they've been missing for years.' *Though not many*, she thought. *And not after so very many years . . .* How many years was it? She'd have to try and work it out. But not tonight. She was too exhausted. There'd just been too many dramatic events today. And too many new people to deal with. Sal. Eddie. Dad, as a beautiful little boy. And, she remembered suddenly, the man that Mum had met – the man wearing antlers . . .

She turned back to face her.

'Mum,' she said. This felt difficult. 'I'm really sorry about what I said, on the train. About you and this . . . this person you've met.'

Mum looked at her and her closed mouth suddenly seemed to wobble. She didn't say anything, so Rose went on, 'I know that you will meet other people, and that I should let you, and I should want you to be happy. I *do* want you to be happy, I mean!' Golly, this was hard. And Mum wasn't helping by staying so quiet. Rose swallowed, looking into Mum's big eyes, then she found herself smiling at Mum and suddenly the words flowed out more easily, all in a rush. 'I want you to be happy,' she said, meaning it. 'I want you to meet someone really nice. And I hope this man, this antler-man, is that person. I want you to gather ye rosebuds while ye may,' she added, remembering the lady in the train.

Mum reached out and pulled her into a hug. 'Thanks, Rosie,' she said. 'We'll see, eh? I must say, what with everything that's happened since we got to Sal's, I've hardly thought about him. But listen, you,' she said, pulling away to grab Rose's shoulders and give them a little shake, 'No one – *no one* – is ever going to take your place; is ever going to come between us. You know that, right?'

Rose nodded, not trusting herself to speak.

Very soon after that, they both fell into a deep sleep, in the soft light of the glowing coals.

Chapter 7

At some point in the night it stopped snowing, and the wind dropped.

Inside the house, on her mattress on the floor, Rose was dreaming. She dreamed that she was in the big supermarket where she and Mum went to do big shops. But this time Mum wasn't with her.

She was standing in the middle of an aisle and before her were rows and rows of tins of tomatoes, stacked higher than her head. People milled about her with their trolleys, picking things up and putting them in, chatting to each other as if everything was normal. But Rose knew that everything was not normal. Everything was far from normal. Why didn't they realise that? Because over the top of the stacks of tins she could see a large pair of antlers – antlers the size of a real, full-grown reindeer – moving slowly, steadily, along the aisles, up and down the aisles, looking for her, heading for her.

She could not move from her place in front of the tins. If she did, it might see her. She had to contact Mum, make sure Mum was safe. Where was Mum? Mum! Pulling out her phone, her fingers stumbled, panicked, over keys. Something wasn't working properly. Either the phone, or her stubby, useless fingers, were not working properly. Then she saw it was a different, unfamiliar phone in her hands, and she couldn't find her contacts. Now she had to remember Mum's number. What was it? She thought she knew. She began to press buttons with slow, numb-feeling fingers and a panicking mind. But as soon as the numbers appeared on the screen they began to disappear again, so she typed the same thing over and over and then watched it fade away before she had the chance to press *call*.

Mum! Help!

She looked up, in terror. Now the antler-man was closer. He was in the next aisle – on the other side of the tins, moving along the row as smoothly and as silently as if he was on wheels. Then he stopped. He turned his head – his unseen head – so that his antlers faced forwards, faced her, behind the tins. Now the antlers were dead still. Waiting. He knew she was there.

She was rooted to the spot in terror, unable to move a muscle now, while shoppers drifted about her, oblivious.

Then Ianto was at her side. 'Ianto!' She turned to him, whispering, fearfully. 'Ianto – *mae dyn y cyrn yma!* The antler-man's here!'

Ianto looked at her and smiled – his familiar, reassuring smile, the sparkle in his brown eyes. '*Dyn y cyrn?*' He followed her gaze and looked at the antlers, standing stationary over the tops of the tins, and then he laughed. '*Na'dy*, bach. No. That's not the antler-man. That's Eddie.'

'Eddie?' whispered Rose.

'Eddie!' said Ianto, laughing again. 'You remember Eddie – of course you remember Eddie. He's our brother.'

Then she saw the wall of tins in front of her begin to shift, to shake. The antler-man, with his dead-still antlers, was dislodging them from the other side, was going to topple them over. Then she would see him – and that must never happen, could never happen.

She moaned aloud, still rooted to the spot. With all her might she struggled to open her eyes, straining to wake herself up. And she moved, she moved from the supermarket back to this cold house, to Mamgu Morris's house. And she was lying in front of the fire, but Mum had gone. Nothing but an empty mattress beside her. And she knew that the antler-man was outside, circling the house. He knew she was inside.

She lay still, eyes closed, horrified that she was still within the dream, still chased by terror. There was no escape. He would get her in the end – asleep or awake, he would get her. Then she heard the back door open, stealthily – the latch click. She heard footsteps on the lino in the little kitchen. She was paralysed now with fear, on the floor, unable to defend herself. He was coming. He was coming for her.

A voice – low, shaky – called 'Mamgu! Mamgu?' and Rose's eyes sprang open – to see a pale, fur-lined face looming over her.

'AAAAH!' she screamed, her arms flailing out. 'Mum! Mum! *Help me!*'

The sound of the coal scuttle, clattering against the hearth; footsteps slapping on lino and the back door slamming shut, while she felt Mum's arms wrapping around her, heard her voice: 'Rose. Rose, love. It's all right. It's all right, darling. I'm here.'

Chapter 8

When they woke again, stiff and uncomfortable, it was
Christmas Day. Mum pulled open the curtains to reveal clear
blue skies above a landscape blanketed white with snow, the
sun lifting sparkles of diamonds from it.

Looking at it from the heap of bedding on the floor, Rose
felt slightly cheered. Slightly. But the best thing about snow
was going out into it and coming in from it to a warm, cosy
house. And this house was anything but. Cruel, stark daylight
revealed the dust, the cobwebs, the grey mould on the old,
dark furniture. It was utterly cheerless in here, and very cold.
Rose felt ragged with the memory of her terrible dream,
chilly, damp and miserable. Mum was doing her best to be
cheery but even she was quiet as they drank a final cup of
watery hot chocolate and ate a slice of cake before the
dwindling fire – Christmas breakfast.

Mum's phone had totally run out of juice. And, with it,
Sal's number had gone. Not that there was any signal up
here anyway, they realised, when they looked at Rose's
mobile.

They were both desperate to be out of this place. They
decided to walk down the road, back towards town. They'd
come across other houses, they thought, and if there was still
no signal they could knock on their doors, apologise and ask

to use their landline. They had some cash on them, so they could pay for it.

Secretly, Rose stuffed Eddie's diary into her backpack.

Then she remembered the photo. She had to take that too. She turned to the seld. But the photo – and the newspaper cutting – weren't there. Neither were they on the floor. Or in the kitchen. Mum must have them. She was upstairs, putting the bedding back. Rose went into the hall and shouted up the stairs, 'Mum, have you got that photo?'

Mum appeared on the landing at the top, lit up by the sun, reflecting off snow through a window somewhere. 'No, love. You bring it – we'll have it framed when we get home.'

'But I don't have it. It's not on the seld, where we left it.' The horrible dream, whose atmosphere still tingled about her, came back to her. At the end of the dream, something – someone – had come in through the back door, had called out 'Mamgu!' What if . . . what if that bit hadn't been a dream? What if the face she'd seen had been a real face? What if they'd taken the photo and the newspaper cutting?

She hurried back to the room. The fire had died completely now, grey ashes in the grate. The coal scuttle was lying on its side next to the hearth. She'd heard it clatter over, last night, as the intruder scarpered. Then they'd dashed out of the back door. She moved into the kitchen. The back door was shut, but the floor before it was wet with partially melted snow. She'd brought snow in last night, with the coal. Was that what this was – or was this snow more recent?

Opening the back door, she saw that the snow-covered steps before her had been scuffed and imprinted with footprints. But these footprints weren't hers. Bending down to examine them, she saw that they belonged to bigger feet, with different patterns on the soles.

She straightened up and saw the footprints extend through the snow for the length of a long garden and disappear over a fence into a tangle of brambles at the garden's end.

Shutting the kitchen door, her heart beating very fast, Rose leaned against it and took a deep breath.

She had no idea what was going on. But one thing was for sure – she desperately wanted to get home and put it all behind her.

When they finally left the house they had to squint in the sudden brightness of the outdoors. Looking beyond the drive, Rose saw that a hill rose steeply behind them, with a flattish top studded by snow-covered lumps. It looked odd, man-made. *Perhaps it's the remains of an iron-age settlement*, thought Rose. They were dotted all over the landscape round here. Any other day, she'd have been up there to investigate – but not today. She turned her back on the strange hill-top and began to trudge down the road with Mum, in the direction of town.

Pristine snow lay across the lane before them – no tyre-marks, no footprints but the ones they left behind them. Whoever had entered the house last night had not left this way, at any rate. Rose didn't want to think about which way they'd left, where they were now.

A *barcud coch*, a red kite, wheeled slowly in the sky above, scanning the white landscape. Its cry, like a ship's whistle – an old fashioned bosun's whistle, from the days when ships were made of wood and had billowing white sails – echoed across the hills around them. The bird was directly above them now, angling its tail feathers to steady itself in the still air, watching them with sharp eyes. The rusty red and white underside of its wings seemed to glow in the light reflected from the snow.

'*Helo!*' called Rose, her heart lifting. She always greeted kites and buzzards. And sometimes they answered her. This one did not. It circled lazily, and then it drifted away.

'*Ffarwél!*' she called after it – 'Farewell.' And this time a ship's whistle, faint now, responded, as the bird sailed effortlessly away across the land and over the horizon.

This encounter cheered Rose. She grinned and linked arms with Mum, and for a little while they skipped down the road, laughing, through the snow, until Mum's foot slipped and she stumbled, nearly falling, nearly dragging Rose down with her. They stopped skipping then.

For the umpteenth time, Rose took out her mobile. Still no signal.

They trudged further. It was a long, narrow lane, bounded by high banks with snow-covered hedgerows, twisting and turning so it was hard to see how far they had to go – or how far they'd come.

And then, through the still air, came a sound. The sound of a vehicle – a diesel engine – chugging up the hill. A very familiar diesel engine. Rose turned and met Mum's surprised eyes. It couldn't be . . . could it?

Chapter 9

It couldn't be – but, oh, hallelujah, it was.

Around the bend in front of them, crunching steadily through snow, appeared a Land Rover, engine whining a little with the ascent. In the front seats were Mr Williams and Ianto, his great-nephew – and, no doubt, Del the sheepdog was standing up on shaky legs in the back, doing her best to see through the gap between the seats.

The vehicle stopped and the three of them leapt out – Del deftly jumping over the front seat and out on to the road with them.

Rose hugged Ianto and as their padded jackets collided and swished Ianto held her out by the shoulders and asked, in a low voice, '*Ti'n iawn?* You OK?'

Showing great restraint (for her), Mum managed not to hug Mr Williams. Somehow she'd learned, over time, that Mr Williams was not a hugger. 'Oh, Thomas,' she said, stretching out her arms to him in a sort of virtual hug, then dropping them again. 'I don't know that I've ever been gladder to see an old friend. How on earth did you know we were here?'

He gestured with his thumb towards Ianto, then he said, in English, 'You can thank this one, and his box of tricks.'

Ianto grinned and held up his phone. It was a new one, Rose saw – must've been a Christmas present. 'Find My

Friend,' he said. 'Saw you'd come up here last night, Rose, well out of town, then the trail ended and I guessed you were out of signal.'

Then he lowered his voice and said to Rose, '*O'n i'n becso amdanat. Ces i freuddwyd – breuddwyd ofnadwy – ac o't ti mewn perygl.* I was worried about you. I had a dream – an awful dream – and you were in danger.'

'Ianto – *ces i freuddwyd ofnadwy hefyd!* I had an awful dream too!' she replied quickly, suddenly desperate to tell him about it. 'Was yours in a big supermarket?'

Ianto shook his head. 'No. We were on a ship. We were standing on deck, looking out to sea then, very suddenly, before I could stop you, you jumped over the rail – just like that. And you were in the sea, amongst these really big waves, and the waves were full of bits of plastic – old bags and nets and stuff, and you were getting tangled up in it all. And underneath you, under the surface, I knew there were big creatures – like fish, but kind of polluted, poisoned by all this rubbish – and that they were going to attack you. I saw you gasping for air, trying to swim, but I couldn't move. I was scared, I was paralysed – I couldn't help you – I thought I'd lost you—

'When I woke up, I felt sure you were in danger. And when I checked my phone this morning, I was really worried. I knew you and your mam were going to see this aunty, then come home again. I couldn't understand why you were up here, in the middle of nowhere—'

'Ahem.' The two of them turned, to find that Mr Williams, Mum and Del were watching them. Mr Williams and Mum were smiling. Del had her head slightly to one side, and was slowly wagging her tail. 'Come on, lovebirds,' said Mr Williams, 'get in the back. I need to get home and tidy up.'

Rose and Ianto pulled apart, grinning sheepishly.

'You can talk, Uncle,' called Ianto, as he and Rose climbed into the back of the Land Rover, closely followed by Del, her claws scrabbling on the slatted metal of the floor. 'Uncle's got a hot date this afternoon, haven't you, Uncle?'

Mum was climbing into the front. 'Now,' she said, as she slammed shut the passenger door, 'I want you all to carry on speaking Welsh, please. It'll be good practice for me, apart from anything. Just bear in mind I won't be able to say much back – though I'll do my best. But what I want to know first of all is,' she went on, turning to Mr Williams, who was reversing the Land Rover across the road, *'beth am y "hot date" 'ma, te?* What about this hot date, then?'

Everyone, even Mr Williams, who'd blushed bright pink at the words 'hot date', laughed with delight to hear Mum join in like this, in Welsh. She'd been doing a Welsh evening course since September and was improving every day.

Now it was Mr Williams who couldn't speak Welsh – or English, for that matter. Rose saw the back of his neck flush even brighter and he cleared his throat, lost for words.

Seeing his discomfort, Mum said, 'Sorry, Thomas, I didn't mean to embarrass you. I think it's just wonderful that you and Gwenllian have taken up again after where you left off, so long ago. Childhood sweethearts! Gather ye rosebuds while ye may – that's what I say!' She turned round to wink at Rose.

Rose smiled back, then looked out the window. They'd just reached the end of the winding, downhill lane and turned on to the main road, which had been cleared of snow, so the Land Rover was able to pick up speed. They were heading home. She felt herself relaxing, at last.

Mr Williams shifted into fourth gear, then 'Gather ye rosebuds while ye may,' he said, in a dreamy voice. *'Dw i'n hoffi honna.* I like that. What is it – a poem, a song?'

'No idea,' said Mum. 'A lady on the train said it to me, on the way down last night.'

Ianto was keying it into his phone. 'It's from a poem,' he called from the back, over the sound of the engine. 'Called "To the Virgins, to Make Much of Time" by Robert Herrick.' He raised his eyebrows. 'Not sure you should hear the rest of it, Uncle – sounds a bit X-rated.'

Poor Mr Williams was still blushing away, still unable to respond. Rose knew that if Mum weren't in the vehicle, he'd respond all right – he'd even reach round to cuff Ianto over the head for being so cheeky. But the presence of Mum was making him shy. She stifled a giggle and Ianto winked at her, before reciting loudly,

'Gather ye rosebuds while ye may,
Old Time is still a-flying;
And this same flower that smiles today
To-morrow will be dying—'

The recitation was cut off abruptly as Mr Williams, watching his left-hand mirror, decelerated rapidly and pulled off the road, coming to a halt alongside a bank of snow.

'It's that boy again,' he said, still watching the left-hand mirror. Everyone strained to look behind them through the mud-spattered, misty windows.

'Yes, that's him all right,' confirmed Ianto.

'Who?' asked Rose, her heart fluttering nervously, all of a sudden. She could see him now – he was running along the edge of the road towards the Land Rover, through the dirty, gritty snow that'd been pushed to the side, slipping and stumbling as if he was afraid they'd pull away and leave him behind. He was wearing baggy trousers and a knee-length parka jacket with a long hood that hid his face – a fur-lined hood . . .

'He was hitching a lift north, when we came down to find you,' said Ianto, watching him approach. 'We thought, no chance – not on Christmas Day. We said, if he's still there when we come back, we'll pick him up.'

The boy had reached the Land Rover now, and he suddenly slowed down. Hesitantly, he stepped through the snowdrift beside the vehicle and looked through the passenger window, his chest heaving with exertion, his breath hanging about his head as steam.

Mum wound down the window and cold air rushed in. Rose shivered.

'*Ble wyt ti'n mynd?* Where you going, lad?' asked Mr Williams.

When he didn't respond but stood there, breathing hard, Mr Williams said, '*Ti'n siarad Cymraeg?* You speak Welsh?'

The hooded boy nodded. There was a pause. Then came a voice from the hood – gruff, frightened, '*Fi moyn mynd i Frynafon.* I want to go to Brynafon.'

'You're in luck, boy – that's where we're heading. Hop in the back,' said Mr Williams.

Rose and Ianto shuffled up – they were sitting on benches on either side of the vehicle, over the wheel arches. Del, who'd been lying between them, stood up and wagged her tail uncertainly, looking to each of them for reassurance. She could tell something was up. Then she turned to face the door at the back, as the handle was turned from the outside.

The door opened and the boy stepped up on to the metal tread and, suddenly, Rose was face to face with him – the tube of his fur-lined hood pointed right at her. He took one look and backed out again, falling backwards into the snow then scrambling to his feet and running from the Land Rover – climbing the snow pile at the side of the road and vaulting the fence beyond it.

In a flash, Mr Williams jumped down from the front seat to chase after him.

'Hey! Lad! Come back, bach!' He struggled up the snow drift, slipping and swearing, and reached the fence, but by this time the boy was halfway over the field behind it, sprinting now, hurdling through snow.

'You want a hot meal, somewhere to stay,' shouted Mr Williams, 'come to the farm on the mountain – Fferm Bigfelen . . .' He broke off, then. The boy had to be out of earshot now.

Mr Williams was mumbling to himself as he got back in the Land Rover. He turned to Mum, with anxious eyes. 'Young lad – got to be the age of these two,' he flicked his thumb over his shoulder at Rose and Ianto, 'out on Christmas Day, hitching a lift. Then running away. Something's scared him. Something's not right . . .'

Rose sat silently in the back, suddenly folded in on herself, her ears ringing with tension. His face – the face in the fur-lined hood – was the one she'd seen, looming over her, in last night's nightmare.

Chapter 10

'*Arhosa funud*. Wait a minute. So that boy yesterday, the hitcher, was the one you saw in your dream? Are you sure?'

It was the next morning – Boxing Day – and Rose and Ianto were on the sofa in her living room. Mum was out, seeing a friend. The woodburning stove before them was giving out warmth and a cosy, orange light and Rose was sitting up very straight, facing Ianto.

'Yes – it was him. But I wasn't dreaming him, I know that now. I'd woken up at that point, when he leaned over me. And seeing him in the Land Rover was exactly the same thing – looking into a tube of fur and seeing his face – pale skin, big dark eyes. It was him. And it was like he recognised me, too – the way he backed out and ran away, as soon as he saw me.'

'So who is he?'

'I don't know, Ianto. But it's like – it feels like he's following me.' It was a relief to put the prickling, uncomfortable feeling into words.

Ianto was silent for a bit, his brow creasing into a frown. Then, 'No,' he said, eventually. 'No – it's got to be a coincidence. He must be homeless – don't you think? He must've run away from home and broken into an empty house in the middle of nowhere, to find somewhere to sleep. Then he saw there were people there already, and he ran away.'

'But he wanted to come to Brynafon, Ianto. That's here. That's where I live – where we live. If he was a homeless person, why would he want to come here, to a little village? Wouldn't it be better to go to a town or a city, where there are shelters and things, or where you can hide? What's he going to do here? He'll get noticed straightaway – everyone here belongs somewhere.'

Ianto stared at her. 'OK,' he said. 'You're right. I – I don't know. But – don't worry about it. Right?' He was trying to smile, now, encouragingly.

'I don't *want* to worry about it,' she said. 'I really don't. But I can't help it. I just wish it – him; he – would just go away.'

'Maybe he will,' said Ianto. 'In fact, I bet you anything we never see him again.'

Rose thought about the boy in the fur-lined hood. It was hard to remember his face, but it was easy to recall the feeling she'd seen on it – full of fear. His voice, when he'd called 'Mamgu?' – tentative, nervous. And again, when he'd muttered that he was heading to Brynafon – trying to sound tough and brave, and not succeeding. 'He was frightened,' she blurted out. She felt a burst of sympathy for him. Out there, cold, full of fear. Hungry. 'I hope he's all right.

'Anyway,' she said, pulling the exercise book with the dusky blue cover from her bag, 'I wanted to show you this. It's a diary,' she added, as Ianto turned it towards him.

'Eddie Morris,' he said, puzzled. He looked up at Rose, and his eyes opened wide. 'Your dad's missing brother! Where did you find it?'

'Under a mattress on a bunkbed in my hen famgu's house. He'd hidden it there – must've hidden it forty-nine years ago, when he disappeared.' She'd worked this out, last night. If he'd disappeared when he was thirteen, and he was nine years older than her dad, it had to be that long ago.

Ianto whistled. *'Forty-nine years ago?'*

'Yes. In 1973.' Rose grabbed the exercise book and flipped through the homework to where the diary started.

Then she realised something. 'Ianto,' she said, staring at the date. 'The diary *starts* in 1973! D'you think it might tell us how he went missing?'

'There's only one way to find out,' he replied, and they began to read it, together – going over the bit that Rose had read already, then starting on the rest.

Saturday, 19 May 1973

This morning little Tony came sneaking into my room, which he's taken to doing lately, first thing, because he's grown just tall enough to reach the door handle. He jumps on the bed and we have a wrestle and I tickle him and he laughs till he hiccups.

But this morning, for the first time ever, I didn't want to see him. I thought I was going to feel great this morning – freedom, freedom at last! But I didn't. I felt awful, like I didn't know where I was any more. Of course, I knew I was in my room, at home, in bed. But I didn't know anything else. Like, what will I do today? What will I do next week, when everyone's at school? And, will Dad ever talk to me again? All the great feelings of yesterday had gone. I wanted them back, but they wouldn't come. So when Tony leapt on to the bed, I just pulled the sheet over my head and lay still.

Tony thought I was messing about. He began jumping on me – it hurt, actually – shouting 'Eddie! Eddie!' Then, when I still didn't move, he went quiet and still. Then he leaned down, and I could tell his little face was right next to mine, under the sheet. I could hear his breathing, with a little catch in it, from the cough he's just getting over. 'Eddie?' he whispered, quietly now. And then I felt small hands, gently stroking my hair through the sheet, like he was stroking a cat or something.

Then I started crying. I tried not to, but I couldn't help it. And I couldn't do it quietly. Soon big sobs were coming from me, and poor little Tony got upset too. 'Eddie!' he was saying. '*Paid â llefen!* Don't cry, Eddie!' Then *he* started crying, din' he. I was wiping my eyes on the sheet, and then I threw it off and grabbed Tony to *cwtsh* him to me.

Now Tony thought it was all a game again, that I'd just been pretending to cry, and he was laughing again, and wrestling with me. But it hadn't been a game when I'd been crying, and it wasn't a game now. I really wanted to hug him, to hold on to him. I had an awful feeling, a lost feeling.

Mad, I know.

Then at breakfast, Dad announced I was going up to Mamgu's for the rest of the summer. Just like that. Said it was the only place for me – away from town, away from the gang, out of trouble.

Mam was very quiet and looked tired and worried.

Little Tony latched on to the idea of going to Mamgu's and he was getting all excited about it – he loves Mamgu – so Dad had to tell him he wasn't going, it was just me. Then of course Tony started crying again and throwing his arms about and wailing 'Want to go to Mamgu's with Eddie! Want to go to Mamgu's with Eddie!' until Mam bundled him into his pushchair and went off with him to the shops. We could hear him crying all the way down the street.

I never even said goodbye to him, or to Mam.

Straight after breakfast, I packed a bag and went outside to where Dad was fiddling under the bonnet of the car. Then I saw that Aunty Nell and Sal were outside too, on the pavement. Aunty Nell gave me a hug and said, 'Oh, Eddie. You look after yourself up there, won't you? Look after Mamgu too. We'll come and see you next weekend – me and Sal.'

Sal stood there, frowning. I don't think she knew what to say. Neither did I. But when I got into the car she came over to the window. I wound it down and she said, 'I'll get Tomo for you, don't you worry.' And she made a fist with her right hand in front of her body, so only I could see it.

Why does she need to get Tomo for me? Tomo's my best friend, I thought. But deep inside, it was like something clicked. Tomo had told me to scratch Armitage's car, and then he'd snitched on me. And everyone knew it.

Sal was trying to make me feel better – but she'd just made me feel much, much worse.

As the car pulled off I watched Sal and Aunty Nell waving, getting smaller and smaller as Dad drove down the street, and I had an awful feeling.

I felt like I'd never see them, or Mam and Tony, ever again.

Rose and Ianto exchanged a look, then Rose turned the page. Eddie didn't sound like such an idiot any more, she thought. She was warming to him – which was good because, whatever happened, he was her uncle, her dad's brother, and she wanted to like him.

Wanted to like him and, maybe, to find out what happened to him. Or, even, to actually find him again, alive . . .

Sunday, 20 May

Today wasn't such a bad day. Spoke to Mam tonight on the phone – and Dad's going to bring Mam, Tony, Sal and Aunty Nell up here to see us next Sunday! Great news. Maybe Dad will have stopped being angry with me by then, too.

While Mamgu was in chapel this morning I played my *Slayed?* album on her turntable and really blasted it out loud, because Mamgu doesn't have any neighbours. I can't do that at home, that's for sure.

When she came back in and heard me singing 'Mama, but weer all crazee now', she stood in the doorway in her raincoat and laughed with delight.

Then she said she'd teach me to play it on the guitar, if I wanted. Spent all afternoon learning the chords and singing it with her.

Practised some more guitar tonight – I'm getting pretty good at it now. Maybe, when I get back, me and Tomo and the rest of the gang can form a band. We could call ourselves – I dunno. What about The Escape Artists? I've always fancied that as a band name. And I could be lead singer – or maybe Tomo will want to be lead singer. Or . . . I just remembered Tomo isn't really my friend, and the whole idea has kind of fizzled out.

Never mind. Seeing Mam, Dad, Tony, Sal and Aunty Nell next Sunday!!!

Nos da!

Monday, 21 May

Something strange happened last night – or very early this morning, I don't know when exactly. I woke up, from a deep sleep. It was still dark outside and the birds hadn't started singing yet. It felt like the sun was almost ready to come up, but not quite. Like the land was waiting. And loads of loud voices, all talking together, like a kind of meeting – woke me up. It was like they were all downstairs, right beneath my room, all noisily discussing something, something that was very important. And there was another sound that came with them too – the sound of a wind instrument, something like a flute, like pipes, that played a strange tune, and I wish like anything I could remember that tune now.

Really strange, right? But the strangest thing of all was that it didn't feel like anything strange was going on. Like it was just completely normal that so many people were somehow downstairs, discussing something very important, and that one of them was playing a beautiful tune on a pipe.

I kind of drifted off to sleep again, despite the noise. Then I woke again, and lay still. The voices were still talking, but there were fewer of them, and it was like they were taking their leave and departing. Like something had been agreed, and they were all satisfied with this agreement. The pipe played on in the background – that tune I can't remember properly – then it faded away, and I went back to sleep again.

And the next time I woke the birds were singing and the sun was coming through the curtains. And I knew what I'd heard hadn't been a dream – that it had all really happened. But at the same time, I knew that there couldn't've been fifty people, one playing a pipe, downstairs in the middle of the night. Only Mamgu and me were in the house. Maybe they were on the road outside, I thought. Maybe a gang were heading home after a party, or after the pub, or something. But Mamgu's house is the last house on this road. It's the end of the road. No one just passes here.

So it's a mystery—

Rose and Ianto got no further. A strident sound – a hunting horn – the thunder of hooves and the excited, bloodthirsty yapping of a pack of hounds cut them off in mid-flow.

Chapter 11

The blue diary fell from Rose's hands as she leapt to her feet and sprang to the window.

'*Beth maen nhw'n gwneud, Ianto?* What are they doing?' she cried, desperately.

The sound of the horn, the sound of the hunt, filled Rose with a mixture of horror and despair, as it always did. She knew almost everyone in the hunt, which made things even harder. All of them lived in the village, or in the countryside about. A couple were friends from school. And every Boxing Day, after the drinks and the loud laughter outside the pub, they were off. And woe betide any living creature that crossed their path.

But the hunt had never come so close to her home before. All around was Mr Williams's land, and Mr Williams hated the hunt as much as she did, because hunts damaged livestock and hedgerows. Usually it was all agreed beforehand, where they went. Something had gone wrong. A shiver ran down her spine.

Before Ianto could answer, something rushed past their vision, right outside the house. A dog. Rose and Ianto ran for the front door and burst into the snow-filled, sound-filled outside world. Now the rest of the pack of hounds were upon them – a blur of brown and white, bounding forward, while Rose and Ianto pressed themselves against the front of the house.

Next came the riders – big horses first, the biggest, heaviest, ridden by the hunt master, the man who lived in the big house just outside the village – and the ground, even the wall at their backs, vibrated with the thumping of heavy hooves on the gravel drive.

'HEY!' shouted Rose. 'What are you doing up here? This is Mr Williams's land! This is our drive! STOP!'

But no one heard, no one even turned their heads – it was as if she and Ianto weren't there at all. Rose had the sudden thought that the creatures on the backs of the horses weren't human any more – not the friends from school, not Ianto's cousin, who lived on a farm on the other side of the village, not the man from the hardware shop – but something else altogether. As if before they'd been wearing masks, pretending to be human. And now they were their true selves – bloodthirsty, brutal, intent on killing.

'*Beth maen nhw'n cwrso?* What are they chasing?' panted Ianto, as they raced into the wood behind the horses, skidding on churned-up snow and mud.

Rose didn't want to think about that. Didn't want to think what would happen when the hounds got hold of it . . . If they could reach it before it was pulled apart . . . 'Stop!' she shouted again.

As she ran, Rose realised with a tiny pang of hope that, as ever, the wood guarded its secrets – and its friends. The hounds and the horses were getting snagged and encumbered in undergrowth. Last summer's brambles caught on legs, forcing riders to make detours, pulling them up short. Humans yanked on bits and shouted, jerking horses' heads, whose eyes rolled wildly as they tried to turn in narrow spaces between trees.

But the dogs were wily and determined, rounding trees and tunnelling neatly through undergrowth, pressing into the heart of the wood and yapping and howling all the way.

Rose and Ianto plunged forwards behind them to find themselves in the clearing in the middle of the wood – the place where the mighty cromlech stood, five stones forming a roofed chamber, throwing its huge shadow on to the snow. There, as they panted to catch their breath they saw, to their surprise, that the hunt had pulled up short, dogs circling, suddenly unfocused, noses to ground; horses reined in by their riders, their snorting breath wreathing as steam around their heads. Breathing hard, all the human heads were now facing a single figure, who stood before them, arms out, wielding a hand-axe and barring their way.

Mr Williams. At his side was Del. Hackles up, she was growling, her lips lifted to expose strong, white teeth. Suddenly, she lunged at one of the hounds, nipping its front leg sharply so it retreated, yelping in pain.

Mr Williams's eyes were fixed on the hunt master, who loomed over him from high up on his horse.

Where the hunt master was resplendent in spotless red, white and black, Mr Williams was on foot, wearing his scruffy waxed jacket with the torn pocket hanging off and a grubby woollen hat.

'*Dych chi'n tresmasu,*' he said, firmly. 'And I do not permit hunts on my land. Control your hounds, and leave. At once. Before something, or someone, gets hurt.'

There was a moment's silence. Then the hunt master chuckled loudly, looking about him for support. Several riders trotted over to stand beside him. As one, Rose and Ianto scrambled from behind the pack to stand either side of Mr Williams, who glanced at them before fixing his gaze back on the hunt master.

The hunt master chuckled again, shaking his head. '*Nawr te, Thomas.* Put your little axe away, boy. You know how it is. Dogs get a scent – and they're off! No one's been harmed.'

Mr Williams did not respond. The hunt master's smile dropped, suddenly, from his face, his eyes hardening. His horse, impatient, shook her head and neighed, rattling the silver harness. Then he dug the heels of his boots into her sides and she stepped forward, lessening the distance between them.

Mr Williams stood his ground, gripping the axe. Rose's heart was beating fast – and not just because she'd been racing through the wood.

And then came a scrunching sound from the edge of the clearing. Someone was striding quickly down the snowy path that led from the village. A man – tall, thin, purposeful – emerged into the clearing. It was Ianto's dad – Mr Lewis, the village policeman. He wasn't wearing his uniform, but there was something about Mr Lewis that meant that whatever he wore (even pyjamas, thought Rose, remembering) he was still a policeman, always a policeman.

She let out a sigh of relief as he stepped swiftly between

Mr Williams and the hunt master, ignoring the dogs that milled about his legs. *Everything will be all right now*, she thought.

'*Beth ydych chi'n gwneud, Wncl?* What are you doing, Uncle? Put that axe away,' he said.

As Mr Williams reluctantly tucked the axe into his belt, Ianto's dad turned to the hunt master, who was already speaking, smiling at Mr Lewis, inviting him to be part of his gang.

'Thank you, Tegwyn. At last, someone sensible! Listen, Tegwyn. This fellow has been threatening us with an offensive weapon, using abusive language. He's trying to sabotage our hunt, trying to stop a sport which has taken place every Boxing Day in this village for—'

'What's your hunt doing here, Mr Thomas?' interrupted Mr Lewis, frowning. 'You're supposed to be over on the common – that is what was agreed. Kindly call off your dogs and take yourselves, in an orderly fashion, out of this wood and off Mr Williams's land.'

He turned back to Mr Williams. 'Uncle,' he said, in a low voice. 'I need to talk to you, urgently.' Then he seemed to take in Rose and Ianto, for the first time. 'What are you two doing here?' he asked, frowning even harder. But the hunt master hadn't finished. He wasn't going quietly.

'As I said,' he interrupted, loudly, 'this fellow was threatening us with an axe, putting all our lives in danger—'

Mr Lewis sighed. Then he turned around. 'Are you still here? If you don't leave the vicinity immediately, I'm afraid I'm going to have to charge you with wasting police time.'

As the hunt master opened his mouth to bluster some more, Mr Lewis continued, 'Yes, I said *wasting police time*. A serious crime has taken place. There's been a burglary at the Canolfan y Gromlech – and our ancient, Celtic staff has been stolen.'

Chapter 12

Next thing Rose knew they were all bundling into Mr Lewis's police car and bumping up the stony, potholed track to Mr Williams's farmhouse, which nestled into the side of the mountain. Mr Lewis and his uncle sat in silence in the front seats and, in the back, Rose and Ianto glanced at each other over Del's head. She was sitting between them, whining faintly. Rose had expected to be sent home, but back in the wood Mr Lewis had eyed her and Ianto then said, 'You two come too. You might be able to help.'

Rose's head was buzzing. Bleddyn's staff, the one that Ianto had broken in half – had been stolen from the Canolfan, where it was kept inside a glass case with the gold-banded helmet and the sword. Had they been stolen too?

When they reached the farmyard and piled out of the car, Rose saw Mr Williams glancing about. She followed his gaze to the haybarn.

Then he rushed ahead of them to open the front door of the cottage, calling out loudly, 'Well, here we are, then,' which seemed pretty odd.

Soon they were all sitting round the kitchen table – Mr Williams having cleared the chairs of piles of newspapers, stacking them on the table-top instead. Rose looked about and was glad to see that, despite all the work Mr Williams had

had done over the autumn – fixing the leaky roof, sorting out the dry rot, rebuilding the chimney – the place felt the same as ever: untidy, cosy, with shelves and shelves of books and the beautiful, honey-coloured seld, full of family treasures. The stove gave off waves of gentle heat. Rose rubbed her arms and realised, with a shiver, how cold it had been in the middle of the wood.

But Mr Lewis didn't seem to notice the interior decor, or the warmth. Pushing aside the pile of newspapers in front of him, he reached into his pocket, pulled something out and placed it on the table top. It was a blue woolly hat with a picture of a sheepdog's head – a sheepdog like Del – on the front in black and white. Rose thought of the lady on the train, with her knitted wolf jumper. But where that jumper had been machine-knitted and bought from a shop, this hat had obviously been hand-knitted – it had that slightly uneven, bobbly look to it.

To Rose's surprise, she saw Mr Williams's face drain of colour as he stared down at it.

Mr Lewis was watching him, keenly. Slowly, Mr Williams tore his gaze from the hat to meet his nephew's – the policeman's – and Rose saw those sharp blue eyes harden slightly, as if he'd drawn a veil over them. Then he sat back in his chair and folded his arms and the colour came rushing back to his cheeks in a pink flush.

Like Rose, Ianto was looking from his dad to his great uncle, puzzled. '*Beth sy'n bod?* What's going on, Dad?' he said. But Mr Lewis ignored him.

'*Dwedwch wrtha i ambyti'r het 'ma.* Tell me about this hat, Uncle,' he said.

Mr Williams was silent for a beat. Then, '*Erioed wedi gweld fe o blaen.* Never seen it before,' he said.

'Never seen it before, eh?' responded his nephew.

'Never seen it before in my life.'

But Mr Lewis wasn't giving up. 'Handknitted, I'd say – wouldn't you?' he went on.

Silence.

'One of a kind, as they say. Distinctive.'

More silence. Finally, Mr Williams grunted, reluctantly.

Then Mr Lewis pushed the hat further across the table, so it was right under Mr Williams's nose. Rose noticed that Mr Williams did not lower his eyes to look at it.

'Come on, Uncle. A serious theft has taken place – a priceless Celtic artefact has been stolen. Are you going to help us get it back, catch the thief, or not?'

No response.

Mr Lewis took in a breath and sat back in his chair, eyes fixed on his uncle. 'All right, then,' he said, finally. 'Let *me* tell *you* about this hat. It was found at the scene of the crime, down at the Canolfan. It was snagged on the frame of the glass cabinet which held the staff, the sword and the helmet. We have to assume that whoever stole the staff was wearing it as they broke the glass.'

Staring down at the hat, Ianto said, 'Whooaaa!'

Then, 'Tell me about the hat,' his dad repeated.

Mr Williams's face had drained of colour again. He closed his eyes and lowered his head into his hands. 'I can't,' he mumbled.

Rose wanted to rush around the table and put her arms

around him. But Mr Lewis had no such sympathy.

He said, 'You know as well as I do, Uncle, that Mam knitted this hat for you last Christmas.'

Mam – that was Ianto's Mamgu; Mr Williams's sister. Rose couldn't help smiling – it was just like kindly Mamgu to knit this special hat for her brother.

'I know she did,' Mr Lewis went on, 'because she made an identical one for me, too.'

Mr Williams looked up, eyes flashing with sudden defiance. 'Then how do we know this one isn't yours?' he said, triumphantly.

Mr Lewis smiled back, tightly. 'This one *is* mine. Do you really think I'd carry an important piece of evidence about with me, stuffed in my pocket? No, the other one's down at the police station. Forensics are giving it the once-over, as we speak. Those boys'll tell us just who was wearing it last night. We'll get the culprit – you can be sure of that.

'Now. Tell me what your hat was doing at the scene of the crime.'

Mr Williams had squeezed his eyes shut again. Mr Lewis glanced at his watch and tapped the table with his long fingers.

Then Mr Williams opened his eyes and looked down, at last, at the hat. He said, in a small voice, 'How do we know she didn't knit more than two? Maybe she gave one to someone else last Christmas?'

'She didn't. I asked her this morning. When she saw that neither of us ever wore them, she realised it wasn't a popular design. She's going to try a new pattern next – with sheep.

No, there were only ever two of these hats, Uncle. And yours, somehow, ended up at the scene of a major crime.'

Then, 'All right, it's my hat.' Mr Williams sounded desperate. 'But I never wear it. I have no idea how it ended up at the Canolfan. Perhaps . . . perhaps I left it there once, ages ago.'

'You just said you never wear it.'

'Well – I don't, of course—'

At that moment, Mr Lewis's phone rang. 'Yes,' he said, frowning as he listened. Then, 'Yes,' he said again, 'I'll be right there.'

He stood, pocketing the phone. 'Look, Uncle,' he said, and his tone was softer, urgent. 'I haven't told anyone it's your hat. Yet. I wanted to speak to you first. Get your story.

'This is your chance to come clean.'

Mr Williams said nothing. His head was in his hands once more.

'I can help you, you know.'

No response.

'Have it your way.' With that, Mr Lewis turned and strode from the room. He left the hat on the table, with the knitted sheepdog staring up at his uncle.

Rose, Ianto and Mr Williams sat in silence as they heard his car door slam, the engine start up then retreat down the drive, crunching through snow.

After a moment, 'Whoooa!' said Ianto, again.

Mr Williams mumbled, 'Stupid hat. *Stupid hat!*'

'So, Uncle. What's going on?' Ianto continued.

His great uncle stood abruptly, looking about his cottage

with wide open eyes, as if seeing it for the first time. 'I've got things to do,' he announced, grabbing the hat from the table. 'And you two need to leave – now.' Hat in hand, he strode for the door – Ianto, Rose and Del leaping up behind him to follow.

'Hey – come on, Uncle! This is us! The four musketeers. You can't keep us in the dark. You can tell us what happened at the Canolfan – we won't tell Dad.'

Mr Williams had ducked out of the cottage and was marching across the yard outside, weaving between the snow-covered, rusting farm machinery towards the haybarn, with Ianto and Rose hot on his heels.

'Uncle,' said Ianto. 'Did you steal the staff?'

This time Mr Williams pulled up short and turned to face them. His cheeks were red with sudden rage.

'Who do you think you are?' he spat. 'Infernal little policeman, that's what you are! Just like your dad – asking stupid questions, swanning about like you own the place. Clear off home now, both of you – just get lost. Some of us round here've got work to do – *real* work. Hard work never stops on a farm, you know – not even at Christmas time. You want to try it – softy like you wouldn't last a minute, I can tell you—'

'Oh – here we go,' interrupted Ianto, equally hotly. 'Feeling sorry for yourself, as ever. But you know what, Uncle? That's not going to wash with us any more. Not after all we've been through together. You can't just, just *dismiss* us! We all nearly *died* in the summer, Uncle – have you forgotten that?'

'Maybe you two softies *nearly* died – but I really *did* die!' shouted Mr Williams.

'Yeah, typical! Always got to go one better, haven't you, Uncle?' shouted back Ianto.

And Rose remembered, with a shiver, just how Mr Williams had died, falling into the chasm deep underground. And how, miraculously, when Ianto broke the wooden staff – the one that had just been stolen – he'd come back to life.

The two of them were facing each other, sparks flying. Then Mr Williams's face softened and distorted, his shoulders jerking up and down in a familiar way, and 'Heh, heh, heh, heh,' he laughed, uncontrollably. 'Heh, heh, heh, heh, heh!'

Soon Ianto, then Rose, were cracking up with him in the middle of the snowy farmyard, while Del looked around at them and yapped in excitement.

'I *really* did *die!*' gasped Ianto. 'Brilliant!'

And they all convulsed in a second bout of laughter, till Rose's sides hurt and tears were streaming down her face.

When they'd recovered enough to speak, Ianto said, 'Can you tell us *anything*, Uncle?'

'No, bach, I can't,' said Mr Williams. He sounded regretful. 'I just can't. Not yet, anyway. And I really do need to do something now – without you two.'

They weren't going to argue with him again. Disappointed, Ianto and Rose turned and crunched down the drive to the track that led to Rose's house. At the corner, where the flag flew, snapping brightly above them in the sharp wind – the red dragon furling and unfurling, again and again – they looked back down the drive.

The small figure of Mr Williams stood in the farmyard,

watching them, with Del at his side. Then he raised his hand to say '*Ffarwél*'.

And Rose knew that he was making sure they were well out of sight before he did whatever it was he needed to do.

Chapter 13

'*Ti'n meddwl gwnaeth e fe?* D'you think he did it?' asked Ianto, as they picked their way down the steep track.

'*Na'dw*,' said Rose. 'Why would he steal the staff? It was him that wanted to keep it safely here – like we all did – in the village where it belongs. No, he didn't do it. But he definitely knows much more than he's letting on.'

She sighed. Then, 'Ianto,' she said, feeling the cold out here, suddenly, and shivering. 'That staff was Bleddyn's. It's what he used to perform his magic – all his terrible, dark magic.'

'I know. That staff, in the wrong hands . . .'

They were just approaching Rose's house when she blurted, 'Let's head down to the Canolfan and see what we can find out.'

'Definitely. But can we get something to eat first? I'm starving. And cold.'

So, Rose realised, was she. Opening the front door, she called out, 'Mum!' suddenly wanting, needing to tell her everything, to hear her reassurance and concern. But the house was empty, silent, still. *Mum must still be out*, she thought. And she felt a pang of disappointment; then another pang, just a little pang, of worry. She'd expected Mum to be back for lunch. Glancing at her mobile she saw it was twelve-thirty already. What had Mum said this morning? Now Rose wasn't sure exactly what she'd said. She was going to meet a friend for coffee – that was it. But that sounded like she'd be home for lunch, didn't it?

Rose hadn't listened properly when Mum had left the house. Had she even said goodbye to Mum? She couldn't remember. She'd just been anxious to get Mum out the door so she could phone Ianto and he could come round to look at Eddie's diary. Another, stressful pang – this time guilt.

As she and Ianto trooped into the kitchen she tried to pull herself together, to stop worrying. *I must be wrong*, she thought. *Mum must've said she'd be out for lunch with this friend, and I just wasn't listening properly.* But the uncomfortable, nervous feeling wouldn't leave her.

Soon, however, they were tucking into hastily-prepared cheese and pickle sandwiches, made with thick slices of Mum's tasty bread. Rose found a bag of crisps too, which they shared at the kitchen table. It was good to have Ianto here.

'You know,' said Rose, 'it's funny, isn't it. It doesn't sound like the gold helmet and the sword have been stolen, too. Why would anyone want to steal two pieces of wood, and leave the much more valuable gold things?'

Ianto took a large bite of sandwich and munched. 'Unless,' he said, 'to them, the staff *is* more valuable.'

'That means they'd have to *know* about it. Have to know that it really is full of powerful magic. And now, they're out there, with it, somewhere . . .' Rose gulped. Then she grabbed a handful of crisps and stuffed them hungrily into her mouth. 'Hey,' she added indistinctly, through the crisps. She'd just remembered something. 'Wasn't Mr Williams supposed to be on a hot date yesterday, with Gwenllian? Remember, you were teasing him about it, in the Land Rover?'

'Yes! I'd forgotten that. She was going round to his yesterday afternoon – Christmas afternoon – that's why he wanted to get home and tidy up. Whoa. If that place had been tidied up, I hate to imagine what it looked like before. So – what do you think? Do you think Gwenllian stole the staff?'

Rose burst into laughter, spluttering drink and crisps out of her nose and mouth, while Ianto chuckled at her. As she recovered, she imagined sweet, shy, seventy-two-year-old Gwenllian pulling on the woolly hat, breaking into the Canolfan and making off into the night with the two halves of the staff.

'No,' she said. 'But – but . . . Gwenllian could at least prove that *he* didn't do it, couldn't she?'

'Yes,' said Ianto, staring at Rose as he mulled this idea over. 'Yes! She could provide an alibi for him – unless she left his place early, of course, and he went out and burgled the staff after she'd gone.'

'So . . .' said Rose, 'we need to know if she spent the night at his, or not.' To her annoyance, she found herself blushing at this thought.

'Ahem,' said Ianto. Then they caught each other's eye and giggled. 'We can't exactly ask her, can we?'

'*Hey Gwenllian – we need to know if you spent the night at your boyfriend's.* No, we can't. But maybe – maybe we could ask her something more roundabout – like, like—'

'Like, does my uncle make a tasty breakfast?'

They snorted with laughter, again.

'Let's just go and see her, when we've been to the Canolfan,' suggested Rose.

Half an hour later, Rose and Ianto stood before a police cordon, staring at the Canolfan in shocked silence. By this time the sky looked dusky and dark, as if the day itself was about to retreat indoors. A bored-looking policeman was standing outside what had been the front door, tiny squares of broken glass littering the ground at his feet. It was shocking to see the police tape, to see the smashed front door and the darkness within. Rose felt saddened. This beautiful, round building was so new. It was the pride of the village, and it had been descrated, pillaged, robbed. Actually seeing the damage made her very determined. *Whatever happens, we're going to find the staff again, bring it safely back here and restore our special Canolfan.*

'All right, kids?' asked the policeman.

'Just looking,' said Ianto. Then, 'Any idea what happened?' he asked.

The man sighed and shook his head. 'We've got a couple of leads. Forensics swept the place this morning and, er, we've got something on CCTV.'

'Oh, yeah? What did you find?'

'If I told you, you wouldn't believe me.'

'Try us,' said Ianto.

'We got someone going in. Wearing a hood, and a hat – pulled down low. But,' the policeman looked about, then whispered, 'no one came out again.'

There was a pause, while the policeman held their eyes and nodded at them.

'What?' said Ianto.

'Just what I said. *No one came out again.*' Then the policeman pulled himself up straight and announced, 'Now then. I've already said too much. Off you go now, kids. Too cold to be standing about out here!'

So they crossed the street to knock on Gwenllian's front door – the little door at the side of her daughter Siân's shop. There was no reply. The whole building – the shop itself and the windows in the flat above – were dark and vacant.

No one was home. So, that was it. Rose felt more puzzled than ever, but Ianto had to get home now, and so did she.

As she set off, through the darkening village and back up the hill to her house, she felt disappointed, empty and, and – *frightened . . .* At last she admitted it to herself – she had to admit it now, because she was heading home.

She was frightened that Mum wouldn't be there when she got back.

Now she was moving beyond the village's streetlights, up the dark, stony track. Snow crunched underfoot, frozen into crusts on this cold, still afternoon.

Though she couldn't remember it properly, Mum would have told her this morning when she was coming home, and she must have said some time after lunch. Maybe she'd said she was going for 'afternoon tea' or 'afternoon coffee' or something like that, and that meant she wouldn't be home till after four, or even five. She glanced at her mobile. It was nearly three. *Everything is all right,* she told herself.

Anyway, Mum is probably home now, waiting for me . . .

Head down now, crunching up the track, she followed it as it came out of a slow curve, hedgerows either side. This was the point where she got her first glimpse of the house.

She rounded the corner, lifted her head. The house stood there, ominous, every window dark and empty. But – wait a minute! The car was there! Standing on the drive. She was sure it hadn't been there when she and Ianto had stopped by for lunch. Mum must be back! Rose rushed now, to open the front door – a feeling of hope bringing a tiny, desperate smile to her face.

But there was no one to see the tiny smile, and it soon faded. As she pushed open the front door she was hit by darkness and silence. Mum was so full of life and sound – somehow, even if she wasn't speaking, Rose always knew straight away when she was in. And she wasn't in. The house was empty. All the lights were out, but the open curtains let in the remains of the day's dusky light, which cast the empty rooms in cold grey, stripping the place of colour.

Mum hadn't taken the car, wherever she'd gone. It must've been outside when she and Ianto came by this afternoon and Rose hadn't noticed. She'd assumed that Mum was going to be home, and she just hadn't noticed. Then she remembered that the car had been out of action for days anyway, because it had failed its MOT.

She slumped on the sofa and closed her eyes, trying to think straight. *I hate this strange, empty, Boxing-Day world,* she thought, *where everyone is inside, but it feels as if there is no one, anywhere.* Even Ianto had been sucked inside, to his family.

And where was she? Alone. Alone in a house that feels full of a sort of quiet horror, without Mum here too.

Now she couldn't hold it back. She was starting to panic. Her heart was beating very fast now, and she was breathing rapidly, helplessly, filled with fear, like she used to after Dad died. Like when she'd felt the ground splitting open up before her and she was teetering on the edge, just about to fall in and be lost for ever . . . *Stop it! Stop thinking! Observe your breath instead!* She closed her eyes, to feel her panting breath – going in, coming out; going in, coming out – as she'd learned at that time, to calm down. And she did calm down, a little.

And time passed. After a while, Rose realised that she'd been sitting in the dark, shivering – though it wasn't cold – for what felt like hours. Outside the window, still, icy night had brought all the stars out, spreading them across the dark dome of the sky. Any other evening, she'd've loved this sight, would have wanted to lose herself in them. Now she saw that the stars were full of strange, cold, indifference. She was just a tiny, useless human down here, in an empty house. Who cared what happened to her? Not the cold stars. No one.

She sprang up from the sofa to find the remote. Grabbing it she pressed the red button and the TV came on, filling the dark room with colour and sound. She watched the screen and registered that it was an ad break – perfume; a sofa sale; holidays in the sun. The noise and colour should have been comforting, but instead they filled her with the same horror as the cold, distant stars. But now the thought of switching off the TV and sitting in silence again was unbearable, so she left it on.

And now she had to do it. She had to try Mum's phone. She didn't want to. The fear was holding her back again. Had it been holding her back all day? Had she known all day, somehow, deep inside, all the time, that Mum . . . that Mum . . .

Pulling out her phone, trying to do this thing before she chickened out, she pressed Mum's number. It rang about six times. Then it clicked to voice-mail. 'Hello – Cath here. *Cath sy 'ma*. Please leave a message after the tone. *Gadewch neges ar ôl y dôn – diolch*.'

Since when has Mum changed her answerphone message to include Welsh? Was it for . . . for the antler-man? Rose closed her eyes. She was supposed to be leaving a message. She opened her mouth and heard herself say, in a high, shaky voice, 'Mum – Mum! Phone me, please. Let me know you're OK. I'm worried. Where are you? Mum . . .' The message beeped. Her time was up.

Now she'd done it. She'd phoned Mum, and Mum hadn't picked up. What she'd been frightened of – terrified of – had happened. Now . . . now what?

Rose clung numbly to her mobile as more time passed and the phone did not ring. The TV babbled on, flickering images – people moving their mouths to make sounds. The curtains were still open, and she could see her pale, TV-lit reflection on the dark glass of the window. Rose did not want to close the curtains. If Mum was out there, she might need to see the light of the TV, to know how to come home. Closing them meant closing Mum out. They had to stay open.

Mum . . . *Muuum!* Panicking again, Rose fought to observe

her breath, to calm down. Hours must be passing, she thought, but she was afraid to check the time. Afraid to see that it was late – very late – and that Mum was still out there, somewhere . . .

How could she not have found out exactly what Mum was doing today? How could she just have let her go this morning, like she did? How could she not have said goodbye? How could she just have wished Mum would hurry up and leave, so she and Ianto could read that stupid diary? How could she not have seen what was important – that Mum was the important thing, the only important thing, and that the diary, Eddie, the stolen staff, everything else, were not important. Were nothing. That everything was nothing, without Mum.

She saw the diary lying on its back on the floor, where she'd knocked it this morning – which felt like for ever and ever ago. Picking it up, distracted, she flicked to the place they'd left off. The TV chattered away as she read it. She didn't know why she was reading it. *Perhaps the answers will be here*, she thought. *Something awful is going on. Something I don't understand.* But reading this, the diary of Eddie – the boy that disappeared (and here she felt, as she said these words to herself, like she might faint) we might come closer to discovering the truth. And at this moment, anything – anything – that might help find Mum was worth trying.

Chapter 14

This morning, at breakfast, I tried to hum that tune to Mamgu – the flutey one I heard last night, with all the voices and everything. I knew that if anyone knew the melody, it would be her.

To my surprise, she joined in, humming away, and she went further than I could go, she knew more of it and she knew it well. I turned to her and grinned, humming along with her. Great! I thought. Now she can teach me to play it on the guitar! But she wasn't smiling back. Her sun-browned face had gone as white as snow. Then she stopped humming and said, in a low voice, 'Eddie. *Dweda wrtha i ble glywaist ti'r alaw 'ma.* Tell me where you heard this melody.'

So I told her what happened last night. About hearing all the voices and the tune on the pipe. She listened carefully, nodding, not saying anything. To my amazement, she didn't tell me I must have imagined it, I must have dreamed it. She just nodded, like she wasn't surprised, but she was . . . something else. Something like very serious, and sad. When I'd finished, she said, 'Stay here, Eddie bach.'

Then she disappeared upstairs.

But soon she was back. And she was holding

something. 'I want you to have this, Eddie,' she said. 'The time has come.' And she pushed it across the table to me. It was a little roll of something, like stiff paper. But when I picked it up, it felt different to paper. It was like . . . I don't know. Actually, it was like old skin – a bit crispy, a bit see-through. And that's what it was – Mamgu explained. It was old calf's skin – what they used to write on before paper. Like, in medieval times. And when I stretched it open and flattened it out, on it was an *englyn*, a short Welsh poem, in strange, old writing. 'Read it to me,' said Mamgu.

I looked up at her. Was she having me on? I grinned, but she wasn't grinning back. I'd never seen her so serious, never.

'Read it to me,' she repeated. So I read it to her – or, shall I say, I tried to read it to her. It was very old-fashioned Welsh, and full of long words that I didn't know. 'This is hard, Mamgu,' I said. 'I left school to get away from this kind of thing, you know.'

But she didn't laugh at my joke.

I stumbled all the way through it then, doing my best. Apart from one or two words that I recognised, it wasn't anything like the way we speak round here. Mamgu said that actually it was written by someone from round here, way, way in the past. But they spoke a bit differently then, and also, the person who wrote it was a bard, a poet. And that was why the words sang together and rhymed so neatly – making a shiver down your spine, even if you didn't understand them all. Like, nine hundred years ago.

Then Mamgu went through the lines with me, helping me understand them. I always speak Welsh with Mamgu, and with Dad, and I don't really think about it – I just know it. But I'm not that good at reading and writing Welsh because we don't do it in school. I've got to say, it was difficult to understand. Even when she'd helped me realise what the words meant I was still in the dark, because it's like a riddle.

'Do *you* get it, Mamgu?' I asked then.

She looked at me and laughed, her little face crinkling up like it does. It was a relief to see her laugh, after all the seriousness. 'No, bach!' she said. 'I understand the words but, like you, I don't understand the meaning. But listen, Eddie, this is very important.'

She stopped smiling then and fixed me with her green eyes, that are always very big because of her glasses. 'One day – and it may be very soon – you will begin to understand what these words mean, and you will need to act according to what they tell you. And, Eddie, I know that you will. I know that you'll manage to do something very difficult and very, very important.'

To my amazement, I could see that she wasn't joking. I wanted to say – 'What, *me*? Sure you haven't got the wrong boy?' but she was going on to tell me some other things – important things. She told me that she has two other bits of parchment, each with different rhymes on them. And, in time, she will give one to Tony, and one to Sal. And they will need to act on those rhymes too.

Of course, I wanted to know more. Like, who wrote

them all? Why? And why me, and why Tony and Sal? And what if . . . what if we *don't* do what the englyn tells us to do? What if we never understand them? What then? But before I could open my mouth to ask, she shot up from her chair, which made me stand too – in surprise – and suddenly, all in a rush and a bit awkwardly, she came round and gave me a big hug. It felt odd, because I'm now a bit taller than her. But she was surprisingly strong, and her arms gripped me tightly and she held on for ages, saying 'Oh, Eddie bach,' till after a bit I felt embarrassed and had to kind of gently push her away – like I was the adult and she was the little kid.

Then I saw that tears were falling from her eyes, and that her glasses had misted up. She gave a hiccuppy laugh then, and took them off and wiped them on her apron. Seeing her without her glasses, her tearful, green eyes, made me feel so very fond of her. For some reason, now I wanted to cry, too. *What's got into me lately?* I thought. *Why do I keep wanting to cry?* And alongside the sad feeling – another feeling. A good feeling – like Mamgu thought I was a good enough person to be given this very important englyn. Made me want, very much, to succeed in this thing, whatever it was, that she was telling me I had to do.

Later on, up on my bunkbed, I thought about old Armitage. And I felt a bit bad. I hoped he was OK. He was all right, really, and I'm sorry now I did his car. Hope he can get that paintwork fixed, and not pay out too much for it. And, suddenly, I had an idea, and it made me feel all warm inside. When I get home, I'm going to get a job. Dunno what – maybe delivering papers, or something. And the first thing I'm going to do with the money is give it to old Armitage, so he can fix his car door.

It's 9.30 and it's still as light as day outside. I'm remembering last time I was here, at Easter, when little Tony slept in the bottom bunk for the very first time. He was so excited to be sharing a room with me he hardly slept at all, and he wanted us to pretend the bunkbeds were a ship.

Tony really thinks the world of me – that's what Mam says. Realise I don't want to let him down – when he gets older, I don't want him to think I'm useless, to think I'm a yob. I want to be a good big brother and look after him, make sure he's OK. Make sure he doesn't do anything stupid – like get expelled from school. Because – and I can tell him this, when he's older – it's actually not as good as it's cracked up to be.

It's so quiet here. No traffic, no voices. When I look out the window I can see the hill and the Cylch Cerrig, the stone circle, at the top – the grey stones sticking up like teeth, like the hill has opened its mouth – opened its mouth so wide that it's flat. I want to run up and be amongst them. But I'll do that tomorrow, maybe.

Nos da!

Rose turned the page. And it was empty. So was the rest of the book. Had Eddie disappeared that night, Monday 21 May, 1973? Or the next day? It looked likely. And, she was sure that, somehow, there were answers here. The englyn – just like the one her dad had given her, that had helped break Bleddyn's curse, back in the summer. Eddie had been given one too. And so had Sal. But what had it said? If only he'd written it down.

So much to think about, but no time to do so. With a suddenly clear head, Rose knew what she had to do now. It didn't matter how late it was. Lifting her phone – her lifeless phone, that had not made a sound all day – she saw that it was twenty past one.

She dialled. After a couple of rings, Ianto picked up. '*Helo?*' he said croakily. She'd woken him.

'*Ianto – fi sy 'ma. Mae Mum wedi diflannu.* Mum's disappeared.'

Chapter 15

Within half an hour, Rose was opening the front door to Ianto – and standing behind him were Ianto's dad and his mamgu, carrying her large, wicker basket. Ianto stepped forward quickly and gave her a brief hug. *'Ti'n iawn?'* he whispered. 'You OK?'

Wordlessly, Rose led them all through to the kitchen and realised, numbly, that Ianto had placed his hand around hers, and was squeezing it. She turned to look at him, and he smiled at her, tentatively.

It was strange having the three of them here. Ianto had been here many, many times – from when he was a little kid. But Mamgu and Mr Lewis had never been in here before. And, of course, the person who *should* be here – Mum – wasn't.

Mamgu put her bag on the table, and said, *'Wyt ti wedi bwyta, Rose fach?* Have you eaten?' Then she pulled a large flask out of her bag, and a loaf of bread. 'Here we are,' she said, bustling about to find a bowl and cutlery. And Rose realised that she hadn't eaten since that sandwich with Ianto, earlier in the day. Was she hungry? She didn't know. But what were they doing, standing about and talking about eating? They all needed to get out there, now, and find Mum!

'Mae rhaid i ni ffeindio Mum! We've got to find Mum!' she

cried, ignoring the steaming bowl of soup that Mamgu had just placed in front of her.

Now Mr Lewis spoke. He looked tired, she thought, and as if he'd just got out of bed – his hair was all squashed on one side and his chin was dusky with stubble. But his voice was as firm and calm as ever.

'Eat first,' he commanded. 'Then we'll find your mam.'

It was good to be told what to do. Rose looked at Mr Lewis, who'd sat down at the table opposite her, watching her with his slightly impersonal, blue-eyed gaze, and she was suddenly very, very glad that he was here. And Mamgu, lovely kind Mamgu, who was smiling gently at her.

And Ianto, of course. Her best friend. She looked at him, at his concerned, brown eyes, and this time she managed a shaky smile back at him.

Then she sat down and spooned the hot liquid into her mouth and ate a slice of bread, without tasting anything. It was hard to swallow. It was just something she had to get out of the way. When she'd finished, she looked up and found all three of them watching her with concern and looking away again, quickly.

Then Mr Lewis spoke. 'Rose fach, I'm going to ask you some questions, all right? Please tell me as much as you can, even if it doesn't seem very important. Anything – absolutely anything – you tell me will be useful. OK?'

As Rose nodded, swallowing nervously, he pulled a little notebook and pencil from his pocket. Rose was pleased to see these things. Mr Lewis, Mr Lewis the policeman, was going to find Mum.

'When did you last see your mam, bach?' he asked, his keen eyes watching her, rather in the way that he'd watched his uncle, yesterday.

Rose's voice was uncertain, shaky. 'I saw her this morning – it must have been about ten o'clock? She was heading out to see a friend . . . and I thought she said she was just going for a coffee. So I thought she'd be back at lunchtime. But now I'm not sure she did say that. I'm not sure what she said – I wasn't listening properly . . .' Rose tailed off and looked at him helplessly.

'Never mind, bach. Did she tell you the name of this friend?'

'No – no, she didn't. She didn't say, but I just assumed it was one of her girlfriends – you know, like Delyth, or someone.'

'Have you spoken to Delyth, or any of her other friends yet?'

'I – no.' Rose felt stupid. Why hadn't she phoned Delyth? She didn't have contact details for Mum's other friends, but she did have Delyth's number.

'I'm going to phone Delyth now,' said Mr Lewis. And he pulled his mobile from his pocket.

'*Delyth – Tegwyn sy 'ma*. Tegwyn here. I'm sorry to phone so late, but we're concerned as to the whereabouts of Cath, Cath Morris.' Pause, and Rose could hear Delyth's voice. She couldn't make out words, but heard her voice rising in pitch. 'We understand that she met with a friend, this morning . . .' Pause again, while Delyth spoke once more. Could Delyth have been the friend? If so, how come she was safely home? Or – or perhaps they were still out together! Perhaps they'd decided to have a night out, in town, let their hair down!

Perhaps she would put Mum on, and Mum would laugh and say she's all right and that we're all silly to worry.

But there was no loud music in the background, or the kind of chatter you'd get on a night out. And Mum didn't come on the phone. Rose felt that her heart had sort of died. It no longer leapt with hope – it was too tired.

Delyth was still talking and Mr Lewis was listening carefully, nodding. Then he looked at Rose with a slightly out-of-focus expression. As if he wanted to hide something from her. 'I see,' he said, finally, into the phone. 'I may need to phone you back, Delyth – is that OK?' Delyth spoke again, briefly. 'Thank you, Delyth. Goodbye now.'

Mr Lewis put the phone back on the table. Rose thought he might tell them what Delyth had said, but he didn't. *That's OK*, she thought. She didn't mind. He could do anything. As long as he found Mum.

'Can you remember what your mam was wearing when she left the house, Rose?' he asked.

'I . . . no, sorry. I can't . . .' Rose stared, in new panic, at Mr Lewis. Then she pulled herself together. 'I mean – she must have been wearing her coat. It's long and padded and black, and it's got black and white fake fur inside it. It's got a hood, and she puts that up when it's really cold. She doesn't like hats, because they squash her hair, and she doesn't like it looking like that . . .' Rose tailed off. 'And I expect she was wearing her boots too, for the snow.' Then it occurred to her – 'I can check!'

She leapt up and ran to the hall, where the two of them hung their coats and kept their outdoor stuff. Sure enough,

Mum's coat, with the fur inside, was gone. And so were her lace-up boots, the ones that looked nice, but were sturdy and warm in the snow, too.

She hurried back and described the boots as best she could to Mr Lewis, who continued to scribble in his notebook.

'Did she take her mobile with her, do you know?' he asked.

'Yes – well, I'm not completely sure she did, but she must have. It's not here anyway, because I phoned it earlier, and it didn't ring here.'

'When did you call her?'

'It was . . .' Rose pulled out her own phone to check. 'It was five past ten, tonight. The phone went to voicemail.'

'Did you leave a message?'

'Yes. I asked her where she was, and told her to call me.'

'I'm going to phone your mam's mobile now. OK?'

Rose nodded, numbly, her heart beating fast again as he lifted his mobile and put it to his ear. They all heard the phone ringing – ringing six times, then Mum's voicemail message came on, indistinctly. After the tone, Mr Lewis said, 'Hello, Cath? It's Tegwyn here. Call me or Rose back immediately, please. Or dial 999, if you prefer. We're very concerned about your welfare. Rose is fine – we're looking after her. Whatever has happened, wherever you are, we need you to make contact.'

Pressing to end the call, Mr Lewis placed the phone back on the table. Then he fixed his gaze on Rose once more.

'Have you noticed anything different about your mam, lately?'

Rose stared back at him. He'd taken her by surprise. She wasn't sure what he meant, and she wasn't getting any answers from his steely blue eyes. 'Um – I don't think so,' she stumbled. 'No, she's the same as ever – you know . . . I don't know.'

'Has she been behaving at all differently? Saying anything different to you? Has she, for example, mentioned a new friend, one she hasn't spoken about before?'

At this, Rose gulped and screwed up her eyes, briefly. As she opened them a new tension seemed to have entered the room. Mr Lewis was watching her.

'Yes,' she said, finally. She felt lightheaded. 'She met a – a man . . . a man that she liked.'

Mr Lewis was nodding, calmly. Then he prompted, 'What else did she say about him? Did she tell you his name, where he lived, what he looked like – anything like that?'

Rose looked at him and shook her head, feeling as if she was drowning. She tried to remember. Tried to remember what Mum had said on the train, and then in the house – her hen famgu's house, on that freezing night. 'She didn't say what his name was, or where he lived. She said – she said he came into the bakery on Christmas Eve. And he had dark eyes. And there was something about him . . . and she just knew . . . And she gave him a loaf of bread, because he was hungry, and he didn't pay for it. And— oh yes! He only spoke Welsh.'

'He only spoke Welsh?'

'Yes – he couldn't speak English. So she did her best to speak to him in Welsh, though she isn't very fluent. And

Delyth helped— Hey! Delyth! Delyth saw him too, she helped Mum speak to him. Delyth can tell us more about him, Mr Lewis!'

Mr Lewis was nodding again, watching her carefully. He didn't seem to find this idea a new or exciting one.

'Can *you* think of anything else about him, Rose?'

'Oh. Yes. Yes.' Rose gulped again. 'He was wearing antlers.'

At last she'd taken Mr Lewis by surprise. He frowned, pulling his head back. 'Antlers?' he repeated.

'Yes. Mum said he was wearing one of those head band things with antlers on them, like people do at Christmas. So she thought he had a good sense of humour. That's what she said.'

Mr Lewis had stopped frowning, regaining his cool. 'Antlers,' he said again, writing the word in his notebook. 'Rose fach,' he went on, 'can you describe to me how your mam seemed when she left the house this morning? Was she happy, excited or, maybe, nervous? Do you think she might have been worried about something, at all?'

Rose tore her eyes from Mr Lewis's and looked down at the table. Her vision blurred as tears gathered in her eyes and then dripped, splashing, on to the wood. 'I didn't notice anything . . . *I didn't notice anything!*' Rose looked up now, wildly, realising that she'd wailed the last four words.

At once, Mamgu was at her side, placing an arm around her shoulders. Mamgu said, gently, 'I think that's enough now, bach, isn't it? Let's get you into bed now.'

Chapter 16

Rose woke while it was still dark, with a heavy head and a mind that felt blank, fuzzy. She was too tired to know anything but that she felt dreadful and she wanted to tell Mum, be comforted by Mum. Half-asleep, she padded to Mum's room, her one thought to sink into Mum's arms. Collapsing on to the bed, Rose noted that Mum wasn't there – and that the sheets felt cold. She struggled with this for a bit as she buried herself under the duvet. But she was too tired to struggle for long. *She must have gone to the loo*, she thought. *She'll be back in a minute* . . . Rose pulled the duvet about her like a cocoon and slept like the dead.

She woke the next morning to bleak, weak winter sunshine, the room still dim. She was stretched out under Mum's duvet, but already her heart was thumping in her chest, propelling her to sit up suddenly, her head pounding at once with pain. Then she heard sounds – the shuffle of feet and the gentle clatter of cutlery from the kitchen. Leaping out of bed, unsteady on her feet, she stumbled into the kitchen, crying 'Mum! Mum! *Mu*—' and there, tea towel in hand, turning to face her . . . was Ianto's Mamgu.

Mamgu's pretty, crinkly blue eyes were watching her with a mixture of alarm and pity, then she threw down the tea towel and stepped forward to draw Rose into a hug. Rose held on to her, speechless, while the horrible mixture of shock and disappointment died down within her, to be replaced by numb misery.

'I'm so sorry,' Mamgu mumbled, into Rose's ruffled hair. 'I gave you a shock, didn't I, bach? I stayed here last night, you see. On the sofa. We thought it best you weren't on your own.'

Rose wanted to shriek now with pain and frustration. But she gulped and swallowed the shriek. She had to stay focused, stay sane. For Mum. For being any use in finding Mum. And it was good that Mamgu was here, of course. Imagine if she wasn't . . . imagine if it was just Rose, all alone in the house again, like last night, without Mum . . .

A few minutes later, Rose was chewing mechanically on a slice of toast and burning her mouth as she swallowed hot tea to try to get it down quicker. She was desperate to get out of the house to look for Mum, now it was daylight. She'd already wasted time, sleeping. Mum hadn't taken the car. And no buses – or trains – were running yesterday. So she had to be somewhere close by, hadn't she? Unless . . . unless someone had taken her somewhere, in their car . . .

Mamgu had been saying something, in a comforting tone, and Rose hadn't been listening. But she snapped to when she heard, 'Tegwyn's organised a search of the village and the surrounding countryside, Rose. It's starting this morning – everyone has come out to help. They're all meeting outside the Lion.'

'What, now?' said Rose, looking up at the clock. It was ten-thirty. She pushed away her plate and stood, abruptly.

'I've got to get dressed,' she blurted, hurrying from the table with Mamgu padding patiently behind her.

Mamgu was speaking again, anxiously. 'Rose fach – I knew you'd want to help with the search. Ianto wanted to as well. But I'm afraid you can't, *cariad*. Children under eighteen aren't allowed to join searches, you see. Best you stay here, with me – till we find Mami again.' 'Mami' was what Mamgu always called Mum.

Rose looked at Mamgu, into her worried blue eyes. Rose would never, ever be rude to this lovely lady. But Mamgu had to realise there was no way – absolutely *no way* – that Rose was staying here, with Mamgu – however lovely she was – while everyone else was out looking for Mum. 'I'm going to join the search,' said Rose, firmly. Then she gently shut Mamgu behind her bedroom door and set about throwing on warm outdoor clothes.

Fifteen minutes later, she and Ianto were sneaking into the village square to stand with their backs pressed against the front of the pub, while adults in outdoor gear milled about them. The atmosphere was very serious, and people were quiet, unsmiling, listening carefully while Mr Lewis, who was standing in the centre of the crowd with a clipboard in his hands, issued instructions and advice. He was wearing his uniform today, tall and smart – but with a black wool cap instead of the usual peaked hat, and a pair of black leather gloves.

The sight of such a crowd in this square, gathered about their leader, reminded Rose of something. Then she remembered what. This was where the hunt gathered – humans on horseback, drinks in hand, laughing and chatting before heading off, after their helpless prey. *Mr Lewis is like the hunt master*, thought Rose. *All that's missing is the horses.* Because many people had brought their dogs, and though they were on leads, they were getting excited, straining to be off, giving out frustrated yaps. She shivered.

Mr Lewis was saying, loudly, 'If anyone finds anything unusual, anything that might be evidence – don't touch it. Take a photo, and phone me immediately. Is that understood?' His eyes roved about the crowd, then they fixed on Rose and Ianto, and he frowned.

'Uh-oh,' said Ianto.

Then something nudged at Rose's hand. Looking down she saw that Del, Mr Williams's sheepdog, was pushing her nose into her palm. 'Del!' As Rose dropped to her knees to wrap her arms around Del's furry neck and bury her face in her rough, black and white coat, she realised that her cheeks were wet with tears. Del, who hated to be fussed over, stood stoically as she clung on. Somehow, Del knew that Rose needed comforting.

Then Mr Williams appeared from out of the crowd and, behind him, Gwenllian. Rose wiped her cheeks and stood up, smiling despite herself at the sight of the two of them, together.

'All right, bach?' said Mr Williams, gruffly, his kind blue eyes watching her anxiously. Then he looked down at his sheepdog – who was now doggedly licking Rose's hand. 'Del is always there for her friends, aren't you, lass?' He ruffled her head.

Then Gwenllian came forward and surprised Rose by gripping her firmly by the shoulders. 'We'll find Cath, Rose,' she said, firmly, in her quiet voice. 'I know we will.' Lifting her eyes to Gwenllian's serious, green gaze, Rose felt a sudden jolt of hope. Gwenllian meant it.

Mr Lewis was moving about amongst the crowd now, a map in his hands, pointing things out to them. The crowd was dividing into smaller groups, each overseen by a leader, and he was addressing them individually before sending them off in different directions.

As the group in front turned around to set off, one figure loomed head and shoulders above the rest. Rose gasped as she recognised the hunt master. At his feet was one of his brown and white hounds – on a lead, this time. Then the man's eyes met hers and he began to hurry, excitedly, in her direction. 'Ianto,' she murmured, tugging at his arm. 'Let's get out of here – now.' But as they turned to leave they found they were trapped by people departing the square and suddenly the hunt master was upon them, towering over Mr Williams – whom he ignored – while Del sniffed disdainfully at his dog.

'Rose – isn't it?' the hunt master said, grinning. 'Don't you worry, bach. We'll find your mami for you. This one's got the best nose in the pack.' Rose looked down at the dog in horror, to avert her eyes from his large, red face.

Then Ianto grabbed her hand and was pulling her away, through a sudden gap in the crowd. Soon they were running, hand in hand, down the street, past the shops, dodging between groups of people, to get away.

Chapter 17

They headed out of the village and down the path into the wood – leaving the crowds behind. As they entered the embrace of the dark, leafless trees, Rose cried, 'Mum!' desperately, and Ianto shouted 'Cath!' Like echoes, through the valley, came the calls of the other searchers.

As they ran, Rose saw that the snow carpet beneath their feet had been churned up by hoofprints, pawprints – evidence of yesterday's hunt. They tracked through the wood, jumping from stone to stone over the stream to the field edge on the other side, lowering themselves into the cave where they'd found Berwyn and Bleddyn's skeletons.

Rose went first, letting herself down hurriedly into darkness, her hands grazing rough rocks, switching on her phone torch to see the way. Shining it about inside, she saw that the cave was empty, rockstrewn, desolate. Soon the beam of Ianto's torch joined hers to bounce about the walls, floor and ceiling of the cave. The next cave – the one you had to squeeze into from the first – was also empty.

Emerging from the caves, they headed next for the clearing in the middle of the wood, where Mr Williams had stopped the hunt yesterday. The cromlech's enormous stones, dusted with snow, stood like a stern, silent master in the very middle of the clearing. 'Mum!' called Rose, spinning about in all directions to call again and again, 'Mum! Mum!'

Then she hurried away to follow Ianto, who was already breaking into the thickness of the trees on the other side of the clearing.

Soon they were bursting out of the wood where it met the mountain and heading up the stony track towards Mr Williams's house – past the flag that flew at the end of his drive and then on, up, to the top of the mountain.

It was wide open up here, and the wind blew strongly out of a grey, cloudy sky. The wind had whipped much of the snow from the surface of Mr Williams's fields and thrown it in piles against hedgerows. Rose and Ianto strode forward with their heads down, fighting the wind that blew strongly at them from the west, only lifting their faces to shout 'Mum!' and 'Cath!', hoarsely now.

They were heading to the top of the mountain. To the place where it sheared away abruptly, falling to nothing over a long, long drop . . .

Rose gripped Ianto's arm. 'Ianto – we have to check the edge.'

Ianto stopped and turned to her. Then he nodded, and on and up they continued.

Soon they reached the large, flat stone that lay at the top of the mountain, a metre or so from the edge. Rose paused, fascinated for a moment, to watch the wind scouring its bare surface with tiny particles of snow – like sand on a windswept beach. Then she joined Ianto to creep on all fours to the very edge of the mountain, until their heads were poking out over the precipice, looking down the drop of the sheer cliff. At first, Rose couldn't see anything below. Thick, windblown mist clung to the mountain. Then the mist cleared, momentarily. Enough for their gaze to drop, dizzyingly, to the base of the cliff – rubble and stones, large and small. Rose remembered, with a shiver, how Ianto, as a giant, had fallen down here, cracking his head on a stone and nearly dying. But there was no one down there now.

The mist returned, shrouding their view of the mountain's base. Edging backwards, they saw that the mist was billowing around them too. It was as if they were perching on a long island in the middle of a fast-shifting grey sea.

And then a barcud coch – a red kite – emerged from the mist before them, like a flying fish leaping from stormy waves. Letting the wind sweep its body before them, navigating neatly with its magnificent forked tail, it schooned low over their heads, and they turned as one to follow its progress. The bird flew so low that Rose could see right into the sharp, yellow eye that was trained on the two of them.

Rose called out, '*Helpwch ni!* Help us! Please help us find Mum!' And above the roar of the wind, she heard a faint ship's whistle and saw that the huge bird was wheeling in the air, flapping with effort now, to come back to them against the wind. The barcud coch had the keenest eyes – laser sharp. He would see Mum and he would whistle, to let them know. He would find her—

Then came another sound, faint against the wind. The ring tone of a mobile. How had it reached them, up here on their windy island in the clouds? Ianto was watching her as if he knew something she didn't. Then she realised why. It was *her* ringtone. She pulled it from her pocket with cold hands and looked at it, dazedly. Unknown caller. Unknown caller! Now her heart leapt with hope – Mum! It had to be Mum, using someone else's phone!

'Mum!' she cried into it.

A gruff woman's voice said, 'Rose? That you? Sal here.'

And her heart plummeted, in the same way it had plummeted this morning, when she'd found Ianto's mamgu in the kitchen.

Sal continued, 'Got your number from some woman at your house. Listen, Rose, I've just heard about Cath – it was on the radio.'

Rose could not speak. But Sal continued, 'I'm going to help find her. You might not know this, but I'm a PI.'

Rose found her voice at last. 'A *what?*' she whispered.

'A PI – private investigator. Always have been. Only thing I wanted to be, after Eddie disappeared. And I've found lots of missing people. But not Eddie. Not him. But I think what's going on now is linked to him, somehow.'

Now Rose clung to her phone, clung to Sal, on the other end. 'Oh Sal, please, please help us find Mum! Mr Lewis is already investigating, and he's organised a search – it's happening right now—'

'Who's Mr Lewis?' interrupted Sal, sharply.

'My friend Ianto's dad. He's a policeman.'

'Policeman,' said Sal. There was a pause. Then she said, 'I don't work with policemen. Listen, I'm heading your way now, and I'm going to—'

Her voice was severed as the phone cut out. Rose lowered

the mobile and looked at it. No reception, suddenly – not one bar. And in the time it took to speak, briefly, to Sal, the clouds had descended even further – or perhaps the foggy sea around them had risen – so it was as if the grey mist was scuffing the tops of their heads. The barcud coch continued to circle above them, tailfeathers dipping and adjusting. Then all at once it turned its head to look beyond them and, with sudden urgency, flapped its long wings to lift and disappear upwards into thick, billowing cloud, followed by something – something shooting out of the mist, something as long as the kite, but swifter – long and thin, that almost caught the barcud's rapidly disappearing tail feathers. Then the head of the pursuer dipped forward, performing a graceful arc and falling, fast, to the ground to stick head-first into the snow on a hummock just in front of them.

Rose and Ianto paused before hurrying forwards and standing before it.

An arrow, fletched with feather, its tip buried in the snow. They glanced at each other, and then, without a word, they broke into a run – stumbling ahead through the fog. *We must steer clear of the edge of the mountain*, thought Rose, desperately, but where was the edge of the mountain?

Reaching out, she grabbed for Ianto's hand and he dragged her along until she, breathlessly, matched his pace, so that at least, whatever happened, they were together. All they could hear now was the roaring of the wind. The mist rushed past them, making them feel as if they were running faster than they were, because they were not running fast, though they were trying their best. The wind was too strong, and they were tiring already, the snow-covered heather and old bracken catching their feet and draining their energy. And the cold was beginning to bite into their bones.

Then they heard sounds from behind them. Very faint at first, growing louder. The thump and thunder of galloping horses – many, many horses. Shouts – harsh, loud, indecipherable. A horn – again and again, strident blasts, and Rose wanted to cover her ears to stop the sound, but she couldn't – she needed her hands to run, to save her when she tripped on an old, rutted root of heather, falling headlong into mud and snow and landing, with a painful jar, on her outstretched palm.

Now came the dogs. Barking, howling dogs, approaching at pace. Ianto pulled her up by the arm and they ran again, chased by sounds. Rose could feel the ground vibrating now with the weight of pounding hooves.

Something fizzed past Rose's ear, landing flat, skidding across the snow in front of her. Another arrow. And then another, and another.

Now they entered a forest. This was not the wood, the known place, but a forest, a dark and unknown place. Tall trees stretched upwards for metres and metres – conifers, whose prickly branches swiped at their faces. The place felt foreign and ancient.

An arrow flew between their heads, almost skimming their ears, so close that Rose saw its fletched tail spinning as it outran them and embedded itself, vibrating, in the tree ahead. Soon they were at that tree, then they were on again, stumbling forwards.

Rose thought to herself, *This is it. We're going to die. Mum, wherever you are, I'm so sorry – I didn't care for you like I should. Then I lost you, and I haven't found you. I can't find you* . . . She felt tears streaming down her face and she turned her head to look at Ianto, racing desperately beside her through the trees.

And then they both tripped over an exposed root and fell on to a bed of dry, brown pine needles.

Chapter 18

A woman's voice, from close behind them, screamed '*Daliwch! Digon!* Hold! Enough!'

Then she shouted, '*A fasech chi'n lladd plentyn eich meistr?* Would you kill your master's child? Leave this place, at once! Return from whence you came.'

Then all sound ceased. Though her eyes were screwed tightly shut, Rose felt the darkness beneath the trees lift.

Snow crunched and her coat swished as she sat up and opened her eyes. The tall conifers had disappeared. She and Ianto were sitting on open, snow-covered ground, and mist swirled about them.

In front of them was a tall woman with long, curly black hair which blew about her face in the icy wind. She was looking down at them, pulling the hair from her eyes and holding it above her head in a small, white fist, the better to see them. Rose looked down and saw, to her amazement, that pale, bare feet, as white as the snow she stood on, poked from the hem of her long, brown dress.

As they scrambled to their feet, the woman spoke again. '*Rose ac Ianto,*' she said. Then she smiled. 'Do not be afraid. You have encountered the Wild Hunt. The Hounds of Annwn. Look upon it as a test, a signal. For you shall soon enter the Otherworld.'

Rose glanced at Ianto, who was staring at the woman, a glazed expression on his face. She swallowed. '*Pwy ydych chi?*' 'Who are you?' she asked.

The woman chuckled and tilted her head to one side, examining Rose's face. 'You know my name,' she answered.

'But I don't.'

The lady laughed again, letting go her fist so that her wild, black hair fell back over her eyes. Then she put her hands to her mouth and called, 'Eira!'

Seconds passed. Then, from out of the mist stepped a magnificent white horse, saddleless, her head held high. As the woman grasped the long mane, the horse trotted forwards and the woman ran with her before leaping lightly on to her back.

'You know my name,' she cried again from high up on her back, 'and soon you'll know my story.'

Then the mist cleared to reveal a long, undulating plateau, studded with huge, white wind turbines that disappeared off into the distance.

'Don't go!' Rose was running after her. She stopped short, breathless, at the horse's side, suddenly nervous to be so close to this tall, shining animal. 'Can you help us – help us find Mum? Do you know where she is?'

The woman blew upwards to dislodge her curls for a moment, revealing the dark, sparkling eyes. 'Look under the seld, Rose,' she said, as the horse wheeled about and Rose sidestepped to avoid her strong, white legs.

'What seld? Whose seld? What do you mean?'

The horse lifted her chin and neighed, loudly. Then she began to canter away.

Rose shouted after them, 'Where is the Otherworld?'

'You will find it, soon enough.' Rose could hardly hear her voice for the wind.

'Is Mum there?'

No answer. The horse was gaining speed now, receding into the distance.

'How do we get there?' she shouted. But she knew it was no use.

Then, almost lost to the wind, '*Ffarwél!*' cried the lady and, although she had her back to them, a slim, white arm appeared, to wave goodbye. Then at last, like a spring uncoiling, the horse broke into a gallop, the long mane and tail and the woman's curly black hair streaming behind the two of them like banners in the wind.

Ianto came to stand beside Rose as they watched them gallop beneath the slowly-turning turbines, until they were no more than a tiny dot, that was soon swallowed up by the white landscape as they crested a snowy hillock and disappeared on the other side.

'Where are we, Ianto?' asked Rose. They turned and saw that the long hilltop extended behind them – with more slowly turning turbines, facing away from them this time.

'Mynydd y Grug,' he breathed, his eyes scanning the horizon.

Mynydd y Grug? 'Mynydd y Grug is miles away, Ianto!' said Rose. 'How did we get here?'

Ianto did not answer. Then, '*Do not be afraid*,' said Rose, slowly. And she felt her heart lifting. Turning to Ianto, she said, 'Ianto, who was she?'

'No idea.'

'She was beautiful.'

'She was,' said Ianto. 'She reminded me of you.'

His tired, brown eyes were fixed on hers. But Rose was still thinking about the woman.

'She said I know her name,' she went on. 'And you know what, Ianto? I feel like I *do* know her, somehow.'

Ianto stood in silence. Rose looked at him – properly, this time. His hands hung at his sides; his eyes were exhausted. The encounter with the strange woman had given her hope, but it didn't look as if that had happened for Ianto.

So Rose grabbed his hands and shook them up and down, grinning up at his face. 'Hey! Ianto! We escaped the Wild Hunt! The Hounds of Annwn! Yay! *Yay*?'

Ianto didn't return her smile.

'Yay,' he said, wearily. 'And next, we're heading for the Otherworld – wherever that is. I, for one, can't wait.'

As ever, when Ianto went into one of his deadpan moods, Rose went the opposite way. She wanted to burst out laughing at this hangdog statement. Then, suddenly, it hit her just what Ianto had been through, all because of her. All because he'd wanted to help her find Mum. So, instead of laughing, she kept her grip on his hands and said, 'Ianto – thank you.'

'For what?' he said.

'For everything. Everything we've just been through. Everything we're about to go through. I really, really appreciate it, Ianto. And I know Mum will too, when we find her.

'Because we *will* find her, Ianto,' said Rose, looking

steadily into his brown eyes. At last, she saw a little spark there. A spark that was lifting the corners of his mouth into a small, tired grin, despite himself. 'But first,' she went on, smiling back, 'let's get off this mountain. We have to find the seld – and I can only think of one, round our way. And that's Mr Williams's.'

Chapter 19

They hitch-hiked back to the village after climbing down off the mountain, taking a leaf out of the strange boy's book. Neither of them had hitched before, and they felt uncertain sticking out their thumbs on the roadside. To their surprise the very first passing car drew in just in front of them and the driver, a middle-aged woman, stared at them in disbelief through her wound-down window.

'*Ewch mewn, ar unwaith!* Get in, you two, at once!' she exclaimed. 'What in the world are you doing up here, alone, in this weather? Where are your parents?'

Good question, thought Rose, as she and Ianto slid, relieved, on to the back seat.

The woman was watching them in the rear-view mirror, waiting for an answer. Ianto cleared his throat. 'Um, they're at home,' he said, 'in Brynafon. Are you heading that way?'

'I wasn't,' she said, 'but I am now.' And she hit the accelerator and drove them the rest of the way in silence, every so often glancing at them in the mirror, then shaking her head. Rose caught her own reflection and understood her concern. She and Ianto were a state. Dripping wet, muddy, pale and shivering with cold.

As the woman's car drew up on the gravel in front of her house, Rose saw Mamgu's face peering from the kitchen window, and the next moment she was pulling open the front door and rushing out on to the drive.

'Rose and Ianto – thank goodness you're safe,' Mamgu said, drawing them both into an embrace. The driver, relieved, gave a little wave, reversed awkwardly then sped off down the track.

And Rose felt terrible. She'd promised Mamgu she'd phone her, on the hour, every hour, to let her know she was safe. She hadn't remembered to do so even once. What time was it, anyway? She checked her mobile as they piled into the kitchen. Four o'clock. And it was almost dark again, already.

Thankfully, Mamgu wasn't asking questions. She was fussing about making them mugs of tea, running baths and instructing them to hang their wet clothes on a dryer in front of the stove.

When they were sitting at the kitchen table, warm, clean and dry, Mamgu said, '*Nawr te*. I don't need to know where you've been today – the important thing is you're both home and safe. But—'

Then Rose remembered. 'Mamgu!' she exclaimed. 'Did they find Mum?'

Mamgu, who'd put on a stern face in an attempt to give them a lecture, softened sadly as she looked at Rose, and Rose knew the answer before she said a word. Of course they hadn't. Mamgu would have told them straight away, if they had.

'No, *cariad*. Not yet,' she said, gently. 'But Tegwyn and the boys at the station are doing everything they can to find her. There'll be another search tomorrow. They're putting the investigation into the stolen staff on hold, so they can devote all their resources to it. Tegwyn can't tell us much, but I believe that Delyth was able to give him some information . . .' Here Mamgu tailed off, looking uncomfortable. Then she continued, 'And Cerys and your mami, Ianto, have been busy too. They've set up a Facebook page and they've been putting up posters everywhere, with Mami's photo on them.'

'Which photo?' asked Rose.

'A lovely one,' said Mamgu. 'From her Facebook page. I think it was taken on her birthday – it's her with a cake.'

Pain twisted inside Rose. She'd taken that photo. Only a few weeks ago – Mum's thirty-ninth birthday. And Rose had baked the cake as a surprise for Mum – her first attempt at cake making, and it hadn't gone too badly – well, Mum had said it was delicious, anyway. Rose had stuck thirty-nine candles on it, lit them, and took the photo just before Mum had blown them all out. She could see the picture in her mind's eye – Mum's delighted face, shining happily in the light of the little flames. The photo was still on her phone.

All at once, Rose was weary, so very weary.

She felt herself wavering and slumping at the table, heard herself mutter, 'Ianto, we have to get up to Mr Williams's . . .' then she fell face forward on to the kitchen table, fast asleep.

Chapter 20

It was the next morning. Rose and Ianto were standing outside Mr Williams's cottage. Behind them, the rusting old farm machinery rested under snow – odd prongs and old, moulded metal seats protruding here and there.

It was very quiet up here. Del's crate, which stood outside the haybarn, was empty – but for her raggy blanket, the edge of which peeped out of the door, and the metal bowl of water standing outside. The battered grey Land Rover was parked in the yard, but the quad bike, that Mr Williams used to get about on his steep fields, was gone, and the place felt deserted.

Ianto knocked at the door. They waited for a bit, shuffling uncomfortably on the flagstones outside. There was no answer. Ianto turned to Rose and whispered, '*Awn ni fewn?* Shall we go in?'

Rose hesitated. Actually, they were about to trespass, on Mr Williams's property. It didn't feel good. But – they had to. 'OK,' she whispered back. 'But let's be quick. And if he comes back, we can explain – everything. And tell him it was an emergency.'

Ianto nodded. Then he put his hand to the door-handle and pulled it down, slowly. It opened inwards and they stepped quietly down on to the flagstone floor.

There was the seld, right in front of them – big, solid and plain. The open, backed shelves at its top were brimming full of plates standing, cups hanging and all sorts of bits and bobs besides. Painted eggs, plastic daffodils, china ornaments, shells, pebbles, each telling a story, a story about a certain time, a certain occasion, which was now in the past.

Looking down, Rose saw that there was a last, low shelf at the bottom, on which Mr Williams kept lots of old-looking brass and copper pots and pans. And below that, only three or so inches high, were six stout legs.

Rose looked at Ianto. He said, 'Go ahead. I'll keep a watch out for Uncle.'

Rose had to lie on the floor to look under the seld. She sneezed, loudly, breathing in the dust of many years. It was dark in the cottage – there was only one small window in this room, but it would have been dark under the seld even if there'd been several.

'I can't see a thing, Ianto. Wait – I'm going to feel under it.'

Edging closer she reached under the seld with her arm and swept her hand about. She sneezed, again, and hoped Mr Williams wasn't about to burst through the door and demand to know what they were up to—

Wait a minute – 'Ianto – there's something here!' What was it? Adjusting her position on the hard, stone floor, she reached in again and pulled something out. Something cold and round and flat. But that wasn't what she'd felt first of all. And so she swept again with her hand, and her fingers closed around something the size and shape of her little finger.

She sat up with the two objects in her hand. Ianto craned over her to see them. The flat, round thing turned out to be a big, brown coin. 'Hey,' said Ianto, taking it from her hand. 'This is an old penny. Look.' Sure enough, along with a seated figure in a helmet, holding a trident, were the words ONE PENNY. And a date, 1967. Ianto whistled and said, 'That's pretty old.'

'Do you think this is what the lady on the horse meant us to find?' asked Rose. 'An old penny? Maybe we have to pay for something with it?'

'Maybe,' said Ianto, doubtfully. 'Or maybe it's just the kind of thing you'd find under an old seld, in a really old house. What's that other thing?'

Rose held the dust-covered object between her thumb and forefinger, a little gingerly. It looked like an old, short brown root, slightly shrivelled. 'What *is* it, do you think?' She looked up at Ianto.

Ianto took it, bent it till it snapped to reveal a pale centre, sniffed at it and said, 'I'd say it's an old chip that fell off Uncle's plate, decades ago.'

Rose gave a short laugh, but inside she was disappointed and anxious. What if they didn't find anything else? She couldn't believe that the old penny was any use. She felt a sudden flash of anger towards the woman with the horse, for not telling them exactly what they needed to find; what they needed to do.

She sighed. 'Look, I'm just going to have another quick sweep under here.' And she reached her arm under the seld once more, feeling along the floor with her hand. Nothing but dust. 'Oh, Ianto,' she said, despairing, 'I don't think—'

Thump! From upstairs. As if someone had dropped a large, heavy book on the floor.

She and Ianto froze, alert.

Silence.

'Uncle?' said Ianto, tentatively.

Then he began to creep, as noiselessly as possible, across the room to the open staircase in the corner. 'Uncle?' he called softly, up the stairs. 'Is that you?'

Silence again, from the beamed ceiling. Rose was still on the floor, motionless. Then Ianto began to climb the stairs, treading carefully on the old wooden boards – when one of them creaked, loudly, under his boots. Wincing, Ianto raised his foot to step back again and, like a small tempest, a figure burst into the room from the top of the stairs as if it'd been shot from a catapult, shoving Ianto aside so his back hit the wall and he yelled out in pain. The figure leapt the final few steps and scrambled over Mr Williams's sofa as it made a bid for the front door and freedom. In the meantime, Rose was drawing out her arm and trying to scramble to her feet when she felt something collide with her legs and heard the terrible, cracking impact of a pair of knees on a hard, flagstone floor, closely followed by a stream of swearwords.

She leapt upright, heart beating fast, to see a boy, about their age, rolling to and fro on the floor, grasping his legs. 'Aah! *Fy nghoesau!* My legs! What the hell are you doing, lying on the floor?'

But he didn't roll for long before he was up again, hopping, wincing, heading for the door. Too late – Ianto got there first. And he stood, arms folded, in front of it, barring his way. Spinning to face Rose again, cradling one of his shins in his hands, Rose saw, in shock, that it was the boy. The boy in the parka with the fur-lined hood. The hood was down now, so she could see his face clearly. He had longish, shaggy brown hair and his skin was pale, emphasising large, dark, darting eyes. As these eyes stared at her he stopped hopping and put down his leg. She saw fear flash in his eyes, then saw it covered up, swiftly, as he frowned and said, in a voice full of bravado, 'You? Not you *again*. You fancy me, or something? Every time I turn round, you're there. Who are you, anyway?'

'Who are *you*, more like?' said Rose, hotly. 'You're the one who's following *me*!'

The boy looked at her, looked round at Ianto, standing in front of the door, and laughed. 'Got your minder guarding the door, eh? So I can't escape? Ha. I assure you that I *can* escape. I can escape from anywhere, me.'

Ianto said, 'Hey, Rose asked you a question. Who are you? And what are you doing in my uncle's house?'

'Tough guy, is it?' said the boy, squaring up to him with a side-stepping boxers' dance, fists clenched at his sides. Then he turned round, winked at Rose and said, 'Noddy. You can call me . . . Noddy.'

'*Noddy?*' Wasn't that the name of a gnome, or something?

'Yeah – Noddy,' he said, nodding. 'What's wrong with Noddy? It's a fine name.' He grinned. 'Noddy Holder – that's my name.' Then he looked from one to the other, smirking. 'Geddit? *Noddy Holder.*'

They didn't get it. 'Noddy Holder. Right,' said Rose uncertainly, to peals of laughter from the strange boy. Now he was shaking his head, in disbelief. 'You two been living under a stone or something?' he said.

'Haven't got much of a sense of humour, have you?' he went on.

'OK, Noddy,' said Rose, giving him the benefit of the doubt. 'I'm Rose, and this is Ianto.'

Ianto said, stiffly, 'And this is my uncle's house. What are you doing here?'

'What are you two doing here, more like? Sneaking in when he's not around, lying on the floor . . . looking for something? What you looking for?'

'We're looking for my mam, that's what,' said Rose, suddenly wanting to cry and screwing up her eyes in annoyance. She wasn't going to cry, not in front of this boy. Her voice shook as she went on, 'She's disappeared.'

She stared, defiantly, at Noddy, though her eyes were brimming with tears. His grin dropped for a moment, and he seemed at loss for words.

Then, 'Lost your mam, is it?' he said. 'Ha! Think you'll find her under the seld, do you?'

Before Rose could react, Ianto leapt forwards from the doorway and grabbed the boy around the collar to shove him backwards on the table, so his head was flat against the table top and his flailing arms were scattering piles of newspapers on to the floor. 'Wha—' he began, his eyes bulging in shock.

'Did you hear what Rose just said?' yelled Ianto, his face tight with anger. 'Her mam has *disappeared*, you complete *moron*.' Then, 'This–isn't–a–joke,' he said, jerking the boy's head up and down on the table top with each word.

He'd taken the boy by surprise, but it wasn't long before Noddy stopped flailing, got his own hands round Ianto's neck and begun to squeeze, hard. 'Aaargh!' cried Ianto, letting go the parka to pull the boy's hands away, while Noddy kept his grip, straightened up, pushing Ianto forward as he did so and then, to Rose's horror, brought his own head forward, swiftly, viciously, to crack his skull into Ianto's forehead.

'AAAAH! You bastard!' cried Ianto, bending double and cradling his head in his hands as Noddy let go Ianto's neck and reached down inside his parka with his right hand.

'Ianto!' cried Rose, leaping towards the boy and grabbing at his arms from behind him. 'He's got something in his coat!' Was it a knife? The next thing she knew, Noddy, swearing loudly, punched his elbow hard into her stomach, and she collapsed, bottom-first, on to the stone floor, winded and gasping for breath.

At the same time, Ianto, bent double, head down like a bull, ran at the boy, connecting with his midriff and, with an 'Oof', knocking the air from his chest. Now it was Noddy's turn to collapse on the floor, his right hand – which had been delving down into his coat – freed just in time to break his fall. Rose saw something flutter to the ground with him, from inside his parka. Something small and rectangular. She and Noddy grabbed for it, but she got there first, leaping to her feet and retreating across the room to keep it to herself.

She looked down at it. It was the photo – the photo of her dad as a baby, Eddie, Mamgu Morris and Sal. Rose felt winded for a second time, breathless, as she stared at it. All went still, for a moment, as she looked up to meet Noddy's eyes, and saw the mixture of fear and hatred in them. 'You give that back,' he said, in a hoarse, shaky voice, reaching out his hand. 'Now. It belongs to me.'

'It does not belong to you,' cried Rose, her own eyes narrowed, holding it behind her back. She was not going to lose this photo, of her dad, a second time. 'You *stole* this. It's *my* photo – my family. It belongs to me. I'm keeping it.'

With a desperate roar, Noddy launched himself at Rose, who stepped back, collided with the sofa and fell backwards on to its cushions. Before she knew it, Noddy had jumped on top of her and was reaching, desperately, behind her back to grab the photo – his parka pressing into her face and the smell of his fear-filled sweat filling her nostrils. She shrieked with surprise and anger, struggling against his strong, wiry body as his fingers found the photo and pulled. She could feel the picture creasing, buckling, tearing behind her back, but she wasn't going to let go. Ianto was pulling at the boy from behind, and then, over the yells and screams that filled the room, they heard a loud voice shout,

'Whoah, whoah, *whoah!* What in heaven's name is going on here?'

Mr Williams.

The three of them fell apart and turned to face him. Rose saw that Noddy was holding part of the torn photo, which he quickly pocketed, and that tears were now streaming down his face. Then, with a turn of speed that took them all by surprise, he dodged past Mr Williams and Del – who was standing just behind him – out, into the yard. As he did so, he called to Mr Williams, 'So long, Tomo – and thanks.'

Tomo, thought Rose. Where had she heard that name before? As they all piled out of the cottage they saw Noddy leaping on to the back of the quad bike, turning the key to start the engine then speeding off with a buzzing roar, dodging old farm machinery till he was out on the open drive, standing up like a charioteer – both hands on the handlebars, hair streaming back in the wind.

'Hey there! Come back, boy!' shouted Mr Williams, sprinting after him with Del, who was barking madly. 'We can sort this out – whatever's happened, we can sort it out.'

The quad bike slowed for a moment, enough for Noddy to turn and shout, in a high, shaky voice – 'Hey, Rose. Sorry you've lost your mam. I really am. But I've lost my whole family. *My whole family* – every, single, one of them . . .' And he turned forward again and, with this movement, something long and dark dropped out of his parka and fell, bouncing, on to the frozen, rocky track. He didn't seem to notice, and his back retreated before them as the quad bike buzzed, bumping, down the rutted drive. Rose and Ianto broke into a run now too. Del, enjoying the chase, was well ahead, sprinting, barking away, keeping pace with the bike all the way to the flag.

'Del!' yelled Mr Williams. 'Get back here, girl!'

And she did, stopping reluctantly at the end of the drive, giving a last bark for good measure. The quad bike turned off down the track and disappeared from view and Mr Williams – who was puffing loudly with exertion – Rose and Ianto halted halfway along the drive and stared down at what the boy had dropped.

It was a piece of wood – about three feet long? – with a shining patina like dark honey. One end was smooth, rounded and almost black, and the other was freshly cut, sharp-edged, giving a glimpse of lighter wood within.

It was one half of the staff that had been stolen from the Canolfan – Bleddyn's staff.

Chapter 21

Mr Williams, Rose, Ianto and Del stared down at the piece of wood. Then Del backed away, whining. None of them wanted to touch it. Mr Williams sighed, shook his head and said, 'I knew it. He denied it, of course.'

'Noddy stole the staff, then?'

Mr Williams frowned and turned to his great nephew. 'What? Who's Noddy?'

'Noddy. Noddy Holder. The boy who's just made off with your quad bike.'

'*Noddy Holder?*' Mr Williams looked between the two of them, then his shoulders began to heave up and down and a moment later, 'Heh, heh, heh, heh, heh!' he gasped, wiping his eyes on the back of his coat sleeve. 'Noddy Holder! Dear, dear, dear. The little rascal. Heh, heh, heh, heh, heh!'

'Yeah, so what's the joke, Uncle?'

Grinning, Mr Williams said, 'Noddy Holder was the lead singer of a band in the seventies – band called Slade. Still is, for all I know. Shouldn't think you two have heard of Slade, have you?'

'We have, actually,' said Rose, looking at Ianto with a frown. Eddie had scratched *Slade* on old Armitage's car. And he'd stuck that poster above the bunkbed where he'd slept, back at Mamgu Morris's house. Then Rose remembered something else. It was Eddie's friend, the one who'd told him to vandalise the car, who'd been called Tomo. 'Mr Williams,' she blurted. 'He called you Tomo.'

'Yes, bach. That's his name for me. I told him my name was Thomas, and he said he'd call me Tomo. Little rascal,' he repeated, shaking his head fondly.

'So what was his real name, then?' asked Ianto. 'And . . . and what's going on? How come you two are thick as thieves all of a sudden?'

'Never got his real name. He didn't tell me it, and I didn't want to pry. Turned up here on Christmas night – took shelter in the haybarn, trying to hide. Del found him. Del took him under her wing – brought out her maternal instincts, he did. You know what she did?'

They both looked at Del and she looked back, slowly wagging her tail. Then Mr Williams cleared his throat, in a very familiar way. *Uh-oh, he's going into story-telling mode,* thought Rose, and she knew this might take some time. She couldn't help glancing sidelong at Ianto, and he gave her a quick wink in return.

'*Ahem.* Gwenllian and me'd decided we were going to go for it, Christmas day. Christmas turkey and all the trimmings,' he began. 'That's why I wanted to get back up here, in good time, to tidy up and get started on the cooking. It was, oh, about six, I should think, and we'd just pulled the turkey crown out of the oven. Looked pretty good, it did – golden, crispy skin, tender white flesh.' Then, 'Sorry, bach,' he said, smiling at Rose. 'Keep forgetting you're a whatsisname. Veggie. Anyway, we put it down on the table, while Gwenllian set to making the gravy and I mashed potatoes, and we were talking and singing a bit, and so on. I'd left the door and window open a little, because the place was getting steamed up with all the cooking, and next thing we knew we turned round and the whole damn turkey crown had disappeared! Nothing but an empty dish! And no sign of Del, the scamp.

'I pulled on a coat and went out into the snow, followed Del's pawprints to the haybarn, expecting to see her tucking in to that piece of turkey, with a very guilty look on her chops. But she wasn't. She was standing in front of a big bale of straw, like a sentinel. No sign of the turkey. And when I came close, she barked! Barked, at me! When she saw I wasn't going to back off she scuttled behind the bale and, when I peered round it, that's when I saw him, cowering against the barn wall, shivering, a half-eaten turkey crown in his hands. And Del stood in front of him, like she was protecting him, and gave another warning bark. I could see he was about to make a dash for it, again – like he had when he was hitching a lift; like he did just now – but I talked to him. Told him he was welcome to the turkey – told him to come inside and get warm by the fire and eat a proper meal, with me and Gwenllian and Del. That, whatever his story was, we would be glad to have his company this Christmas.'

At this, Rose felt a huge pang of shame. She hung her head, unable to hold Mr Williams's blue-eyed gaze. Mr Williams had, so naturally, been so generous to this boy. The boy without a family – because Rose knew, though he hadn't told the truth about his name, that his tears and his fear and what he'd said about losing his family were true. And what had she and Ianto done? They'd questioned him, harangued him, fought with him . . . Two against one. She glanced at Ianto, wondering if he felt bad too. Like her, he was looking down. Then he raised his head and she saw him wince and touch his forehead – the place where the boy had nutted him.

He'd hit her too, dug his elbow into her stomach and wrestled with her on the sofa. She pulled the photo from her pocket. It was creased and ripped, but she'd managed to hold on to the bigger part of it. She could see Sal, Mamgu Morris, baby Dad – but no Eddie. The boy with no family had the little bit of photo with Eddie on. All that remained of him on this piece was his arm, embracing his mamgu's neck. Perhaps, thought Rose, the boy stole the photo because he had no family, and he wanted to pretend that this was his family. That thought made her feel even worse. She looked up again, heavy-hearted, as Mr Williams continued,

'That night, after we'd all eaten, we made up a bed for him in the spare room, upstairs. He was exhausted by that point, talking nonsense. Wanted to know why there was snow on the ground, how come it was so cold, odd things like that. We told him he'd be welcome to stay here as long as he liked, warm and fed, till he got himself sorted out. I found some winter clothes for him because, do you know, all he had on under that parka were a pair of old jeans and a T-shirt. Sorted him out with long-johns, jumper, thick socks and that woolly hat – the one that Mary knitted for me – the one that got me into all that trouble with your dad, Ianto. Heh, heh, heh!

'Next morning, his bed was empty. Upped early, I guessed, and I thought, maybe, we wouldn't see him again.

Was just putting my feet up with one of my papers – Saturday's, it was, that I hadn't got round to reading – and a cup of coffee after checking on the sheep, when Del came to the door, whining to get in. But she wouldn't settle when I opened it. Kept barking and turning in circles, distressed. "What is it, lass?" I asked her, and off she went, running down the drive, expecting me to follow. I pulled on my coat and I grumbled a bit, I'll own. Then I heard the hunt, down in the wood – right where they shouldn't be. So I grabbed my hand axe – you can never be too sure, with that lot – and headed down there as fast as I could. Caught up with it all by the cromlech, there. Saw the dogs, haring after something or other – couldn't make out what. Then the horses arrived, and the whole mad circus was upon me. And, well, you know the rest.

'I had a feeling, a little, nagging feeling, that our young visitor had something to do with all this. That he was still on the scene somewhere – hadn't gone far. Then when Tegwyn confronted me with the hat, I knew he must have stolen the staff. Why – I just couldn't imagine. Still can't.

'So when you two left, I set out to find him and, sure enough, there he was, hiding in the haybarn again. Denied having anything to do with the staff.' He paused, and the three of them looked down at the piece of wood lying, motionless, on the icy track. 'That was two days ago,' Mr Williams went on, 'and he's been around and about ever since. Been gaining in confidence,' Mr Williams chuckled, fondly, 'getting cheeky. Little tearaway, really. Like having a squirrel in the house. Look out! Went through all my old records and put them on. Showed him my guitar and, fair play, he wasn't too bad on it. But I had a feeling he wouldn't be here long. Had a feeling that, underneath it all, he was afraid, badly afraid; and that there was something he had to do, something he had to find. And I guess, from what he said just now, that's his family.'

There was a pause. Rose thought, *He's doing the same thing as me, then. Looking for his family. Maybe we can work together—*

Then, 'But what are we doing standing about, looking at this old stick?' interrupted Mr Williams, staring accusingly at them as if they'd been wasting his time. He took a breath in and seemed to brace himself before leaning down and picking up the half-staff.

Straightening, he weighed it in his hand then stuck it inside his coat. 'That boy's just stolen an expensive bit of kit,' he went on. 'But he'll not get far on it. Come on, let's track him down.'

They hurried back to the house, then Mr Williams stopped on the drive, suddenly, and turned to Rose. 'If that's all right with you, *cariad*,' he told her, gently. 'Because our priority is finding your mam. But I've got an odd feeling. An odd feeling . . . that this boy, and the missing staff, have something to do with it all.'

Rose stared into Mr Williams's anxious, kind blue eyes. 'So have I,' she said.

She turned to Ianto, who nodded. 'Yeah,' he agreed. 'Yeah. Let's go.'

Chapter 22

Rose and Ianto helped Mr Williams attach a flat-bed trailer to the back of the Land Rover. They'd need this to bring the quad bike back – if they found it. Then, when they were about to set off, Ianto said, 'I've just remembered something,' tearing back through the door of the cottage while Mr Williams and Rose waited in the Land Rover, the engine idling. Behind them in the back, Del barked, restlessly, trying to peer through the seats to see what was going on. She didn't like it when they split up.

Ianto hurried back and slammed the door shut behind him, buckling his seatbelt; Del barked again, as if to say, 'Come on, then!' and Mr Williams set off, rolling down the drive with the trailer bumping and bouncing lightly behind them.

Rose looked, intrigued, at what Ianto had fetched from the house. It was a book – an old, thick, hardback book. There was no name on its plain, brown cover, but as she gently took it from him and turned it, she saw that its spine was marked, in faded gold letters, *Gwyddoniadur Celtaidd* – A Celtic Encyclopedia – and that the name of its author was Thomas Williams. 'Old Thomas Williams!' she exclaimed. 'Good Old Thomas Williams!'

Old Thomas Williams was Mr Williams's great, great, grandfather – author and historian.

'Ha!' said Mr Williams, glancing down at the book then raising his eyes to the road once more. 'Anything you want to know about the Celts, about Cymru fach, just ask Old Thomas Williams. He's your man. Never mind Google – or whatever it is you kids do these days.'

He turned off the drive at the flag and started down the track, while Ianto, head down, riffled through the book's pages.

They got as far as Rose's house when Mr Williams said, '*Beth yn y byd*— What the—' and stepped on the brake, bringing the Land Rover and its clattering trailer to a halt. The small figure of Mamgu was standing in the middle of the road, arms waving to flag them down.

Hastily, Rose looked at her mobile. Argh! Two hours had passed, and she'd forgotten to call Mamgu, *again*. Mr Williams was rolling down his window. 'Yes, Mary?' he called wearily to his sister.

'Rose – are you all right?' asked Mamgu, hurrying to the side of the Land Rover, ignoring him.

'So sorry, Mamgu,' said Rose. 'I forgot.'

'Have you eaten yet?' Mamgu went on, looking round at them all now. 'It's coming up to one o'clock, you know.'

Rose said, 'Um, not yet, but someone's stolen Mr Williams's quad bike and—'

'Never mind that,' said Mamgu. 'Wait here.' And she hurried inside Rose's house again. Rose could see her buzzing about in the kitchen, through the window. Mr Williams drummed with his fingers on the steering wheel, then looked at his watch. Soon Mamgu was back again, passing a handful of bulging, silver-foil-wrapped packages through the window, together with a big Thermos flask. 'That should keep you going,' said Mamgu. 'Now. Are you all warm enough?'

Mr Williams ignored this one. Ianto sighed and said 'Yes, Mamgu,' and Rose nodded, smiling at her. Then Mamgu turned to her brother. 'Thomas – you look after these two,' she instructed, firmly. 'Rose, Ianto – I know there are important things you need to do to find Mami. And I have no doubt that you'll succeed – as you have in the past. I'll be here, when you all get back.'

Then she stepped back on to the drive, raised her hand and called '*Ffarwél!*'

Mr Williams wound up the window, Rose and Ianto waved back at her, and then they continued down the track, trailer bumping along behind them.

After a bit, Ianto said, 'D'you think Mamgu knows something we don't?'

'Mary *always* knows something we don't,' replied Mr Williams, with a sigh.

They were driving through the village now. It was Friday, one of those odd days between Christmas and New Year that can't make up its mind whether it's a normal, working day or a holiday. Most of the shops were shut. Dirty snow littered the streets, and only a couple of people were out and about – Mr Williams raised a hand to one of them: an old guy in a cloth cap who was ducking into the Lion. No sign of the quad bike, or the boy.

The sky above was dark already and cold rain was beginning to spit down. Mr Williams flicked on the windscreen wipers and the headlights. Soon the Land Rover was heading out of the village for the main road – the road that took you north, or south. And then Rose saw it, taped to a lamppost.

'Stop!' she cried.

Mr Williams drew in sharply and Rose and Ianto jumped out. Hurrying to the lamppost, Rose stared, numbly, into Mum's face. The poster was inside a plastic folder, to protect it from rain. In big letters, above her beaming face, lit by cake candles, were the words AR GOLL – MISSING then, in smaller letters, HAVE YOU SEEN THIS WOMAN? Last seen Boxing Day. Then came her age, her height, her weight. Rose didn't even know that Mum was five foot five. That she weighed nine stone. She felt sick and dizzy, and found herself gripping Ianto's arm. Below this were contact numbers, which, it said, were free and confidential.

Again, Rose wondered at everything everyone else was doing to find Mum. While she pottered about, uselessly, exhausting herself with the Wild Hunt and the strange, beautiful woman who spoke in riddles. And this boy, this stupid boy they were chasing after now. What was she doing? Nothing made sense. The poster blurred as her eyes filled with tears.

She felt Ianto tugging at her arm. 'Come on, Rose,' he said.

'What?' she asked, tearing her eyes from the poster to look at him. Too late, he averted his eyes from where they'd been, lower down the lamppost, and she followed his gaze and gasped in horror.

Beneath Mum's poster was another. On this one was a photo, but then again not quite a photo, something put together, with the edges smoothed off, of a man's face – a man's head and shoulders. Shaggy, dark hair hung around his face. Straight dark eyebrows, black, oval eyes, eyes that stared right into your soul. A mouth that did not smile. Rose shivered. Above the face it said *YDYCH CHI WEDI GWELD Y DYN HWN?* HAVE YOU SEEN THIS MAN? And below, contact numbers. The same ones, she realised, as for her mam.

They had put them together. This was him. This was the man. Someone – Delyth, she guessed – must have described him. A shiver rippled down her spine. 'He had antlers,' she heard herself saying as Ianto, gently pulling at her arm, steered her back to the Land Rover. 'They've left off his antlers . . .'

As she climbed back into the Land Rover she found Mr Williams looking at her. 'All right, bach?' he said, softly.

Rose nodded. Then Mr Williams released the handbrake and the Land Rover moved forward again.

'What do we reckon, then?' he said, as they approached the junction. 'Which way did he go?'

'South,' said Rose, sniffing back her tears. Really, she had no idea. But maybe the boy would want to head back the way he came – back to Mamgu Morris's? *He knows there's an empty house there.* Had she left the back door unlocked? She hoped she had, so he could get in and shelter. Then she remembered how he'd crept into the house that night, his frightened whisper – 'Mamgu! Mamgu?'—

Rose's phone was ringing. She closed her eyes, briefly, unable to stop her heart beating fast with hope. When she opened them she saw that it was an unknown caller, again. The hope died. Because this time she recognised the number, recognised the abrupt voice.

'Rose? Sal here.' A pause. She could hear Sal taking a breath in. Then, 'Do you believe in spirits?'

'I— *what?*'

'Spirits. Ghosts. Phantoms – whatever. I don't. Or, I *didn't*. Load of rubbish, I thought. But I do now. Oh, yes, I do now. Look, Rose, I'm heading your way – I'll explain when I get to your place—'

'Sal!' Rose said loudly, breaking into her stream. 'We're not at my place. We're heading south, to your neck of the woods. We might end up at your mamgu's house – I'm not sure. I'm with Ianto and his great uncle. See, someone stole his quad bike—'

'Quad bike!' shouted Sal.

What is wrong with Sal? Rose went on, 'Yes, Sal. There was a boy, you see, a boy in a parka, who was staying—'

'I've seen the quad bike,' interrupted Sal, a little more calmly, as if she'd taken another deep breath. 'Just now. Saw it coming in the opposite direction. Nearly came off the road, I did – the shock was so great. Sitting in a layby now – don't trust myself to drive.'

Mr Williams had just pulled out on to the main road. 'Sal, don't move,' said Rose. 'We're heading your way. We'll stop when we see your car, OK?'

The phone cut off. Sal was one of those people, Rose

thought, who never say 'hi' or 'bye'. Fair play to her.

'What's going on?' asked Ianto.

'It's Sal. My aunty,' said Rose. And despite everything, it felt good to say 'my aunty'. 'We were right,' she went on. 'The boy's heading this way – Sal saw the quad bike. It's got to be him. But she was talking about spirits – she was pretty distressed. She's in a layby somewhere here . . .' Rose scanned out of the window. 'There she is!' she called and Mr Williams indicated to cut across the lane and draw up in the layby behind a familiar, slightly battered blue car.

As Mr Williams pulled up the hand brake they saw Sal get out of the car and slam the door shut behind her. Rose was struck again by how tall she was, how awkwardly she moved. She strode urgently towards the Land Rover, as the four of them jumped down to greet her.

'Eddie's spirit,' she blurted at once, her arms spread out in agitation. 'Eddie's spirit was driving that quad bike.'

Chapter 23

No one knew what to say. Cars sped loudly by on the main road, tyres spitting grit and wet, and Rose shivered in the cold, drizzly rain.

Sal looked round at them with wide, distressed eyes. 'The first time was bad enough,' she continued. 'But at least then I could say to myself, *No. No – I must have imagined it. I must have been hearing things.* But when I saw it again, just now . . .'

'When did you see it the first time?' asked Rose, gently.

'On Christmas Eve. Not long before you and your mam showed up. I heard a commotion next door. Remember, Eddie used to live next door. I believe that Eddie's spirit returned home and, of course, found strangers there. This would have angered him, upset him. I could hear something going on on their doorstep – shouting, the guy next door telling someone to get off the premises. Then I heard more shouts, and a loud banging on their front door. Next thing I knew, a police siren was going off and I heard it stop right outside. I could see the car's light flashing through the curtains. Stayed inside, I did – I wasn't going to get involved. It had just started to snow then, I remember.

'Next thing I knew –' Sal swallowed. Her large eyes looked around at them all – 'Next thing I knew, something was trying to get in through my back door, which I keep locked, these days. Something was rattling at the handle. Then it was knocking on the glass. Course, I didn't think it was a spirit, at that point. I thought it was just a local kid. Something to do with the trouble next door. So I headed for the kitchen, to tell them to get out of my garden. I could see a shadowy shape, the size of a young boy – behind the frosted glass. Just an outline, with the dark garden behind it. Then I heard a voice. And it sounded just like Eddie. Just like Eddie, way back, when he was thirteen. Before he disappeared. And it said, in a loud whisper, "Aunty Nell, that you? Let me in!"'

Sal swallowed again. 'I froze. I literally froze, like a statue, to hear that voice again – after forty-nine years. The shape behind the glass was rattling the handle again. Then it called, "Sal!" And it was his voice. Eddie's voice. I'd know it anywhere. Now I really knew it was him. His spirit.

'I stood there in the dark kitchen, watching the moving shadow at the back door. *If I open the door,* I thought, *if I open that door – what will I see?* My heart was beating so fast and so loud I thought I might have a heart attack; so loud I thought the spirit would hear it, would break through the glass and open the door for itself. Then I saw the shape behind the door go still. It kind of slumped, and stopped rattling the handle. "Sal," it said, again, pitifully. "Help me, Sal. Let me in, will you? It's so cold out here . . ."

'It broke my heart to do it, but I tiptoed back, out of the kitchen, and quietly, quietly, closed the door behind me, so I couldn't hear the voice any more. Couldn't hear the knocking on the glass, the rattling of the handle. And I sat on the sofa, my hands over my ears, heart beating like mad, trying to make sense of what had just happened. But I couldn't. All I knew – and this broke my heart even more – was that Eddie really must be dead. To have come back as a spirit, like this, the spirit of a thirteen-year-old boy – he had to be dead. And it felt like my world had crashed down all around me. That everything I'd done since he disappeared, all my efforts to find him, were useless, meaningless. I had failed. Totally failed. I hadn't found Eddie, and now it was too late. And I hadn't protected Eddie, back when we were kids. I should have stopped him going up to Mamgu's . . . or I should have insisted on going with him, so I could look after him. But I'd just let him go. Let his dad drive him off. And now, he was dead – and, even worse, maybe – a restless spirit. An unhappy spirit . . . And then the doorbell rang.

'I thought it might be him, again, at the front door. This time, I thought, I'll answer it. I'll face it – him. I'll try to lay his spirit to rest – somehow. Rest in peace, as they say. I screwed up all my courage and opened the door . . . and you and Cath were standing there.'

Sal stared at Rose, clutching her hands together, just as she had on Christmas Eve. There was silence now, but for the roar and swish of passing cars.

Rose felt stunned. Poor, poor Sal. She wanted to hug her, but she knew that was not what you did, not with Sal.

Mr Williams cleared his throat and placed his hand on Del's head. Rose realised that, to him, none of this would make much sense. Ianto cleared his throat too, sounding just like his great uncle, and shuffled his boots.

It was up to her to respond.

'Sal,' she said. 'I'm not sure what's going on. None of us are. But one thing I – we; all three of us here – can tell you for sure, is that the boy on the quad bike – the one you think is Eddie's spirit – is real. I mean, he's a living, human being.' Rose remembered when he'd jumped on her, on the sofa back at Mr Williams's – his weight, his strong arms, the smell of his sweat. 'He's real,' she repeated, firmly. 'He's not a spirit. And we're going to find him again – and understand what's happening here.'

Chapter 24

Now they were turning right, suddenly, pulling off the track up the hill and crunching down a wet, overgrown drive. They'd decided, without any real evidence, to head for Sal's mamgu's place and look for the boy there.

There was no quad bike on the drive. No boy. Mamgu Morris's tall house loomed over Rose once again as Mr Williams stopped the engine and rain, which was falling heavily now, rolled freely down the windscreen, melting and blurring the detail in the stone of its walls. Just like the first time she'd come here, Rose didn't want to get out of the car.

Sal was already kneeling to retrieve the key from under the front mat – where Mum had left it, four, long days ago. During another, carefree life.

As Rose, Mr Williams, Ianto and Del jumped from the Land Rover the rain hit them, hard. Sal was standing outside the front door, key in hand, facing them. The familiar, anxious frown was on her face, but there was something more there now. Her eyes had shed that dead, lost look, and glittered purposefully. Rose thought, anxiously, *I hope we find the boy. I hope somehow, amazingly, he really is Eddie. Or that we find sixty-two-year-old Eddie. Either will do.*

Sal was speaking now, taking no notice of the rain that soaked into her hair and ran down her face.

'Right,' she said. 'No quad bike, but never mind. If he's in here, he'll have entered by the back door. So what we'll do is this. I'm going round to cover the back now. You –' she nodded at Mr Williams. 'What's your name?'

'Thomas.'

'You cover the front door. Close it behind you and stand just inside, in the hall. And you two –' she glanced at Rose and Ianto – 'go upstairs and flush him out, if he's up there. If he isn't, come downstairs and search every room. If he jumps out of a window, shout, and we'll all give chase.'

Mr Williams raised his eyebrows. 'Well, now,' he said. 'Steady on there! This isn't a hunt, you know – we don't want to frighten the lad . . .' But Sal wasn't listening. She was already disappearing round the side of the house. Mr Williams, shaking his head, stepped through the front door, as did Rose, Ianto and Del, who was whining anxiously.

Then they all did as they were told. Rose climbed the wooden stairs and felt a shiver run down her spine. It was very odd to be in this house again.

There was no one upstairs. Or downstairs. Nothing but old furniture and neglect.

They ended up in the back room, with the table and chairs, the iron range, full of dead ashes, and the seld.

The seld, towering over everything in the room. Dark wood, ornate carvings . . .

Rose whipped her head round to look at Ianto. He caught her eye and nodded. Again, there was a little space between the base of the seld and the floor. The faded red rug that sat in the centre of the room didn't reach this far – under the seld were rough, bare floorboards. She got down on hands and knees once more, then lay, stretching out her arm beneath it.

'What are you doing?' hissed Sal from the back door. 'He's not under there!'

Rose ignored her and felt about under the seld, aware that her wet coat sleeve and hands were getting filthy. But there was nothing there – nothing but balls of grey dust and little shoals of coal grit. Disappointed, she slumped, her arm outstretched. Then she turned her hand the other way, to feel upwards, her fingers exploring the unpolished, wooden base of the seld. Almost immediately, she felt something sticking downwards, only an inch or so thick – something solid, wooden, about a foot wide. Feeling around it, she realised that the front of it, set back from the face of the seld, was open.

A shelf! A secret shelf, unseen from the front. Gently, she put her fingers inside and felt something slim and flat. She pulled it out. Then she sat up, on the floor before the seld, with the object in her dusty hands. Looking up, she saw four faces staring down at her – Mr Williams, Sal, Ianto and Del.

It was a book – a thin book. But it was ancient, no doubt about that, because it was made of parchment, or vellum – the skin of a young animal. What they used to write on before paper was invented. Rose knew vellum, because the englyn her dad had given her had been written on a scrap of it.

A brightly-coloured picture of a woman, head held in profile, in a long, brown dress, adorned the cover. She had small, white feet; long, curly, black hair and, on her head, a crown. She was holding a hand up, with one pointed finger, as if she was asking them to stop and take notice. Around this picture were ornate, coloured patterns. And within these patterns was the title of the book, in Welsh.

Llyfr Erwain – or, *The Book of Erwain*.

Rose recognised the picture. It was the woman on the mountain with the wind turbines. Now she knew that she had been Erwain and, more than that, she knew that this Erwain was one of her ancestors – a princess, the sister of Berwyn and Bleddyn. She knew this because Ianto's mamgu had told her about her, in the summer. Had told her about this book – which was also called *Llyfr Coll Erwain* or *The Lost Book of Erwain*, because historians had been searching for it for centuries.

Now she had found *The Lost Book of Erwain*. Erwain herself had told her where to look.

She opened the book to learn Erwain's story, and read the whole thing aloud. It was written in Welsh, old Welsh, but they all understood every word.

Llyfr Erwain

Listeners! Hear this, the Story of Erwain.

Let it be known, then, that a Long Time Ago, a great king, whose name was Baruc, had built a magnificent hall in this kingdom. To Baruc and his queen were born three children – the princes Berwyn and Bleddyn, and a princess. Of Bleddyn and Berwyn, there are yet more stories to tell. But not here. For this book tells of their sister.

This sister was named Erwain, that is, Meadowsweet. Myrddin, the druid or wise man, came to their court, to see the baby Erwain. He told her tynged, that is, he told Erwain's fate. He said to her, as she lay in her cradle:

'You will do a stranger a great kindness. For that, you will become queen, twice. And for that, you will leave this land, and you will not return in our time.'

When her mother heard this, she wept, for she did not want to lose her daughter. So she took the baby from

its cradle and locked her up in a hut on the mountain,
with only a nursemaid to keep her company.

As the child grew, the nursemaid left. Erwain saw
only her mother, once a day, bringing food.
'Mother,' she asked, 'why do you keep me here, a
prisoner?'

'I keep you here because I love you.'

'You do not love me, Mother. If you loved me, you
would let me be free.'

At this her mother ran from the hut – weeping bitterly.
But she could not free Erwain, for fear that she would
leave the land. And so she kept her daughter a prisoner.
In truth, she was imprisoned too – by fear and sadness.

Erwain grew to be a young woman. Her father, the
great king, died, and her brother Berwyn took the
throne. A good king was he, also. And there are
many tales of his deeds. But this is the Book of
Erwain, his sister, so we shall not tell them here.

From Erwain's window, in the hut on the
mountain, she saw the sun rise and the sun
set, and she longed to be free. One friend had
she, and that was a drudwen – a
starling. Every day, the drudwen
came to her window, and when
Erwain fed her with crumbs she
chattered and whistled in thanks.

'O Drudwen, that I were
free as you,' she said.

The next day, Drudwen came to her window. In her beak was a key, and this she dropped on to the floor. That night, Erwain opened the door and escaped into the night. She ran through the dark forest in the valley below, going she knew not where, until she saw a man that was hanging in the air, his feet snagged in a hunter's trap. What did she but sever the rope to free him.

The man stood before her, and he was tall and handsome. 'Fair woman,' he said, 'I thank you. Will you go with me to a wonderful land where music is? Woman, if you come to my mighty people a torque of gold shall be about your neck: honey, wine, ale, fresh milk and beer you shall have there with me.'

Erwain went with the man to this land, and the land was called Annwn. There she found all that the man had promised, and more. For he was King of Annwn, and his name was called Cernunnos. He gave her a golden torque to wear about her neck, and he made her his queen.

One day, Erwain and Cernunnos reclined in a stately garden, rich with roses and the merry laughter of a company of fair men and women. 'Are you happy, my queen?' asked Cernunnos.

'How could I not be,' replied she, 'as queen in this fair land, free as a bird to go where I will, and with my beloved husband at my side?'

Then she remembered her *tynged*, that had been given by Myrddin, the druid. 'Perhaps,' she said, 'I shall be happier yet! For it is foretold that I shall be queen not once, but twice.'

At this, Cernunnos turned his face from her. For he knew that Erwain could only be queen once, in Annwn. To be queen twice, she must leave this land. And Cernunnos could not bear to lose Erwain. So, he locked her in a tower that was in that garden, and there he kept her, like a bird in a cage.

In the tower, Erwain wailed and rent her hair, shouting from the window, but it was as if the fair company did not hear her, for they continued to enjoy their pleasure garden – talking, dancing, laughing – and now the sight filled Erwain with horror.

After some time, a child was born to her – a baby boy. For fear that Cernunnos would take the child from her, she kept him hidden beneath her bed.

'I shall call you Eirwyn,' she whispered to the baby. Eirwyn, snow white, like a snowdrop. Because in this perfect land there were many splendid flowers, but no tiny, white snowdrops. No snowdrops, because there was no snow. No winter. Only long, balmy days, as if it were the month of May the year round. And Erwain longed for home. For Cymru – where lived her people, where the seasons could be harsh, and where there were dangers and heartbreaks, but yet, it was home. Hiraeth, a great longing, was upon her, and she hugged her baby to her and wept, and the child cried too – not knowing any better.

She had seen the truth. That even this beautiful land was full of suffering.

And then, she heard a twittering at the window. Looking up, she saw that Drudwen, the starling, was sitting on the sill outside. And in her beak, a key.

As before, she took the key and opened the door to the tower. It was night in that land, but the stars shone almost as bright as day. Running from the court, little Eirwyn wrapped inside her shawl, she followed Drudwen, who flew before her. A creature of both worlds, only she could guide her out of Annwn.

Within the forest, she spied Cernunnos in her path, sitting high upon a tall horse. 'Go back,' he commanded. 'If you will not, I will set my hounds on you and they will kill you.'

'I will not return to you. Let me go home.'

She turned her back on her husband and ran the other way. At this, Cernunnos roared with rage, and presently she heard the baying of hounds. Huge hounds they were, fearsome – the Hounds of Annwn. And behind them was Cernunnos, thundering on his great horse. Through the forest they chased her.

Though Erwain was fleet of foot, and though she was led by Drudwen into the densest part of the forest, she stood little chance. Presently, the hounds closed on her. Her last hope was to show baby Eirwyn to Cernunnos, that he would save his son. She scrabbled with her shawl to free him as she ran. But in her haste she tripped and fell. Drudwen screamed in fear as the hounds leapt upon Erwain.

At that very moment came from her shawl the tiny cry of a baby.

Cernunnos roared, 'Daliwch! Digon! Hold! Enough!' and the baying of the hounds ceased.

Then Erwain stood, holding her shawl tightly about her.

'What have you there?' asked Cernunnos, pulling up his horse before her.

'My son,' she replied.

'Give him to me,' said Cernunnos.

'I shall not,' she said. 'Let us go.'

'He is not yours to take. Give him to me.'

Erwain turned and fled again, holding her baby to her, Drudwen leading the way through the trees.

'Woman!' roared Cernunnos, galloping close behind. 'I cannot kill you, wretched woman. Nor can I kill our son. Go, then. Take him back to your miserable land. But hear this. I will have my son – he will come back to me.'

Erwain did not turn around.

She did not stop running as fast as she could, following the bird.

'Did you hear me, woman?' And Erwain, as she ran for her life, heard the loud sobs of her husband, Cernunnos. Through his tears, he repeated, 'My son will come back to me. If not this son, then another son. If not this time, then another time.'

hen Erwain came to the edge of Annwn. Before her was a large stretch of water. And on that water was a wooden boat. In the boat was a little man. Drudwen fluttered over the boat, and so Erwain knew she must step inside it.

'What will you pay me?' asked the little man.

Erwain pulled the golden torque from her neck and handed it to him. 'This,' she said.

The man accepted it, and he rowed Erwain and baby Eirwyn across the water. And, when they disembarked on the other side, the man rowed his boat away again.

resently, Erwain saw that she was standing upon the edge of Llyn y Fan Fwyn, in her own country. Weeping with joy and relief, she knelt to kiss the ground. Then she began the long walk over the mountain and back to the court of her kingdom, her baby prince clasped to her beneath the shawl.

Erwain found a different land to the one she had left behind. Many centuries had passed, in the short time she had been in Annwn. She learned, with a heavy heart, that her brother, Bleddyn, had murdered Berwyn and so had lost their precious kingdom.

Her own, royal line had died out – in its place a lawless state, a people cowering in fear before cruel, foreign overlords, a place where bandits ran amok.

But Erwain, aided by her people and by the will of God, laid claim to the throne of her land. Many battles were fought, and many died for their cause. But Erwain and her people overcame all. She was crowned queen and a golden time came upon the land. Farmers farmed, blacksmiths made tools and fine things, horsemen raised magnificent horses, and bards and musicians flourished and were well rewarded. The court of Erwain was a merry, peaceful place, and so was the kingdom.

In this way, Myrddin's *tynged* came true. For Erwain had been queen twice and, for that to come to pass, she had left her land and returned in a different age.

In time, Erwain died. And her son, Eirwyn, took the throne. And a fine king he made. But his is another book, and this is the Book of Erwain.

That is my story! If there be a lie in it, be it so! It is not I who made or invented it.

Chapter 25

Rose looked up, drawing in a deep breath.

No one spoke. She carefully closed the book and stared down at the image of Erwain on the front. She might have seen something interesting, if she'd turned to the very last page. But she didn't.

Mr Williams cleared his throat. Then he said, 'Well, well, well.'

Rain spattered and hit at the window.

Sal was frowning, hard. Then she said, 'OK. We've found an old book – about the *tylwyth teg*, the fair people, or somesuch – that, for some mad reason, Mamgu hid under the seld. It can't be true – and even if it is, it can't help us find Eddie; help us find Cath. And that's the only thing that's important now.'

She looked around at them, expecting them to agree with her, to put away this nonsense. Her gaze grew more and more incredulous when they didn't. As a last resort she fixed her dark eyes on Mr Williams. 'Come on, Thomas . . .' she began.

But Mr Williams was looking down now, at the open book that Ianto had just pulled from his bag and thrust in front of them. Old Thomas Williams's book – the Celtic Encyclopedia. He was pointing, silently, at one of its pages.

'Ha!' said Sal. 'Another old book. How's that going to help?'

Rose saw Ianto's finger shaking slightly as it pointed to the entry in bold type: **Cernunnos**. Under this was a paragraph of text in small writing. But what caught her eye and held it was the picture below the text.

The black-line illustration of a man, sitting crosslegged and surrounded by wild animals – something like a lion, a bull, a stag and a horse. A strange, antique image. The man was holding a snake in one hand, a torque in another. Another torque was around his neck. And, sprouting from the top of his head, were two, large antlers.

Chapter 26

Ianto was reading aloud in Welsh: 'Cernunnos is the horned god of the Celts – the god of fertility, life, animals, wealth and the Otherworld. He rules the land of Annwn, and is master of the Wild Hunt, also known as the Hounds of Annwn. In images from Celtic times, Cernunnos is depicted with the antlers of a stag, and is often seen holding or wearing torques. *The Lost Book of Erwain* is said to tell the story of the abduction by Cernunnos of Princess Erwain – daughter of Baruc, sister to Berwyn and Bleddyn – to the land of Annwn. Hundreds of years later, Erwain returned to Cymru together with a son, to successfully reclaim the throne of her land.'

Mr Williams cleared his throat. Then, 'Mum's been abducted, too,' blurted Rose. 'Abducted – by the antler-man.'

The room fell silent. No one had anything to say – not even Sal, this time. The cold, dusty air heaved with menace, as the day darkened outside the window. Another day almost gone, thought Rose – and no closer to Mum. Erwain's story, this new information about Cernunnos, made her feel even more impossibly distant.

'We have to get to Annwn!' she cried, urgently.

Again, no one said anything. Mr Williams's anxious, blue eyes stared at her helplessly. Then her stomach rumbled, loudly. She felt an empty twang within and realised that she was hungry – very hungry. Too hungry to think properly. 'Er, can we eat now?' she said.

Mr Williams twitched in surprise. 'Of course, bach!' he said. 'I was forgetting myself. Ianto – where are those sandwiches, boy?'

Ianto took his backpack to the table and pulled the foil-wrapped packages out. And there were four. One for each of them.

'How did Mamgu know there'd be four of us?' wondered Rose.

'Haven't you realised yet that Mamgu knows everything?' said Ianto, as he poured steaming, milky tea from the Thermos into cups that Sal brought over from the seld.

Soon they were tucking in at the table. Rose drew a little, welcome warmth from the hot tea. No one spoke.

Mr Williams gave half his sandwich to Del, who took it from him delicately, then carefully ate everything but a slice of tomato, which she left on the rug. Sal munched mechanically, glazed eyes staring at the wall above the range. She was either deep in thought, or in some meditative trance. What went on behind Sal's dark, troubled eyes?

Rose glanced at Ianto and he returned her gaze with a tentative smile. Then he reached over to hold her hand, but missed – she'd just stretched it out to receive the last of the tea, that Mr Williams was pouring from the flask. Ianto's hand dropped back to the table, then, head down, he wearily pushed about a folded piece of silver foil, having finished his sandwich in four swift bites.

The silence continued – anyway, what was there to say?

There was at once too much to say and nothing to say, thought Rose. And she knew, too, that the others were afraid to voice their thoughts about Mum, because they were afraid of hurting her – of raising her hopes, or of dashing her hopes.

If Mum was here, thought Rose, with a tiny, inward smile, she'd keep the party going. She'd be chatting away, finding ways to make us laugh, to make it fun, despite the situation. Rose felt a terrible mixture of loss and panic, and did her best to swallow it. *We're going to find you, Mum*, she thought, desperately, though with every second that passed it felt as if Mum was moving further and further away from her . . . *We'll find you soon. I know we will—*

'So,' said Sal, loudly, and everyone jumped in shock. She was still staring straight ahead. 'Tell me what you know about Eddie.' Then she closed her eyes and shook her head. 'I mean, tell me what you know about the boy on the quad bike.'

It wasn't clear who she was addressing. Mr Williams looked at Rose and Ianto. But neither of them wanted to speak – Ianto was fiddling with the silver foil, again; Rose looked away, smarting with guilt about the way they'd treated him, back at the cottage.

So Mr Williams cleared his throat and, at this sound, Rose sighed inwardly. I hope he won't take too long, she thought. *We can't sit around here all day. We have to get going again, to find Mum – or, I suppose, find Eddie? Will that help us find Mum . . .?* Meanwhile, Mr Williams was speaking.

'Ah, well. Turned up Christmas Day, he did, at my farm. Hiding in the cowshed. It was obvious he was on the run from something – someone? Yes, indeed. Stayed a few days. Nice lad. Full of beans. Never told me his name, of course. Or where he was from, what he was after. Ahem!' Mr Williams cleared his throat again, and fell silent.

Rose and Ianto stared at him, incredulous, but he avoided their gaze and Sal's frowning glare by looking down at the table, tightening the lid of the empty flask.

Was that really all he had to say?

'Plus, he stole the staff,' prompted Ianto.

'The staff? What do you mean?' Sal jerked her head to look at him.

'Ah,' said Mr Williams, eyeing Ianto with an inscrutable expression. Rose wondered what was going on. Was Mr Williams trying to protect the boy? From whom? Why? The room prickled, suddenly, with hidden motives and secrets. 'Well now. It seems the lad may have broken into the Canolfan in our village and taken a Celtic artefact. The staff that belonged to Bleddyn.'

'Bleddyn, Erwain's brother?' asked Sal.

Rose looked at Sal. Though she'd heaped scorn on the story, she'd taken it all in. She was clever, was Sal.

'But then, we don't have definite proof he took it,' went on Mr Williams. A frown was growing between his brows.

Ianto snorted loudly. 'Not much!' he blurted. 'Only the fact that the hat he was wearing was found at the scene of the crime; plus the staff dropped out of his coat.'

'The staff dropped out of his coat?' repeated Sal. 'What do you mean? When?'

'When he ran off. This morning. Actually, only half the staff fell out. So he's still got half of it.'

'Oh, yes?' asked Sal, her eyes glittering. 'So where is the other half?'

Rose and Ianto looked at Mr Williams, who was frowning hard now, at Ianto. He did not reply.

'Come on, Uncle,' said Ianto. 'What's the problem?'

Mr Williams took a deep breath and shook his head, still watching Ianto. Then he sighed and said, 'Here,' fishing it out of his coat.

Rose watched Sal's hooded hazel eyes. Watched as she reached out and took the worn, dark piece of wood from his hands, examined it with a frown, looked carefully at both ends, and twirled it experimentally. 'Huh,' she said, laying it down on the table.

And that was it. But the room felt tense as a sprung bow – as if something – or someone – was going to snap, any minute now.

To try to calm her racing heart, Rose glanced out of the window at the top of the hill behind the house, where, now the rain had let up a little, she could see a set of stones in a curving line – some rounded, some jagged – dark against the grey, rain-soaked sky. Rose remembered seeing them, covered in snow, on Christmas Day, when she and Mum were leaving the house. Suddenly, Eddie's words came into Rose's mind: *the grey stones sticking up like teeth, like the hill has opened its mouth – opened its mouth so wide that it's flat.* What had he called these stones, again? Oh yes –

'Is that the Cylch Cerrig, Sal?' she blurted, pointing at it.

Sal looked up, out of the window. 'Yes,' she said, and her gaze went soft. Like she did, sometimes, Sal had returned to another, happier time. 'We used to go up there and play, as kids,' she went on. 'Me and Eddie. Stay out till it got dark, in summer. Our favourite place. Feel like you're on top of the world up there, you do. On a good day, a clear day, you can see all the way down to town. We'd try and spot our houses, from up there. But we never could. They'd have been hidden by the steelworks, of course. And everything else. Just little houses, they were. Two little houses out of many, many houses, all together in rows.

'Home felt so far away, up there.'

Everyone stopped for a moment to gaze at the stones – grey, windswept, ancient.

Then, 'We found Eddie's diary, Sal,' said Rose, carefully. 'From 1973. From when he disappeared.'

'Did you?' said Sal, still staring up at the stones. Then she turned, sharply. 'Tell me. Where is the diary? You got it on you?'

Rose winced, sorry to disappoint her. 'No, Sal,' she said. 'Sorry. It's at home. When we get back, I'll show it to you.' Then she felt guilty – perhaps it wasn't hers to keep? – so she added quickly, 'I mean, I'll *give* it to you – when we get back.'

'I'd like that. Though I'm hoping I'll have Eddie to tell me everything in person, very soon.'

Oh, gosh, thought Rose. What if this new Sal – this new, hopeful Sal – is disappointed. How would that be? A woman who'd lived her life in despair and in searching . . . If they didn't find Eddie— But then a voice inside cried, *Never mind Eddie – what about Mum? We have to find Mum!*

She frowned, closing her eyes. What had they been

talking about? Oh yes, the Cylch Cerrig. She forced herself to continue, 'Well, Eddie talked about the Cylch Cerrig in his diary. He talked about it in his last entry.'

Sal stared at Rose. 'Did he?' she said.

'Yes,' said Rose. 'I can't remember exactly what he said, but he definitely talked about wanting to go up there.'

'Right,' said Sal. Then she stood, abruptly. 'Excuse me, all,' she announced, and set off into the living room.

Rose guessed she was heading for the bathroom, upstairs.

As soon as she was out of the room, Mr Williams leaned across the table to hiss at Ianto, 'What the heck were you doing, telling her about the lad – telling her about the staff?'

'Hey! She's his cousin, isn't she? She needs to know! We've got to work together, haven't we? Pool our resources—'

'Keep your voice down!' Mr Williams hissed again, looking up at the ceiling and ducking his head, as if he was afraid Sal would burst through it. 'She's only upstairs! Listening to us – probably. Seeing what we say when she's out the room. Listen, boy. You say she's the lad's cousin. She is, of course, if he's Eddie, the boy that disappeared in 1973. And maybe he is – stranger things have happened, as we all know. But maybe he *isn't*. And maybe he doesn't want to be found by her.' Mr Williams eyed the two of them and whispered urgently, 'Because all I know, see, is that, despite his bravado, the boy was all alone and desperately frightened – of something, or someone. What if . . .' he lowered his voice even further, nudging his head towards the ceiling, 'it's *her?*'

Rose felt sick, suddenly. But Mr Williams hadn't finished yet.

'You talk about *pooling resources,*' he hissed at Ianto, who looked almost as stunned as Rose. 'Fine. But I don't see *her* pooling resources. Knows how to keep things close to her chest, she does. Takes it all in, gives nothing out, then goes her own way. I know her type.'

Finally Rose found her voice. 'But . . . but what about the spirit at the door, then? And what about her looking for him all her life?'

'Could have made all that up. Made it up to connect her to the boy.'

This was, suddenly, too much. 'Noooo!' Rose wailed, clapping her hands over her ears, squeezing shut her eyes.

Ianto's chair toppled back as he rushed round the table to her. She registered his arms about her and clung to them like a liferaft, breaking into uncontrollable sobs.

Still hugging her, Ianto turned to Mr Williams and whispered, angrily, 'Shut up, Uncle! Just shut up, with your insane conspiracy theories! Can't you see it's hurting Rose? D'you think she needs this, right now?'

Muffled by Ianto's coat and her own, loud sobs, Rose heard Mr Williams's chair fall to the floor. Then she heard his voice next to her. He must have been kneeling by her side. 'Rose, *cariad*,' said Mr Williams in a low, shaky voice. 'I'm sorry, bach. The last thing I want to do is hurt you. But I don't want that boy being hurt, either. Like I say, he was very afraid. And he had no one in the world, but me. I owe it to him to protect him. To keep his secrets. To make sure he's safe.'

'But Sal is his family . . .' began Rose, and then she stopped, suddenly. Because she'd just remembered something. 'Dad never said anything to me and Mum – not one thing, ever – about having a brother.'

'So . . .' said Ianto, frowning. 'So maybe Eddie didn't exist – is that what you're saying?'

'No – yes. Oh, I don't know! But it's really hard to understand, isn't it? Why didn't Dad mention him? Mum nearly fainted, when Sal told us about Eddie – it was such a shock.'

Then Rose remembered something else. She whispered, looking up at the ceiling – Sal was certainly taking her time – 'Sal said she didn't like policemen. She didn't want to work with your dad, Ianto.'

'So what?' said Ianto.

'I don't know,' admitted Rose. 'But it might, maybe, mean that she's done something . . . bad.'

'Something against the law, eh?' said Mr Williams, then he whistled, low, under his breath.

Following his gaze, they all stared at the ceiling. What on earth were they going to say when she came back into the room? They couldn't possibly act normal now. In a flash – the space of just a couple of minutes – Rose's feelings towards Sal had changed. Now she felt full of creeping, crawling, distrust . . . and a sort of horror.

'Hey!' said Mr Williams then. 'Where's it gone?' He ducked his head to look under the table, then stood up straight, panicked. 'Have you two taken it?'

'Taken what, Uncle?' said Ianto, wearily.

'The staff! She left it on the table. I thought she left it on the table!'

'She did,' said Rose, standing herself, then ducking to check under the table herself. Nothing but the dusty old rug. 'Did you put it back in your coat?'

Mr Williams patted his coat with nervous, hurried hands. 'No,' he said. 'No. I didn't put it back in my coat. She's stolen it.'

Chapter 27

Then, 'Look,' said Ianto. He was pointing out of the window at the hill behind the house. The hill with the Cylch Cerrig crowning its top.

Taking wide, determined strides, a tall figure was battling the rain and the wind to mount the steep side of the hill. Their short, thick hair was being pushed violently this way and that in the roaring wind.

Without a word the four of them rushed for the front door and ran towards the foot of the hill, crunching gravel beneath their boots. Del sprinted ahead then turned to bark at them to hurry up, her ears blowing back in the wind.

'Sal!' shouted Rose.

The figure stopped for a moment, spun round and looked down at them. Then she turned back to the hill and broke into a run, falling over tussocks of rushes and rocks as she fought her way towards the brooding, grey stones above her. They could hear her shouting now, screaming into the wind.

'*Eddie!* EDDIE!'

Soon Rose, Ianto and Del were scrambling up the slope after her, leaving a puffing Mr Williams behind. As she stumbled onwards, Rose felt utterly alone, as if she was in a frosted-glass bubble of panic. *We've all split up*, she thought, feverishly. *Sal is looking for Eddie. Mr Williams is looking for the boy. I'm looking for Mum. Is anyone else looking for Mum?* 'Ianto, do you want to find Mum,' she blurted. And she found that she was crying, again.

'Of course I do!' Ianto stopped and turned to her, frowning. 'Of course I do, Rose! That's why I'm here, with you—'

Rose hardly heard him as she went on, 'Because I feel like I'm the only one who really does,' she cried. 'I feel alone. And the more time goes past, the further Mum slips away from me, and the more other things, and other people, wanting other things, get in the way, to stop me finding her . . .'

Ianto grabbed her shoulders. 'Rose. Listen to me. I want to find your mam. Right? But, but . . . I want to find *you* again, too.'

'What does that mean?'

'I – don't know. Sorry. I don't know what I mean. I think,' he went on, searching her face with his eyes, 'what I mean is, I feel like we're so apart. You're so far away. But of course you are, because this awful thing is happening to you, and it's not happening to me – or not in the same way, anyway. And I feel like I can't help. Like I can't do anything. I can't do anything to help you!' Ianto was shouting into the roaring wind and tears were running down his own face.

Rose lifted her hands to gently wipe his cheeks. He smiled, shakily, took his hands from her shoulders and did the same for her. Then they caught each other's eyes and together, all at once, they started to laugh. They couldn't help it. And then they drew each other into a hug.

'All right, you two. There's a time and a place, you know,' came a voice from behind them. They turned to see a grinning Mr Williams, pulling himself up to stand with them, catching his breath while Del looked down on them from further up the hill.

As they set off again Rose was just in time to see Sal crest the top of the hill and disappear from sight amongst the stones. 'Sal!' she screamed again, uselessly.

This last bit was very steep. Rose was on all fours now, clinging to the side of the hill as she climbed. A few minutes later, she, Ianto and Del had reached the flat top of the hill, and before them was the Cylch Cerrig, the stone circle.

An uneven set of large, grey stones stood up and lay toppled over in what looked like a perfect circle, enclosing a space about as big as a tennis court. Some stones were tall, taller than Mr Williams; some were low enough to sit on. All were deeply embedded in the short turf.

In the middle of the Cylch was a sort of crater, or *pant*, full of wet, wintery grass and rushes. And right in the middle of this pant stood the empty quad bike – looking very still and slightly unreal. But there was no sign of the boy, or of Sal.

Rose pressed forward to pass between the huge stones then felt a hand grab her arm from behind and heard a shout of '*Wait!*'

She stepped back and Mr Williams let go her arm. 'Sorry, bach,' he said, loudly, against the buffeting wind. 'You get to my age, you have instincts. Powerful instincts. And you learn to trust 'em. If we enter the Cylch, we do it together. Right?'

'Right,' said Rose.

'OK,' said Mr Williams, squaring his shoulders. 'No time to waste.'

The three of them held hands and Mr Williams grabbed hold of Del's collar. Then they all stepped forward through the gap in the stones.

Nothing happened. Still holding hands, they walked through the wind and the drizzle to the quad bike in the middle of the pant. Mr Williams reached out a hand to touch the handlebars, then he exclaimed and bent to pick up a screwed-up piece of paper from the rain-spattered plastic seat. With one hand, he flattened it out against his knee, and Rose saw an untidy scrawl, smudging and blurring in the rain. Familiar writing . . .

Tomo – if you find this, then I'll have found a way back there. And going back is the only way I can try and sort things out. Sorry, I did steal the staff. But I needed it. And it belongs to me, anyway – to my family. So I didn't really steal it. It's going to help me. It's helped me already . . .

Should have explained all this better when I was at your place – but I was a bit confused. And afraid. I'm still afraid, to be honest with you, but facing him and finding my family again is the only way to stop being afraid.

So, thanks again, Tomo, for everything. You been a real friend. And I hope that maybe I'll see you again . . .

but who knows.

So long, Tomo.

Eddie

Then Rose found her hands slipping from the others, as if she was disappearing down into the earth. She grabbed at them to find them again, touched finger-tips, then her hands closed on air.

She could hear muffled noises – someone shouting 'Rose!' and she thought it was Ianto. Other, distorted sounds, breathy, flute-like, came and went in the time it took to blink. Darkness surrounded her then and the Cylch Cerrig was gone.

The next moment she was standing in full sunshine on the edge of a broad stretch of water. Alone.

There was no wind here. No rain. The only sound was of gently lapping water. Before her on the shore was a long, narrow wooden boat, with three rows of wooden benches across it.

Seated at the front of the boat was a small man. A man about the size of a six-year-old child, thought Rose, watching him as he watched her. But though his body was small, his head was as large as a grown man's. His face was creased and sun browned, his eyes sharp and dark and his mouth twisted in a way – impatient, unpredictable – that made Rose nervous. He was holding an oar and using it to keep the boat steady in the pebbly shallows.

She cleared her throat. Instinctively, she spoke in Welsh. Her voice shook a little. '*A'i Annwn yw hon?* Is this Annwn?'

'*Ynys yw Annwn,*' he replied in a raspy voice, pointing across the water with a small, crooked finger. 'Annwn is an island.'

Following his finger, Rose saw a dark, wooded island – beachless, the trees extending all the way down the shore. She shivered.

'I want to go there,' she said.

'You want to go to Annwn,' said the little man.

'Yes. I want to go to Annwn.'

'*You want to go to Annwn,*' he repeated, loudly, and he cackled with laughter. Then, 'It does not matter what you *want*. You think you can do what you *want*, here?'

Rose said nothing.

'Yes!' said the man. 'You think you have found me, yes? That you have travelled here. You have not. It was not in your control. You were *allowed* to come here.'

'Who allowed it?'

The man smiled, looking up at her slyly. 'My master allowed it.'

'Who is your master?'

The man did not answer but watched her carefully, raised his eyebrows and widened his eyes. Then he nodded, as if prompting her.

'Is it – is it, Cernunnos?' As she stumbled over the name, Rose realised that she'd never said this word out loud before, and she shivered again.

'Is it, is it, *C-c-cernunnos?*' sneered the man.

Then he burst into loud, harsh laughter. 'You thought that holding hands would bring your friends here with you,' he said.

'No,' he went on. 'No. You were wrong. You are all alone here. No friends.' He grinned.

Rose looked at him. Whatever he was trying to do, his words actually made her feel stronger. Because she knew better than him. She knew, from Erwain's story, that the antler-man did not control everything here. No. Erwain ran away from him. She got away. And Rose was going to get away too – get away, with Mum. And I *do* have friends. Many friends. Especially my best friend, Ianto. And even if they're not with me, they're still here, in spirit.

Two can play this stupid game, she thought. She stood up as tall as she could, looking down at him.

'Enough of this!' she said imperiously. 'Take me over the water. Take me to Annwn.'

To her surprise, the man grunted, surly-faced. 'What will you pay me?'

'I . . .' Rose panicked for a moment, delving into her pockets. She felt her phone. She wasn't giving him that.

Then her fingers closed around something large, cold and round. She pulled it out. The penny, from beneath Mr Williams's seld.

'Here,' she said, handing it to the man, shuddering as she touched the rough skin of his palm and saw that his fingernails were thick and curved, like little claws.

Placing it carefully inside the pouch that he pulled from around his neck, 'Get in,' he said.

Chapter 28

After a short, wordless journey, they reached the island. As the boatman paddled away, Rose stepped into a vast forest.

A familiar forest. Rose inhaled its smell – damp, piney, ancient. It was just like the one she and Ianto had been hounded into, by the Wild Hunt. 'So this is Annwn . . .' Rose whispered to herself. She wished Ianto was with her. He was always at her side – her best friend, since they were little kids. They'd been together through all the adventures in the summer. Now he wasn't here. It didn't feel right – as if half of her was missing.

The sound of her footsteps was muffled by the thick, mulchy ground. No birds sang, no small mammals stirred in the layers of pine needles at her feet. The trees soared above her head as she walked and walked between their trunks, in what she hoped was a straight line. It felt like a straight line, but she couldn't tell. She couldn't see the position of the sun, from beneath the canopy.

She pulled out her phone and saw that she had no signal. That was not a surprise. But the time was. It said 99.59. As she watched, it clicked over to 00.00. Then she waited, to see what would happen in a minute's time. And she waited, and she waited, but the numbers did not change.

So she put the phone back in her pocket and continued to walk.

Then she pulled the phone out again and, before she could talk herself out of it, dialled Mum's number, despite the lack of bars. Nothing happened, of course. But, light-headed, Rose spoke into the phone, anyway. 'Mum,' she said, in a low voice. 'Mum, I'm here. I'm in Annwn. Don't worry, I'm going to find you. And then I'm going to bring you home. And I will never, ever again not say goodbye to you, when you go out. Or find out where you're going. And I'll make sure that you're with good people, who want only the best for you. And I'll always be interested in you, and everything you do and think and feel. I will never take you for granted again. I promise.'

Then she pocketed her phone and walked on.

Time passed. Rose tramped through the forest and thought about things, for the first time in what felt like forever. Who was Sal, really? What did she want? She wanted to find Eddie, that was clear enough. But was Mr Williams right about her motives? Why hadn't Dad said he had an older brother? And what had Sal done to make her hate the police?

Eddie's note. That note, on the quad bike, meant that the boy really was Eddie. Was he here too, in Annwn? The boatman would've known – she could have asked him. She should have asked him about Mum too. But she had a strong feeling she wouldn't have got a straight answer in return.

Then there was Erwain, the woman who'd come to Annwn then escaped back to Cymru. Her own great, great, great – how many times great? Who cares. Loads – grandmother, who'd appeared to her and Ianto on Mynydd y

Grug. How could her story help her now? 'It's already helping, Erwain,' Rose muttered. 'Thank you.' For wasn't she in the forest, surely the same forest that Erwain had fled through, to escape from Annwn, escape from—

Rose couldn't say the antler-man's name, even in her thoughts. It felt as if, if she said his name, here, she would summon him, alert him to her. Or something—

And then she heard a sound, and stopped dead in her tracks. Around her, dark trunks seemed to stretch forever in every direction. But she could hear music, music floating on the air. That flutey music; the beautiful tune . . .

And she walked onwards, pulled towards it.

Then she began to run, because she could hear voices now and tinkling laughter, mingling with the music. And amongst it all – woven in, as if they were all dancing together – Mum's voice. What was she saying? Rose couldn't make it out.

'MUM!' she shouted, stumbling forwards. 'MUM! Where are you?'

No answer.

It was dark under the trees but Rose sensed a lightness ahead, from where the sounds came. As she ran she saw there was a wall before her, made of large, rectangular grey stones, stretching high into the sky. Had Erwain's book mentioned a wall? She couldn't remember.

Soon she was standing right before the wall and, hesitating, she stretched out her hand to touch it. Her fingers met rough stone, dry and warm. Now she could see the sun again, above her, through the break the wall created in the forest. But she couldn't see what was over the wall.

And all the time the chattering, laughing voices were growing clearer, louder. And the music . . . and, yes, there was Mum's voice again!

'*Mum!*' she screamed. Moving round the wall, filled with desperate, fearful joy, she began to make out words, snatches of conversations. Men and women. The voices were soft and mild, full of warmth, speaking Welsh. Then came tinkling laughter, a shuffle of feet and a swishing sound, the sound of rich material moving against itself, to the flute. Were they *dancing*?

Then she heard Mum's voice once more. And she realised that Mum was speaking Welsh too – or trying to. '*Dw i'n hoffi'r ddiod 'ma. Beth yw hi?* I like this drink. What is it?'

'MUM! Don't touch it! Don't drink anything! Mum – I'm here! On the other side of the wall!' she screamed.

But there was no response. Mum was talking again. She sounded happy. '*Dw i'n hoffi*— I like—' she went on, then she broke into English – 'oh, I'm sorry, my Cymraeg isn't very good yet. But I'm working on it!' Mum laughed, and the company laughed with her. 'Of course!' she exclaimed. 'You don't understand English, do you?' More soft laughter, Mum laughing with them, until Rose could no longer tell which laugh was hers and which was theirs.

'MUM!' Rose shouted again.

Now she was running alongside the wall, looking for a gap, a gate, a door. It ran into the distance ahead of her and it seemed to curve, slightly, as she ran. *What if there's no way through it?* she thought. Could she climb it? The stones were tightly mortared together. No toe-holds. Nothing to grip. It was impossible.

Then Rose heard something else. Something on this side of the wall. The thumping of rapid footsteps. Coming her way.

And then a figure appeared. A tall figure, awkwardly striding, with short, thick hair.

Sal.

Rose stopped. But Sal didn't break stride. As she came closer, Rose saw no surprise on her frowning face.

Approaching Rose, she announced, 'There's no way in. No gate. No door. It's a circular wall. Been all the way round it once already. We need to try something else.'

As Rose opened her mouth to speak she remembered the dark, horrible feelings back there, in the house, about Sal. But now, looking into her brown, restless eyes, Rose made a decision. *Sal is my aunty*, she said, firmly, to herself. And I have to trust her. I *want* to trust her. Just as she has to trust me. We are all we have, at this moment. So she closed her mouth again, and nodded.

'I can hear Mum in there,' she said. 'Mum's voice.'

'You hear Eddie?'

'No. No Eddie. Just Mum, and lots of other people.'

'Me too,' said Sal. 'But they can't hear us, can they.'

Rose shook her head.

Sal stared at Rose, then, suddenly, she pulled the half-staff from inside her coat. 'I've been trying to use this,' she said, 'but nothing's happening—'

'Sal!' said Rose. She couldn't help it. 'That's not yours! You stole it from Mr Williams!'

Sal frowned at her, staff in hand. 'What are you on about?

This staff belongs to our family. He stole it from Eddie, if you want to get technical about it.'

'But . . .' Rose struggled to hold on to her outrage. 'But you *stole* it, and ran away. I thought we were a team. We were supposed to be working together, making plans and, er, pooling resources – finding Mum and finding Eddie, but you ran away, like it was every man for himself—'

'It *is* every man for himself, Rose,' interrupted Sal, looming forward so that Rose stepped back in alarm. 'Don't you know that? It's every man for himself, in this world. Well, in our world, anyway. And here. Annwn, or wherever we are. You don't put yourself first, you get trampled on. Fact.'

'No! No! Not fact, Sal. Not fact,' Rose retaliated, facing Sal. What had happened to Sal, to make her like this? The answer came to her at once. *Losing Eddie has made her like this. And maybe other things too . . .*

And then Sal turned, staff in hand, and began to lope around the wall in the opposite direction.

'Hey! Where are you going?' shouted Rose, giving chase.

Sal had the advantage of surprise, and her long strides were taking her ahead. Rose sprinted after her – she wasn't letting her get away again. The staff was swinging to and fro in Sal's hand like a baton in a relay race. Panting with effort, closing on Sal, Rose grabbed at it as it swung backwards and then, all at once, the two of them were flying through the air and over the wall, their feet wheeling, their hands holding on to the half-staff for dear life.

Chapter 29

They drifted over the wall then downwards, gently, and all at once they were part of it all: the music, laughter and chatter, the most beautiful smell of roses and the warmth and light of a sunlit, summer morning. Once their feet had touched the soft, short grass of the greenest lawn Rose had ever seen, they found themselves amongst a small crowd of milling people in beautiful, floaty clothing, apparently unperturbed by the appearance of two people wearing coats and boots, arriving from out of the sky. Then, eyeing Rose with a glance she couldn't decipher, Sal yanked the staff from her hands and ran off. But this time, Rose didn't follow her.

Rose didn't follow her, because she'd seen Mum.

In fact, Mum was standing right before her. And she looked beautiful: cheeks flushed pink, her bright, clear eyes open wide in astonishment. She was wearing a golden torque around her neck and her feet were bare and pale on the lush green grass. In her arms she held a large bunch of fragrant, red roses.

'Rosie love!' she exclaimed. 'What a lovely surprise! Look – I'm gathering ye rosebuds – literally!'

Then she opened her arms and enclosed Rose in a hug.

And it really was Mum. Real Mum. In the flesh. Rose closed her eyes, breathed her in, and sighed, long and hard, as if she was letting out the breath of days of darkness and utter misery. For a long moment she clung to her mother, afraid to let her go. Mum's body was shaking slightly, and Rose could hear her laughing with delight.

The roses smelled so sweet, crushed between them. All Rose wanted to do was to cling on to Mum, melt into her, never let her go again. But there was no time for that.

Stepping apart, she said, grabbing at the torque, 'Mum, take that off. Now. We're going home.'

'Ow! Rose, what are you doing? You're hurting me!' The roses scattered on to the lawn as Mum's hands closed over Rose's. 'It was a present, love! I'm not taking it off. What's the matter with you?'

Mum pushed her away and looked carefully into her face. 'Hey, are you OK? You look awful.'

'Thanks, Mum.'

Mum laughed again. 'Come here!' she said, pulling Rose towards her for another hug. This really is Mum, thought Rose, gripping her tightly. *This really is Mum!*

'How on earth did you find me, anyway?' Mum went on.

'With a lot of trouble.'

Mum looked thoughtful. 'Ah,' she said. 'It's that app, isn't it. The sat nav thing. On your phone.'

'It doesn't matter how I found you, Mum. What matters is getting you home again. Now. Please take that torque off, and then . . . then we're going. Quick – before—'

'Now, Rosie,' said Mum, smiling at her. 'I'm having a lovely time. A really lovely time. And I've only just got here – I'll be home for lunch, like I said. Why don't you stay? These are such nice people. There are a few about your age, too, I'm sure you'll get on—'

'Mum! You haven't just got here. You've been gone for days!'

'Days? What do you mean?'

'I mean, days! Since Boxing Day.'

'But it's Boxing Day now!' Mum was dancing to the flutey music, twirling about and dragging Rose with her. 'Dance with me!' she laughed, attempting a waltz. 'You know, Rosie,' she went on, as they staggered about, 'I think we've both been guilty of taking life too seriously. Worrying about things, and so on. We need to have more fun! I'm having the time of my life here. And I'm not going to let my spoilsport daughter put a damper on it.'

At this point Mum gave a naughty grin and reached out to tickle Rose's sides, and Rose, squirming, doubled up, managed to blurt, 'Aargh! Stop it, Mum! This is serious!'

Mum chuckled and carried on tickling. 'Come on. Let's see that smile! Honestly, Rosie, I haven't felt so happy since . . . since . . .' and then she stopped tickling and her smile fell a little.

Since Dad, thought Rose.

'Where is he?' Rose said then.

'Who?'

Rose gulped, looking about. Nothing but pretty women and men, talking, dancing, drinking a golden liquid. 'The man. You know. The man with . . . antlers.'

Mum's face lit up again.

'Oh, you mean Ceri! He's been called away. There was

189

some sort of commotion. Someone gatecrashing the party, I think. He had to go and sort it out. But his lovely friends have been looking after me.'

'Ceri, eh? Is that what you call him?'

'Well, his full name is something else, but I call him Ceri – it's friendlier—'

'Mum. Listen to me. Please listen now. There are things I need to tell you. Loads of things. But we'll start with the basics. You think you've been gone for half an hour – actually you've been gone for days. This . . . this is another world. The Otherworld, in fact, or Annwn. Time works differently here. And this man, the antler-man, well, he's bad news.'

Mum stopped smiling now. A second passed. Then she sighed, and said, 'No, Rose. We've been through this before, remember? On Christmas Eve. We talked about it – about me, me meeting other people—'

'Mum! This isn't about you meeting other people. I want you to be happy! But just . . . just not with the antler-man, the King of Annwn. I know it sounds mad, but that's who he is. And he wants to make you his queen, and keep you here. He abducted you—'

'Rose!' said Mum sharply. 'Now that's just ridiculous. Of course he didn't abduct me. I wanted to come to this party! I wanted to spend time with him, to get to know him better. What we need –' Mum looked about, above the heads of the people in the crowd – 'what we need is for you to meet him too. I know you'll like him, when you do. Do you know, he reminds me a bit of . . . of Dad!'

This was painful. But it had to be done. 'I don't want to

meet him, Mum. He's the last person I want to meet. You're not the first, you know. He abducted someone before, and—'

'Rose, if you're talking about his ex-wife, I know about her – he told me,' interrupted Mum, in a shaky voice. 'It's hard to understand everything he says, because my Welsh isn't great, but from what I can gather he was very upset at the time about losing her, and still is. In the end, though he loved her very much, he had to let her go. She was a free spirit, I think, and, at that time in his life, he said, he was a bit, sort of, insecure and clingy.'

'*Insecure and clingy?*' That was one way to describe it. 'Mum,' said Rose urgently, grabbing her shoulders and shaking them, 'did he tell you what he did to her?'

Mum's eyes had filled with tears now, and her lips were shaking with unsaid words. Rose felt terrible, horrible inside, but she continued, 'He locked her in a tower, and then, when she escaped . . .'

But, suddenly, she'd lost Mum's attention. Mum was staring beyond her, above her head, her eyes wide in fear. Rose turned herself and looked, properly, at the garden. Within the circle of the tall wall was a wide, green lawn, dotted with fountains that played sparkling water and beds full of roses. And in the middle, the very centre, there was a tall, tall tower, taller even than the walls. There was a single, barred window in the tower, at the very top. From that window, a pale face peered.

'There's someone in there!' whispered Mum.

'Yes. He's locked someone else up now.'

Silently, they moved closer to the tower, their eyes fixed

on the face at the window. The face was watching them back, mouthing words they couldn't hear, waving its arms. Then Rose saw who it was.

'Eddie!' she screamed loudly, without thinking.

The garden fell silent, and everything seemed to freeze. She looked around to see that the beautiful people had turned and were staring at them. Closing her eyes in horror, she turned back to Mum.

Mum was frowning in confusion. 'You know him? Eddie . . . Who's Eddie?' she whispered. 'Wait – you mean – you don't mean . . . Dad's brother?'

'Yes. That Eddie.'

Slowly the music started up again and the chatter and the dancing began afresh. Eddie was still up there, gesticulating desperately. Now he was waving his half of the staff. Pointing to the end of it.

Rose waved back, shaking her head. What was he trying to tell them? She mouthed 'Sal!' to him, and tried to make the sign of a staff, measuring it out with her hands. Where was Sal anyway? What was she up to now?

Mum, meanwhile, was still digesting this piece of information. She tore her eyes from the tower to look at Rose. 'Dad's brother . . . He's *here*? Well, that's wonderful— or, or is it?'

Rose had no answer to that. Mum continued, turning back to the face in the window, 'But . . . why's he so young?'

'I think because he spent some time here, before now,' said Rose, watching him. He was far above them, but close enough to see that he was crying, his shoulders heaving with sobs. Now he banged with his fists against the window behind the bars. Still no sound came. He looked as if he was drowning in there, clinging on to Rose with his eyes, until she could bear it no longer. She turned to her mother. 'Look Mum, there's loads to tell you. And I will tell you it all, when we're safe, back home – but right now, we just need to get out of here.'

At last, Mum was listening to her. She whispered back, 'Rosie, love, I think you're right. I mean, about getting out of here. Now. Before . . .'

Before the antler-man gets back, thought Rose.

'But . . .' began Rose.

'. . . we can't leave Eddie behind,' finished Mum, nodding.

For a fleeting moment, Rose remembered Sal's words – *You don't put yourself first, you get trampled on. Fact.*

It would be so easy to run away now, with Mum. To get home again. To forget about Eddie, forget about Sal. But how could she live with herself, if she did? *No, Sal*, repeated Rose to herself. No. *Not fact. Not fact.*

As the two of them moved closer to the tower, they found a wooden door at its base. Rose grabbed the iron ring in its centre and pulled. Then she pushed. It didn't budge.

'Drudwen,' murmured Rose, looking at the keyhole. 'Where is she? We need her.'

'Who's Drudwen?' asked Mum.

'The starling. The starling that set Erwain free. Twice. She has the key.'

'Drudwen!' called Mum, loudly, into the air, startling Rose. The torque around her neck sparked in sunshine as she put her hands to her mouth and shouted again, 'Drudwen! Drudwen! Drudwen!' in every direction.

At the sound of her voice, the chatter of the fair men and women and the piping of the flute was cut short again. But this time, it didn't restart. This time, to Rose's astonishment, the people turned their backs on them and drifted towards the outer walls of the garden, then gently disappeared through the stone. So that the only ones left in this strange, round garden were Rose and Mum. And the only sound, as the echoes of Mum's shouts died away, was the tinkling of water in the fountains. And the air seemed to change, to become charged with a sense of unease. Rose shivered, suddenly, despite the warm sunshine.

Then, '*Pwy sy'n galw am Drudwen?* Who calls for Drudwen?' came a deep, slow voice from behind them.

Rose hesitated, drawing in a breath. She felt Mum's hand around hers, and clung on tightly. Together, they turned. Turned to face him.

There he was. Tall and broad, like a great statue, a monolith. He was standing very still. Watching them, with dark, dark eyes. From a face that looked young and ancient, all at once. Not quite human. And from his head came two huge antlers, making him even taller, making him seem like a giant.

Mum's face drained of colour. 'Ceri – *dw i* . . . I . . .' she stuttered.

'*Fy mrenhines.* My queen,' he said. 'It was you. Why? And who is this?' The antlers shifted slightly as he turned his head to Rose and his eyes bored into hers.

'Um,' Mum glanced with wide, frightened eyes at Rose.

And then she grabbed hold of her, strongly, pulling her head into her shoulder to shield her from the man's view.

But Rose wasn't going to hide. She pulled apart to stare back at this man. The man from her dream – that awful dream. She was looking at him now. Facing her fear. Looking him right in the eye . . .

Eyes that were black and bottomless. It was like sinking into deep, dark galaxies of space. Suddenly her head spun. She felt unsteady on her feet. She struggled to pull herself out, as if battling to surface from a profound pool.

'Urgh . . .' she gasped, breathless, tearing her eyes from his.

'*Dw i'n gweld pwy ydy hi.* I see who it is,' she heard him say. 'It is my daughter.'

She dared to glance at him once more, and saw that he was still staring at her. Her insides seemed to turn over. 'You have come to me,' he went on. 'Like my son. You will stay here now. You will all stay here now.'

'I'm . . . I'm not your daughter,' she managed to gasp. Looking into his eyes, her brave words didn't ring quite true. She knew now, from Erwain's book, that she *was* related to him, on her dad's side. Suddenly she saw her dad's eyes in his, and it made her feel weak and helpless. Instinctively she backed away, squeezing her eyes tight shut.

'And I won't stay here,' she said, wrenching out the words and watching the water in the fountain behind them, twinkling in the sunlight. 'Nor will Mum. Let us go.'

She dared look back at him now. He was still, very still, as if he was holding himself in. 'My daughter,' he repeated. 'You will stay here. Gold shall you have here. Fine raiment. Honey, wine and sweetmeats will be yours. In time, you will marry. A handsome match will be found.'

Rose recoiled. 'I don't want a handsome match!' she cried, at last finding her voice. 'And I don't want gold and stuff. That stuff doesn't matter! I just want to go home.' She grabbed Mum's hand. '*We* want to go home. Now. Please let us go.'

He inclined his head to one side a little, still watching her. The antlers shifted too, as if they were weighing him down. A line appeared between his brows and his eyes seemed to harden. To become impenetrable, thick glass, where before they'd been deep pools. He turned to Mum.

'My queen,' he said. 'You find fault in this land? With these people? With . . . me?'

'Ceri, *cariad*,' said Mum, stumbling on, in her imperfect Welsh. Her voice shook, and tears began to roll down her cheeks. '*Dych chi . . . dych chi ddim wedi . . .* You, you haven't displeased me. But, oh, Ceri, I'm so sorry . . .' she wept, in English now. 'I can't stay with you if Rose isn't happy with that. And I can't stay here, if that means I'm away from the village, from my friends, from Cymru . . .'

'Then I have no choice! *I have no choice!*' he cried out, his face grimacing wildly, his eyes bulging. Rose backed away in alarm.

Then 'Do it!' he bellowed. 'Do it! *Now!*' And he took a pace forward, towards them, stretching out his arms, opening his huge hands, throwing back his head and roaring. The sound was awful – deafening, wild.

Rose covered her ears, her eyes wide with alarm. She felt

Mum's hand pulling at her arm, heard her scream, '*Run!*'

As Rose stumbled and turned, from the corner of her eye she spied movement. A figure had risen up from behind the fountain. It was Sal, standing legs akimbo. She was holding something small and black. Something that she raised swiftly with both hands, arms outstretched, levelling it.

Then a gunshot exploded like a thunderclap, extinguishing the roar, leaving behind a deathly absence. The only sound was the tinkling of the fountains, echoing about the garden's walls. And before them the antler-man teetered slowly, then fell swiftly, heavily, flat on his face. His antlers dug into the soft turf. And bright red blood flowed from a hole in the back of his head on to the green, green grass, like the petals of the roses that Mum had gathered, then dropped to the ground.

Chapter 30

For a moment there was total silence, and nobody moved. Then Rose saw Mum collapse to her knees. And Rose heard high, hysterical screaming. Was it Mum? No, it was coming from her own, open mouth. She shut it, dizzy, and the screaming stopped. Dropping to the ground, she reached out to touch Mum's arm. Mum did not react. Rose saw that she'd lifted the antler-man's wrist. It looked heavy, and his fingers hung down like dead weights.

Then Mum looked round at Rose, and Rose gasped to see that her face had drained of blood – it was as white as snow. 'He's dead,' she said, and her voice was strangely calm. 'He's dead, Rose.'

They looked over the long, prostrate body before them at Sal, who was approaching from the fountain, still holding the pistol in her right hand. She stopped in front of them and looked down.

Rose searched her face. She could see nothing there. Nothing that she could read, nothing that made sense. Rose opened her mouth to say something, but her voice wouldn't work.

Sal said, 'Eddie's in that tower,' nodding her head towards it. 'We need to get him out. There isn't much time, now.'

Rose swallowed, feeling nauseous. She had to keep it

together. Had to keep it together . . . For Mum. For getting out of here. Because they had to get out of here right now. Get away from Sal. Sal was capable of anything – Rose knew that now. But Mum wasn't moving. She was still holding the large hand as she looked up at Sal and whispered, 'Sal . . . what have you done?'

Rose saw that the pistol, still clasped in Sal's hand, was shaking. Sal's eyes were blank, as if she was somewhere far, far away. 'I've done what I had to do, Cath,' she said. 'What I've been waiting to do, for forty-nine years. It was the only way, believe me. And it's what he wanted.'

With this, she threw the gun from her, as if it was suddenly burning hot. It skidded, spinning about its trigger, across the shining, green grass.

'What who wanted?' asked Mum, her eyes following the weapon.

'Cernunnos. I'll explain later.'

Sal is mad, thought Rose, shivering. *Sal is stark, staring mad.*

'What are you waiting for?' Sal was shouting now. 'Get up, you two! I told you – we don't have much time.'

Rose got to her feet. With a sigh, Mum placed the antler-man's hand on to the grass beside him. Then she stood too.

Sal pushed past them to the base of the tower. She hammered on the door with her fists, screaming, 'Eddie! We're here! We're going to get you out!' Then she reached into her coat and pulled out the half-staff.

Turning, wild-eyed, she shouted, 'Rose! Hold this with me. We'll fly up to the window. Get him out.'

'No.'

Sal paused, staring. 'What do you mean, no?'

'No, Sal. I won't help you. Not till you've answered my questions.'

'There's no time for this!' Sal yelled, striding forward and grabbing her arm with a strong, hard hand, forcing Rose's hand on to the staff. Sal's grip was like a vice and Rose was screaming again now, wordlessly, as she grappled at Sal's arm with her free hand and kicked wildly at her shins. Sal swore, but she didn't let go – her face strained as she slowly lowered Rose's fingers on to the staff.

'Take your hands off my daughter!' Mum swung wildly at Sal, her hand connecting with Sal's cheek in a hard, sharp slap.

'Aargh!' screamed Sal, dropping Rose's hand, dropping the staff as she brought both hands up to her face. Quick as a flash, Mum snatched up the piece of wood and stepped back.

Grasping the side of her face – which had turned bright red but for the snow-white imprint of Mum's palm and fingers – Sal lunged at Mum. 'Give it back!' she screamed.

Mum held it behind her, backing off, and Rose stepped between the two of them. Sal was not getting that staff back. Not till she explained, properly.

Sal stopped then, as if she could read Rose's determined mind. Her shoulders dropped and she stood there panting, still holding her bruised face. Her lips, on the side where Mum had hit her, were starting to swell already.

'What's the matter with you two? Don't you understand? There's not much time! We have to work together!' she said.

'We have to work together now, do we?' said Rose. 'I thought it was every man for himself.'

'No. You answer my questions, Sal. Answer them truthfully. Then we'll work with you – maybe.'

Sal was silent for a moment, eyeing her. Then she sighed. 'OK,' she said, finally. 'But get on with it – make it quick.'

Rose swallowed and rubbed her forearm, where Sal had gripped it. It hurt. She closed her eyes to gather her thoughts. Where to start? But there was only one place to start.

'Why did you kill the antler-man?'

Sal squeezed her eyes tight shut, distorting her red and white face. When she opened them she looked tired, lost.

'I told you. It was what he wanted. What I had to do. I know it doesn't make sense, but it was the only way to save Eddie – to save us all.'

'But why?' Rose repeated.

'Because of the englyn Mamgu gave me. Before she died. She told me I had to do what it told me. And the englyn told me to do it. It told me it was the only way.'

'Where's the englyn? Show me it.'

Sal sighed again. But she reached into her coat pocket and pulled out a scrap of folded vellum. Rose took it from her and opened it. Like the one she'd been given by her dad, it was covered in old writing, in old, old Welsh.

The poem's title was '*Ei Blentyn Hynaf*' – 'His Eldest Child'. Rose read it aloud, and it went something like this, although, in the orginal Welsh, it was much stronger, much cleverer:

'Ever seeking love; never keeping love – so blunders the king
From love to love; see him destroy, see him cling.
Even he has had enough. Now he has lost all love; lost all will
To live. Free him; to reunite his kin. Find him, stop him . . . kill.'

Rose swallowed. 'So,' she said. 'It's addressed to you, is it? You're the eldest child – or the eldest surviving relative, more like?'

'Yes,' said Sal. 'I was a few months older than Eddie. Now I'm forty-nine years older, of course . . . anyway, whatever – I'm the eldest surviving member of Cernunnos's family, of *our* family. So – I did what I had to do. I don't know about freeing Cernunnos, but I'm hoping this will reunite our family. Well – reunite me with Eddie, anyway.'

Rose wondered if Mum had understood the poem – the Welsh was difficult, after all. She looked at her. Tears were trickling down her cheeks and she gave a small sob. Yes. Mum had understood it. Rose sighed.

Then Sal said, 'Happy now? Give me the staff, Cath.'

'No,' said Rose, and Mum, who held it firmly in her hands, shook her head, grimly. 'Not yet. Another question. Why didn't Dad say anything about Eddie, about having an older brother?'

This question seemed to take Sal by surprise. Her eyes opened wide, then, to Rose's surprise, they filled with tears. 'Right,' she said unsteadily, swallowing. 'Right. OK. Well, Tony didn't say anything to you about Eddie, because . . . because he didn't know that Eddie existed.' A tear spilled from an eye and rolled slowly down her cheek.

Rose heard Mum gasp behind her, in just the same way she'd gasped when Sal had told them, way back on Christmas Eve, that Eddie was Dad's brother.

'But, but they grew up together!' said Rose. 'Eddie talked about him in his diary – Dad loved Eddie; they loved each other – they were always playing together! And – surely their mam and dad talked about Eddie to Dad, after he'd disappeared? But anyway, Dad must have remembered him – he wasn't a baby, he was a toddler! He must have remembered!'

'No. No, Rose. See, Aunty Beryl, Uncle Billy – when Eddie disappeared, they couldn't bear to tell little Tony. It was too hard for them. Tony adored his older brother. And, of course, he kept asking about him. Wanted to know where Eddie was. When he was coming home. They didn't know what to say. Didn't know how to answer. And they thought it would be best all round, easier for everyone, if they just pretended he'd never existed.

'So . . . so they told Tony he'd imagined Eddie. That Eddie wasn't real – that he was an imaginary friend, and Tony needed to grow up now and stop playing silly games. Little Tony didn't get it. He kept on asking where Eddie was, saying Eddie was real, he wasn't pretend. And Tony'd get really upset and he'd cry, cry for hours – cry himself to sleep. We'd hear it all, through the wall. It was awful. Tony used to go into Eddie's old room, you know, and lie on the bed, and cry. So Aunty Beryl took all Eddie's clothes away, all his stuff. Threw it all out. Broke her heart. Broke both their hearts. But they'd started with this lie, see, and they had to keep it up.

'Sure they regretted it. But how could they change their story now? How could they tell Tony they'd lied? How could they tell him the truth? That his brother had disappeared and, despite the searches, despite the appeals, he'd not been found and, as time passed, the likelihood of his being found was getting less and less? They wanted to protect Tony from that. They wanted to put it all behind them. So they kept up the lie. And after a while, after a year or so, Tony stopped asking about Eddie. Stopped talking about him. Went quiet. They all went quiet. We had to as well, of course. Me and Mam. We couldn't talk about Eddie to Tony, and pretty soon I couldn't talk about Eddie to Mam, either. She just couldn't bear to. Couldn't cope with it. Too much pain. Too much terrible pain.'

Then Sal sobbed and hid her head in her hands, and her sobs grew and grew, uncontrolled now, tears dripping from between her fingers as her broad shoulders heaved convulsively.

'Oh!' said Mum. Rose looked round to see that she was holding her own face in her hands, the staff gripped against her cheek.

And Rose felt tears running down her cheeks, too. Poor, poor little Tony. Poor Dad. In a flash, an image came to her. How sometimes, she'd come into the kitchen and catch him unawares in his seat by the table, next to the stove. He'd be staring into space, his eyes lost and desolate, deep in memories. 'Dad?' Rose would say, and she'd climb on his knee and hug him and he'd snap out of it, clear his face of pain, smile and hug her back.

She'd known, even then, that there was something very painful inside him, something very sad – something that, as a child, she'd longed to put right for her daddy.

Now she was crying too – sobbing like Sal.

'How could they do that to him?' she wailed.

'Rose. Listen,' said Sal. 'Aunty Beryl, Uncle Billy – they were good people – right? They were good people. They just didn't know what else to do. That's what it was like in those days. People didn't talk about everything then – all their problems, all their worries. You kept it all to yourself – you just kept going. And they were just ordinary people. Ordinary people, struggling with something terrible, struggling to carry on. But it killed them, in the end. The grief, the covering up, the pretending to Tony – it killed them. They died within a year of each other, you know. Cancer. Both of them. When Tony was still a teenager. Only eighteen, he was, and he lost them both.'

The three of them stood in silence. Sal's head was downcast, but she wasn't sobbing any more. Rose rubbed her eyes with her hands and drew in a deep breath. There was one last question.

'Sal – why don't you like the police; why won't you work with the police?'

Sal lifted her head. 'Because of something that happened. Something that happened after Eddie disappeared.

'I . . . attacked someone.'

Rose, heart beating fast, said, 'Did you kill them?'

Sal frowned. 'No. I didn't kill them, but I beat them up. Pretty badly. I didn't know what I was doing. I hit him and hit him and hit him – it was in the school yard. Eventually a teacher pulled me off him. And then the police came, and took me away. Called me a "problem child". Took me out of school. Took me away from Mam. Mam came to the station. Pleaded with them to let me go – let me come home. Told them I was all she had. But they didn't listen. They put me in borstal.'

'What's borstal?' Rose asked. It sounded horrible.

Mum said, 'It's what they used to call a young offenders' institution, love. Go on, Sal.'

'They sentenced me and locked me up for a year. It was awful in there. Scary kids; scary staff. It didn't feel safe. No one was kind . . . And when I came out – well, things were never the same again. I felt like I'd lost everything. I'd lost Eddie. I'd lost Uncle Billy and Aunty Beryl – because it was like they weren't there any more. Walking around like ghosts, they were. Tony like a little ghost too. But worst of all, Mam wasn't the same. Her heart had broken too. And you know, she didn't live long after that.

'I broke her heart. I broke her heart. And I've never forgiven the police, for taking me away, for taking me away from Mam – taking a *child* away from her mam. But more than that, I've never forgiven myself. Never forgiven myself.' Sal looked up, wiping her face with her palms. Mum's imprint was still there on her cheek.

'Who was it,' asked Rose, 'that you beat up?'

'Hah!' Sal snorted, then sniffed, loudly. 'A friend of Eddie's. Except he wasn't a friend. He was a sneaking, treacherous, snake in the grass. It was him that got Eddie expelled. Him that meant Eddie went up to Mamgu's. Him that meant Eddie disappeared.'

'Tomo,' said Rose.

'Tomo,' said Sal.

'Tomo,' repeated Mum, though Rose knew that she didn't know who they were talking about.

'Any more questions?' Sal said then.

'No. No, Sal. No more questions. And, I'm sorry. So sorry. About everything.' And with that, Rose reached behind her to take the staff from her mother's hands. Then she extended the old, dark piece of wood to Sal.

Sal swallowed and gripped the staff with her right hand. And this time . . .

Nothing happened.

Chapter 31

They didn't fly upwards, as they had before. They stayed on the ground, gripping the staff, staring at each other.

And then Rose's knees gave beneath her, suddenly, and she cried out in alarm as the earth shivered. Then came the crack of another gunshot. Letting go the staff, Rose spun around in terror. But there was no one behind them. The only people here were her, Mum, Sal and the antler-man's long, motionless body, the front of his antlers anchoring him in the turf.

Then came a groaning sound and more loud, rapid explosions and Rose saw a long, zigzagging crack open up in the garden wall – from top to bottom. And something stopped. The background hum of running, tinkling water stopped, abruptly. The fountains weren't playing any more.

In this brief silence she heard Mum gasp and saw her running towards the antler-man's body, whose solid form was disappearing, melting into the grass, the antlers falling, suddenly, as dust. Mum dropped to her knees, reaching out to touch him, but already there was nothing left but a dark imprint on the grass, and then not even that.

Then came another loud crack. This time it came from behind them. It was the tower. A powerful, meandering fracture was snaking its way, rapidly, down its stony length. Then a large stone fell from high up, crashing against the tower's wall then thudding into the turf, sinking deeply in. Rose cried out in alarm, backing away and shouting 'Sal! Get away from the tower!'

But Sal didn't move from the tower's door. Staff in hand, she screamed, 'Eddie!' Then she whipped round to Rose. 'We've got to get him out of there—' she shouted, her voice drowned in an avalanche of creaks, groans, cracks and thuds as the stonework above them seemed to come alive, to detonate. Huge chunks of stone fell from the tower and dust spiralled down through the air, coating Sal's short, wild hair. She was pulling at the iron ring on the door, bashing the wood with the half-staff, her mouth open, screaming, as heavy stone rained around her.

'Drudwen!' Rose heard Mum shouting, from behind her. 'Drudwen! We need you!'

Then, 'Look! Look – Rose!' She was pointing at the sky beyond the garden.

A black dot was approaching, flying over the forest through the cloudless blue sky. As it drew closer, they saw that it was a little scrap of a dark-coloured bird, with shining feathers that caught the sun. It was speeding silently with short sharp flaps towards the window of the tower – the window that was still intact, though stones all down the tower's length were exploding outwards, filling it with dusty holes.

Eddie is in there, thought Rose. *How will he survive? How long has he got?* Even with a key to the door – *doors*: as surely there was a door to the room he was locked in, then to the door at the base – how could he make it out before the tower self-destructed completely?

Drudwen reached the window. Was there something in her beak? Rose couldn't tell from down here, through the dust and debris.

The bird rocketed past the window bars and into the glass. Rose cried out and closed her eyes tight. Surely the impact would kill this little bird?

But when she opened them there was no crushed, feathery body, spiralling from the sky.

Instead, through the holes blasted in the side of the tower – even as its top groaned, toppled and fell – they saw, intermittently, a dark shape rushing down spiral stairs, running a race against the destruction of the tower above it. 'Come on, Eddie!' Rose cried. 'Hurry! Hurry!'

Sal was at the door, pulling desperately. Then it swung outwards, knocking her over, and a small, shining bird burst from inside, followed by a flash of dull-green parka as Eddie leapt from the tower and hit the ground running, tripping on a half-buried stone but managing to stay upright, stumbling on at speed, not breaking pace.

They all ran, Rose covering her ears as the tower's walls exploded outwards in a final, deafening act of self-destruction. As if it was roaring in frustration that Eddie had escaped its clutches.

The four of them, breathless, had reached the garden's ruined outer wall. Behind them, the tower settled as a huge pile of rubble, glimpsed vaguely through a seething cloud of dust.

Then Eddie looked round at his companions. His dark, flitting eyes landed first on Rose. 'You,' he said. 'Not you again.' He looked at Mum. 'This your mam, is it?'

Rose nodded, dumbly.

'You found her, in the end. That's good.' Then Eddie turned to his cousin – to Sal, who was staring at him with wide eyes, wringing her hands before her, still trying to catch her breath. *She looks as if she's holding down an over-wound spring,* thought Rose.

Eddie stared at her, a frown growing between his eyes. Then, stepping towards her, tentatively, his face broke into a smile. 'Aunty Nell?' he said. 'That you? Aunty Nell!' He held out his arms to her. 'What you doing here?' He looked around. 'Are you all here? Where's Sal?'

Sal stared back. Then the spring unwound and she rushed forwards, arms outstretched, enveloping him in a hug – sobbing wildly, leaning on to him. 'Eddie,' she said, her voice muffled by his hair. 'Oh, Eddie.'

Eddie laughed, trying to extricate himself. 'Whoah there, Aunty! Steady on, girl. I'm not used to this kind of adulation, you know—'

'Eddie, I'm so glad to see you. So glad to see you . . . Let me look at you.' Sal held him out at arms' length, then hurriedly wiped her eyes on her sleeve, gripping his arm tightly with her other hand.

'It's you. Oh, my goodness. It's really you.' And with that she hugged him to her again. He looked so small, so young, Rose thought, against her large body – it was almost as if she was swallowing him up.

'Course it's me,' he said, pulling away again and grinning. 'The one and only. The escape artist! Did you see me running down inside the tower, back there? Whoah! Race against time, that was. A race against time. Would have floored a lesser man.' Then he noticed her tears, and said, more gently, 'Hey, don't cry! I haven't been gone that long . . .' He tailed off, frowning. 'Have I . . .?' Then he narrowed his eyes, examining Sal's face. 'You OK, Aunty? You look . . . different. And – what happened to your cheek?'

'Ah,' said Sal, flicking her gaze to Mum then back to Eddie, her fingers touching the bruise. 'Someone hit me. Doesn't matter.'

'Someone *hit* you? Why?'

Sal just stared at him, mutely. He stared back, and the old fear, the old confusion, drifted across his face again. Then he shook his head and grinned. 'So, Aunty,' he said. 'Where is everyone? When I went back, couple of days ago now, no one was there. Where were you all? Strange people round our house, wouldn't let me in; no one answering the door at yours. Even Mamgu wasn't home. Trudged up to her place, all the way, through the snow, and she wasn't in. Instead – *she* was.' He pointed at Rose, frowning. 'She was. Still don't know what she was doing there.'

'Eddie –' Rose stepped forward, urgently – 'I'm part of the family, I'm—'

'Yeah, that's Rose,' interrupted Sal loudly, putting an arm round Eddie to steer him away, turning sidelong to Rose with a narrow-eyed frown.

What was Sal doing? She wasn't going to let Eddie think she really was Aunty Nell, was she?

Eddie said, 'Where's Sal then? I know she'll be with you – you wouldn't have come on your own.'

'I . . . I . . . no, Eddie. She's at home, bach. She's, er, waiting to see you.'

'With Mam and Dad and Tony?'

'Ah,' Sal looked wildly about and her eyes met Rose's. Rose was frowning at her, shaking her head, vehemently, from behind Eddie. Sal closed her eyes as if to blot her out. 'Er, yes. Yes, Eddie,' she said, in a strange, high voice. 'With . . . with your mam and dad and Tony.'

Rose gasped – 'Sal, what are you doing? You can't—'

'Shut up. Shut up! You – you don't know anything. You just stay out of this,' snapped Sal, stabbing her finger at Rose.

Eddie's dark eyes flew between the two of them. Then he grinned uncertainly, reaching up to sling an arm round Sal's shoulders. 'That's the best news I've heard all day. What we waiting for then? Let's go home!'

He looked up, put a thumb and forefinger to his lips and whistled sharply. Rose heard a whistle in reply and saw Drudwen, perched in a tree just outside the wall. At Eddie's call, she dropped from the branch, chattered excitedly and swooped to land on Eddie's extended finger. There she sat, small, upright and magnificent, drawing her beautiful, shining wing feathers through her golden beak, one by one.

'She got me out last time, Aunty,' said Eddie, looking down at the bird with a smile. Rose had never seen him look so gentle, and for a moment they all stared at Drudwen, mesmerised by the magical sheen of her coat.

Then Drudwen took to the air and fluttered further into the forest beyond. Following her, they scrambled over a gap in the crumbling wall. Rose looked back and saw that the grass was growing, lengthening as she watched, coming to seed then falling over under its own weight, and that brambles were spreading prickly tentacles across the ground, over the roses, over the ruins of the tower, the dried-out fountains and the breached, uneven wall.

Drudwen led the way through the forest, hurrying them along, flitting between low branches, whistling encouragement. Sal and Eddie went first, weaving around tree trunks; Rose and Mum trudged behind. It was dim and shadowy here, beneath the trees.

'See, there's this big guy here – man with antlers,' Eddie was telling Sal. 'Did you see him?' He turned round to include them all in this question.

Mum was mute, staring miserably at Eddie. Rose kept quiet too. What could she say to Eddie now? What could she say, when he thought he was heading home to his family – a family that were all dead? All dead, apart from Sal – or would that be Aunty Nell, now?

Eddie went on, eagerly, 'Aunty Nell, I've got so much to tell you all, I don't know where to start. I went up to the Cylch Cerrig, see, a week or so ago – no, more like, a month ago? – I don't know. Anyway, doesn't matter. I was following some music – like flute music. It was this tune, this tune that went . . .' He hummed a snatch. Then, 'No,' he said, 'not like that,' and he tried again. 'I can't remember. Never mind. Mamgu knows how it goes – we can ask her. Anyway, then I came into this world. A little man with a big head brought me over the water in a boat – I had to pay him. I gave him all I had in my pocket – half a pence, Aunty Nell!' He laughed at this and touched Sal's arm. 'Half a pence! All I had on me – but he seemed happy enough with it. Then I got locked up by the guy with the antlers. It was mental. He started out being all nice, like he was my dad or something, giving me stuff, anything I wanted. I couldn't believe it. I thought – what's he after? And I got bored. Got bored pretty quickly. And I said, Thanks, and everything, but it's time I went home now. Then he turned all odd, and—' He stopped, and his eyes grew wide.

'Can you hear that?' he went on.

Everyone paused and listened, including Drudwen, who tipped her head to one side as she perched silently on a branch before them.

The thunder of distant, heavy hooves. Getting closer, louder, every moment.

Oh, no, thought Rose, grabbing Mum's hand and starting to run. *Oh, no . . .*

'What is it?' cried Mum.

'It's the Wild Hunt,' gasped Rose. Then she shouted, 'Run! Run for your lives!'

Chapter 32

Drudwen flitting urgently before them as they raced through the forest, dodging tree trunks, feet pounding the soft, pine-needle ground.

The rumbling behind them was growing in volume and the ground was vibrating with hammering hooves. Other sounds, horribly familiar, came too – shouts of men, strident, blasting horns and the crazed baying of hounds that had spotted their prey.

Sal and Eddie ran silently in front of Rose and Mum, their arms held out before them to fend off low branches. Eddie's foot slipped and he righted himself and sprinted on, Sal kept pace; and Rose thought how light on her feet, how fit she was.

Mum ran at her side, grasping her hand, and Rose could hear her gasping for breath. Stealing a glance she saw her frightened eyes and the thick, golden torque around her neck. *The heavy gold is weighing her down,* thought Rose.

Surely the water wasn't far off. But even if they reached it – would the little man and his boat be there? Would the hunt pursue them into water?

Arrows sped through the air now, whizzing past their ears, thudding, vibrating, into trees. The chaotic sounds behind them were so loud that Rose knew if she looked back now she'd see it all – horses, riders, hounds. Sal and Eddie were sprinting well ahead. *Do they realise they're leaving us behind?* Was it every man for himself, again?

Then Rose saw Eddie and Sal pull up short, turn and come sprinting back towards them. At this point Mum stopped too, hands on knees, wheezing to catch her breath. Rose watched as two pairs of terrified, dark eyes, set in two pale faces – so alike – rushed towards her. 'Go back!' shouted Sal, overtaking her and Mum. 'They're coming this way!'

Rose turned, pulling at Mum's hand to drag her along, and saw huge, heavily-muscled grey dogs, curled-back lips revealing rows of sharp, white teeth, leaping through the trees in front of them. Everyone reared back in horror, turning to find more dogs, encircling them, advancing at a crouch; so they could only back up rapidly until they found the bark of a wide tree digging into their backs and they could go no further.

Then Rose remembered. Erwain had saved her and Ianto, back on the mountain. Maybe she would save them now. 'Erwain!' she screamed. 'Erwain! Help us!'

Now Rose could see the horses and their hooded riders in the dim light beneath the trees, like wisps of deadly smoke. At their head, a huge, riderless moon-silver horse stood forward, its bridle hanging loosely over its mane. It fixed them in its fearsome, wild-eyed glare then reared so that its great hooves pawed above their heads.

Rose shrank back as the hooves thumped back, shaking the ground.

This is the antler-man's horse, thought Rose. *The hunt is masterless – leaderless.* And Erwain had not come to their aid. *There's no one to call them off now . . .*

Drudwen perched high above their heads, screaming in panic. Rose gripped Mum's hand hard. Then she felt a large, strong hand find and encircle her other hand. She looked up in surprise into two large, hazel eyes and felt a tiny spring of joy inside her, despite everything, as she met Sal's steady gaze. *Sal is my aunty . . .*

They were all holding hands, backs pressed against the tree trunk.

Rose closed her eyes as the pack of howling dogs leapt forwards as one, as if released from a trap.

Chapter 33

'*Ewch o 'ma! Gadewch nhw fod!* Get out of here! Leave them be!'

A man's voice, determined, strong, rang through the forest like a bell, sweet and true amidst the baying of the hounds and wild horsemen's shouts. Then a series of thumps shook the forest floor – was that hooves on turf or falling bodies?

Rose was cowering against the tree trunk, gripping Mum and Sal's hands for dear life. She heard dogs howling and whimpering. More heavy thuds, together with the swift, slicing sound of metal through flesh. Men and horses screamed in panic. Drudwen screamed too, from above. All this took moments, seconds. Then, through closed eyelids, Rose saw bright, flashing lights.

Her eyes burst open to behold a knight, crouched low and circling the tree in the dim, sunless space beneath the firs. He wore a helmet with dazzlingly bright, golden bands across it. In his hands he held a flashing iron sword with a golden handle which slashed and stabbed at the dogs with easy grace.

Beside her, Mum gave a cry of recognition and so did Rose, for they knew the helmet, the sword. They were King Berwyn's – the symbols of his rule, that were kept, alongside the staff, in the Canolfan. But they did not know the knight who wore them.

Then Rose saw that another figure was protecting them, arms spread to make himself wide. He was dressed in drab colours, a cloth hat on his head, quite eclipsed by the golden warrior. She heard his ragged breathing and realised he was holding a small, silver-bladed axe that he wielded before him, slicing at the hounds, catching them sidelong, sweeping them up, knocking them out. And there was a dog with these two figures and this dog, though small – much smaller than the others – bared its teeth at the attackers, snapping swiftly at their forefeet then retreating to bark and threaten, guarding the four with their backs pinned to the tree.

And each time the golden sword or the silver axe hit a dog, it screamed in agony – mouth wide, teeth bared – then it disintegrated, like Cernunnos, into the forest floor, while the horses behind reared and cried out, their hooded riders shouting, pulling at reins, digging in boots, to keep control.

All this was happening so fast that Rose didn't have time to think. All at once, she heard Sal shout something, release her hand and step forwards, saw a huge hound leap over the dog into the protected circle, mouth open, head slewed to one side, to grab at her neck. Rose screamed, reaching out to pull Sal back and, at that moment, the golden knight turned, his sword sweeping, flat, through the air before him, slicing the rearing hound in two, right before their eyes.

Stumbling, Sal threw herself backwards while the animal fell to the ground and disappeared. Tearing her gaze from this sight, Rose looked up to meet the knight's eyes.

Beneath the helmet, which encircled his dark eyebrows and came down over his nose, brown eyes sparkled at her and his graceful dance stopped, for just a second. But in that moment, the riderless horse leapt through the circle at him, rearing to lift massive front hooves high over his head as if galloping in air, black eyes rolling in deep, dark sockets.

'Ianto!' Rose screamed.

Ianto spun, sword in hand. Then the hooves came down and he sidestepped, lost his footing and fell to the ground, his sword knocked, flying, from his grasp as the horse reared again and its hooves fell, like massive hammers, on to his head.

Without thinking, Rose cried out and dashed forwards, past Mr Williams – who was swinging his axe to drive the horse back – ducking to grab the sword by its handle.

Meanwhile Ianto was crouching on the forest floor, shaking his head unsteadily. The gold-banded helmet had saved his life.

But he was still in danger. 'Watch out!' Rose screamed, drawing the heavy sword through the air as the horse reared once more. The flashing blade missed its hooves by a whisker and it jumped back, awkwardly, on its hind legs, front hooves paddling, loose harness jingling, screaming in fear of the sword.

Now Ianto was up and dancing again, quick as a flash, reaching high for the horse's bridle and long mane as the animal reared, backing away, wildly shaking its head to dislodge him. Ianto held on tight, legs flying through the air, pulling so that the horse's head twisted to one side, its white-rimmed eyes frantic.

Then he slung a leg over the horse's back. And he held on, lopsided, though the horse was bucking now to throw him off, hind legs flying backwards, scattering the horses behind him, causing the whole hunt to mill and circle in panic, men shouting fearfully.

By now, Ianto had found his seat and was sitting upright, back straight and reins tight in his hands – and the horse was suddenly still, its sides heaving with exertion.

Rose and Mr Williams stood back now and Rose let the tip of the sword fall to the earth. Beside her, Mr Williams tucked his axe into his belt, muttering '*Jiw, jiw!*' to himself.

Then Ianto turned to the other riders, and the golden bands on his helmet flashed. '*Ewch o 'ma nawr.* Get out of here now. Leave!' he shouted.

The shadowy, hooded huntsmen pulled at reins to turn their horses' heads, then they thundered away through the trees; black tails, black capes ribboning out behind them, until, very soon, they disappeared amongst the thick trunks and all that remained of them was the diminishing thunder of hooves.

Then Rose stepped forward and reached up to hand back the sword, while the horse shivered in fear and attempted to wheel about. Quickly, Ianto tugged at the rein to bring it under control, and Rose was glad, now, that she had not injured this beautiful creature.

Ianto leant forward to take the sword from her, saw that it was clean and replaced it in the scabbard at his side. Then, looking down at them all, he grinned.

'*Pwy sy moyn lifft?* Who wants a lift?' he said.

Chapter 34

'Mum,' said Rose, at once. 'Mum wants a lift.'

She turned to her mother and Mum managed a shaky nod. Gripping her by the hands, Rose and Mr Williams helped Mum up on to the tall horse, where she sat behind Ianto and clung to his back, her face pale and exhausted. Rose realised that she was still barefoot, her small white feet hanging down against the horse's broad, dappled sides. It made her think of Erwain.

'Sal?' said Ianto now, turning to her. 'You want a lift too?'

Before Sal could answer Eddie stepped forward, frowning. Rose saw that he was shaking, but his words came out strongly enough. 'Who're you calling Sal?' he said. 'You don't even know Sal. This is Sal's mam. Mrs Morris – to you.' Then he turned to her. 'Aunty Nell,' he said, gently. 'You want a lift, Aunty?'

'Er – no, bach. No. I'll walk,' she replied. Then she looked down at her feet, avoiding everyone's eyes.

There was a moment's silence. Ianto was returning Eddie's frown. 'You what . . .?' he began, looking from Eddie to Sal. Then something seemed to click. 'Oh, right,' he said. 'Yeah, of course. Sorry.'

'Why you sorry?' snapped Eddie.

'Sorry because . . . because I misjudged you. Back at Uncle Thomas's. I'm sorry for that.'

'So am I,' said Rose, glad to get this off her chest.

Eddie whipped his head round to look at her, still frowning, but his eyes – large, dark and expressive – were giving him away, as usual. In them, Rose saw the old uncertainty, the old fear.

At this point, Del, who'd sidled up to him unbeknownst, nuzzled forcefully at the side of his leg with her nose. He looked down then dropped to his knees, taking Del's long head in his hands, looking into her eyes – one blue, one brown – as she gazed up at him. 'Hey, Del!' he said, ruffling her head and her silky ears. 'Hey, girl! I've missed you, you know?'

Without taking her eyes off him, without moving her head, Del gave a short, sharp bark, wagging her tail.

'She missed you too, lad. Been moping about the place, she has. Looking out for her friend. No time for her old master any more, oh no.'

At Mr Williams's voice, Eddie jumped upright, and now his eyes were shining with joy. 'Tomo!' he exclaimed, grinning widely, turning to him with arms outstretched.

Rose watched Mr Williams grin back and step forward, then hesitate. But Eddie wasn't hesitating. Abandoning Del, he rushed to enclose Mr Williams in a hug.

Rose held her breath. Mr Williams wasn't a hugger. He wasn't going to like this. But, to her amazement, he put his arms round Eddie and held him tightly and, as he did so, she saw tears start from his blue, blue eyes to run, sparkling, down his cheeks.

Some instinct, some prickling feeling from behind her,

made her turn. Sal's eyes were fixed on Eddie and her mouth was open in a kind of silent scream. 'Eddie!' she said loudly, stepping forwards frantically with her own arms outstretched, and Rose knew she wanted to tear him away from Mr Williams, to keep him all to herself. 'Eddie . . .' she finished, quietly, dropping her hands and clutching at them instead.

Eddie broke away from Mr Williams and turned to her. 'Aunty Nell! Aunty Nell – this is Tomo.'

When she didn't reply but continued to stare dumbly at him, he went on, eagerly, 'Not to be confused with the other Tomo, the one at school. No, this Tomo's a *real* friend. Put me up, he did, when I was on the run. Him and Del and Gwenllian.'

Mr Williams was frowning now. 'Aunty Nell, eh?' he said slowly, watching Sal.

Sal was wringing her hands again, as if she might burst with anxiety. At that moment a loud squawk came from above.

All eyes flew upwards. Drudwen was sitting on a branch above their heads, watching them with a sharp, dark eye. When she had their attention, she took off from her perch, flapped her wings and flew ahead, chattering impatiently.

Chapter 35

The moon-grey horse walked on beneath the trees with Mum sitting silently on his wide back, her arms gripping Ianto. Ianto held the reins loosely, the gold-banded helmet still on his head, the sword at his side. Rose walked alongside her mum, with the horse's shiny flank looming above her. She could smell his rich, warm, horsey smell, mingled with the fresh scent of the still forest.

Following Drudwen, Mr Williams and Eddie led the way. Rose could only see the back of them, but she could sense the ease and comfort of their companionship. In between them and the horse, Sal stumped, head down, and Rose felt pure misery coming from her slumping back.

Poor Sal, thought Rose. Then she realised, *Sal has done this to herself*. She'd lied about who she was, about what had happened to the rest of the family. In doing so, she had, in some strange and hidden way, cut herself off from everyone and made them turn from her.

Del circled them all, keeping them together, checking that everyone was present and correct. But Rose wasn't sure that everyone was quite present and correct . . .

Mum was staring straight ahead. The mouth that was always smiling wasn't smiling. The eyes that usually sparkled looked extinguished. Rose had never known her to be so quiet. She reached up to gently put a hand on her knee.

'All right, Mum?' she asked, in a low voice.

Mum looked down at her and managed a nod. 'We're going home,' Rose said.

'Yes,' said Mum, in monotone.

Now Ianto looked down at Rose. '*Ti'n iawn?* You OK?' he asked her, quietly, with a tentative smile.

'*Ydw, Ianto*. Yes,' she replied. 'Thanks to you. And Mr Williams, and Del. Thanks.' She felt strangely shy and could not hold his earnest gaze. But then she smiled to herself. And looked up once more to see that he was still watching her. This time they shared a grin and Rose felt herself relaxing. Yes, he'd been amazing. But he was also the same old Ianto. Her best friend.

At that moment, 'So,' announced Eddie, turning as he walked to include them all. 'How did you three find us?'

'Well now,' said Mr Williams, and he cleared his throat '*Ahem!*' in a very familiar way, then took a deep breath in.

Uh-oh . . . Ianto glanced down again at Rose and winked. This might take some time . . .

'*Roedd hi'n dipyn o sioc* . . . It was a bit of a shock when you disappeared, Rose fach, back at the Cylch Cerrig,' Mr Williams began, speaking loudly so everyone could hear. 'An awful shock. But we knew where you'd gone – knew that Cath and Eddie and, er . . . you,' he turned his head to address Sal, 'had all gone there too. So we had to decide what to do. First things first, we rescued the quad bike and headed home.

'Then we made plans. Me, Ianto, Mary, Gwenllian – we all sat down up at my place, and we made plans. We knew we had to find a way to get to Annwn, so we could get you all out of here. And quickly – as quickly as we could – what with time being . . .' Mr Williams glanced at Eddie, 'Yes. *Ahem*. So Ianto got out Old Thomas Williams's book, *Gwyddoniadur Celtaidd*, didn't he. *A Celtic Encyclopedia*. Read it to us – the section on Annwn.

'Well. I tell you, it was as if Old Thomas Williams was with us too – one of the company around that kitchen table. Giving us information – vital information, as if he knew it was going to come in handy, some time in the future. Found out from Old Thomas Williams about the different ways people get to Annwn. Some follow music – sweet, entrancing music. Some fall in love with the the fairy folk, and go with them—'

At this, Mum sobbed, loudly and suddenly. 'Sorry, bach,' Mr Williams murmured, grimacing in sympathy.

'Ahem!' he went on, striding forward again. 'Some get called because they're family, family to the *tylwyth teg*, the fair folk themselves. That'll be you, Rose, Eddie, and er . . .' He waved his hand at Sal. 'Because, as we all know, this Cernunnos is—'

'*Was*,' interjected Sal in a loud voice. All eyes turned to her. She'd lifted her head and looked defiant, for a moment.

'*Was*, eh?' Mr Williams's blue eyes opened wide. He shook his head and whistled then glanced, quickly, at Mum, who sat rigid behind Ianto, her eyes screwed tight shut. '*Was*,' he went on, in a lower voice, 'your many, many times over, great grandfather.

'Then,' he went on, a bit more brightly, 'some meet with the Wild Hunt, the Hounds of Annwn – and when they do, it's only a matter of time before they go back there . . .'

'That's what happened to us,' Ianto said to Rose. She looked up at him, sitting high on the horse. Was she imagining it, or had he grown taller?

Suddenly, she had a little, warm feeling. A little, warm feeling that she watched, fearfully, waiting for it to disappear. But it didn't disappear – it grew, just a tiny bit. And with it came the thought that maybe, just maybe, everything would be all right, now. OK, they weren't out of Annwn yet, but they were all together again – and, best of all, best of all – she gently squeezed Mum's knee again – Mum, Mum was here too!

'But I couldn't afford to wait,' Ianto was continuing. 'There was no time to waste – we had to find you all, get you back. Mamgu was pretending you were still safe and sound with her, Rose, but you know what Dad's like. It's hard to keep secrets from him. Any moment he was going to find out you'd gone too.'

'Wait a minute,' said Rose, her heart beating suddenly fast. 'How long have we been gone?'

Mr Williams and Ianto looked at each other. 'Tonight is New Year's Eve, bach,' said Mr Williams, though it was still daytime here beneath the trees.

New Year's Eve, thought Rose. *Three days have passed – or is it two?* She was losing track.

'So we tried to work out how to get here, quickly,' said Ianto. 'All we could come up with was the family option. Getting here by pretending we were part of your family – somehow. And then Mamgu had a brainwave. The brainwave to steal Berwyn's sword and helmet.'

'Mamgu wanted to *steal* them?' Rose was shocked.

Ianto smiled down at her. 'Not steal. *Borrow*. That's what she wanted to do. Borrow them – use them, then put them back again, before anyone's the wiser. Because they belonged to one of your ancestors, of course. And we already knew they were magical, after what happened in the summer. So we thought if we borrowed them, and one of us actually wore them—'

'Ahem,' said Mr Williams, loudly. 'Who's telling this story, boy?'

Ianto grinned. 'Sorry, Uncle. You are.'

'Well now,' he said. 'We all agreed that the helmet and the sword were our best bet. But how to get at them; how to *borrow* them – that was the thing. There's still a twenty-four-hour police guard around that Canolfan till they get those doors fixed properly. How the heck were we going to get past that? But that's where those wise women, Mary and Gwenllian, came in. Together, they cooked up a scheme of their own. See, Gwenllian has already befriended the guard who does the evening shift. You know how kind she is?' Mr Williams was beaming, proudly. 'She's taken to bringing him a hot drink every evening, to warm him up. Has a little chat with him too, so he doesn't feel all alone. So, of course, there was nothing unusual about tonight, when Gwenllian went down to see him with a mug of steaming, milky hot chocolate in her hand. Nothing out of the blue when he took from her and took a grateful sip; had a little chat with her, about this and that – his new year's resolutions and so on, I expect. But little did he know – little did he know, that tonight, there was a special, new year's ingredient in his drink.'

Rose saw Mr Williams's shoulders begin to jerk up and

down and soon, sure enough, 'Heh, heh, heh, heh, heh!' he went, his face screwed up with mirth.

'What was it?' asked Rose. 'Whiskey?' She was a little shocked, again.

'No, bach. Not whiskey. We wouldn't have done that to him. Might lose him his job – and we don't want that. No, those two ladies gathered some herbs and suchlike – not sure what, to be honest – and cooked up a sleeping potion. Found the recipe, handwritten, in an old, old cookery book that Mary had stashed away somewhere. You know how she never throws anything out?' Mr Williams looked around at them, wide-eyed. 'Not like me, of course,' he went on. Rose opened her mouth to laugh, before realising that Mr Williams was completely serious. She looked up at Ianto, he caught her eye and winked again, grinning.

Meanwhile Mr Williams was continuing, 'Well, sometimes, just sometimes, it turns out some of these old things are worth saving. That policeman gulped down the rest of his hot chocolate – loved it, he did – and the next thing we knew (we were watching him from Gwenllian's window) he was slumped against the front of the Canolfan, behind the wall, fast asleep. Felt a bit bad about it, did Gwenllian. But she and Mary were very careful to get the measurements just right, and with a bit of luck he'll only be out for a few hours.

'So then we had to get to work, and quickly. The place was deserted. But we couldn't take any chances. Me and Ianto put on hoodies and wrapped scarfs round our faces, so only our eyes showed. Crept down, out of Gwenllian's flat, and slid past the snoozing policeman. Got inside. They'd taken the helmet and the sword out of the smashed glass case, of course. Locked them in a safe, instead.'

Rose's heart fell. 'So how did you get into the safe?'

She looked up to see Ianto's eyes twinkling at his uncle. Mr Williams said, 'Aha. Well. This clever one . . .' Jerking his thumb over his shoulder at Ianto, Mr Williams allowed him the limelight for a bit.

Ianto said, 'I guessed what the combination was.'

'How?' Had Ianto suddenly developed magic powers?

'Because it was a computer password, and Dad had set it. See, Dad always uses the same password for everything – he doesn't know that I know, but he does.'

'What is it?' asked Rose at once, without thinking.

'I can't tell you that, bach,' he said, smiling down at her.

'No, course you can't.' She shook her head and smiled back. 'But it worked? It was the right password?'

'I couldn't believe it myself,' admitted Ianto, 'but yes, it was. I keyed it in, there was this little click, and the safe opened. And there were the helmet and the sword. Shining in the darkness, like they wanted to come out, wanted to be worn, wanted to help find you all. But as soon as we get home, I'm having a word with Dad about his password. He's got to change it – and start using different ones too.'

'Ahem!' said Mr Williams loudly, wrestling the story back from Ianto. 'So we made off into the night with the sword and the helmet. Past the sleeping policeman and back up to my place, for phase two of the plan. Which was, of course, for us to head back to the Cylch Cerrig, with the helmet and the sword. Because we'd learned something else from Old

Thomas Williams. That is, that people tend to get to Annwn from special places. Like stone circles and cromlechs and caves. There's a word for them – it's on the tip of my tongue. What's the word, boy?'

'Portals,' said Ianto.

'Portals – there we are. And, of course, we'd seen for ourselves that the Cylch Cerrig was just such a portal. So we were going to head up there, put on the helmet and sword – then, well, hope for the best.

'But as it happens, we didn't go anywhere. We got back up to my place, shut the door behind us. Ianto tried on the helmet, unsheathed the sword; I got out the little old axe, thinking it might come in handy; Del stuck close by us, then . . . hey presto, we were in this forest! And well – we had to be on our toes – had to hit the ground fighting! No easy job, dispatching the Hounds of Annwn – I can tell you.

'If this *is* Annwn, of course,' he added.

'It's Annwn,' said Rose. 'It's definitely Annwn.'

As she spoke, she saw light between the trees ahead of them – glimpses of sparkling water and snatches of blue sky.

And presently they were all standing, blinking, on the shore of Annwn.

On the shining waters before them, in his wooden boat, sat the little man with the big head, paddle in hand. And he was glaring at them with such vicious malevolence that a shiver coursed down Rose's spine, as if she'd been stabbed in the back.

Chapter 36

The horse shook his head and stamped his feet and Ianto dropped easily from his back. Then he and Rose helped Mum down too. So that soon they all stood in a line on the edge of the water, staring silently at the boatman.

The little man stared back and the hatred in his dark eyes seemed to grow in intensity as he moved his gaze from one to the other, lingering lastly on Del. Rose saw a ridge of fur rearing rapidly along Del's neck, and she let out a long, low growl.

The grey horse shied backwards and rolled its eyes, then it spun rapidly and took off at a gallop into the darkness of the forest. And Drudwen, who'd been fluttering above their heads, sped to follow him, disappearing swiftly amongst the pines.

Silence. Rose looked at the others, then pulled herself up tall and took a deep breath.

'*Ewch â ni i'r ochr arall,*' she said loudly, trying to sound confident. 'Take us to the other side.'

But she knew, as soon as the words left her lips, that he wasn't buying it this time.

Instead, he focused his hate-filled stare on her. The shiver coursed down Rose's spine again and she had to drop her eyes.

Then, suddenly, she knew what to do. Turning to her, she

whispered, 'Mum, he wants payment, to take us over the water.'

Mum frowned in confusion, then she opened her eyes wide – 'Oh! I left my bag behind, in the garden! Everything was in it – phone, purse . . .'

'Don't worry, Mum.' Rose squeezed her hand then went on, 'I think . . . I think he'd probably be happy with the,' she looked at Mum and touched at her own throat, 'the, um . . . torque.'

Mum's face cleared then she frowned again, hard, clutching at the torque, backing away from Rose and shaking her head.

'No,' she said. The lines between her eyes deepened even further. '*No!*' she cried. 'This was a *present*. A present, from the man I love. How *dare* you ask for it? How dare you suggest that I let it go? It's all I have, of him. All I have!' She was shouting now, shaking with anger.

Rose's hands flew to her cheeks, as if Mum had slapped her hard about the face. 'I . . .' she stumbled. 'I'm so sorry, Mum. Of course.' Unable to hold her mother's eyes, she stared down at the clear, clear water lapping at the shore.

Then, 'Ahem.' Mr Williams. 'Anyone got any cash on them?'

Rose knew she didn't. But the others felt in their pockets. And came up empty.

Then Rose remembered her phone – perhaps he'd like that? 'Look—' she began, forcing herself to meet his eyes, pulling it from her pocket at the same time as Ianto whispered, 'Do you think he wants the sword and the helmet?'

'*Do you think he wants the sword and the helmet?*' spat the man, suddenly, sneeringly. 'You think I want *objects*? That *objects* are important, at this time?

'I have objects. Objects, I have aplenty.' Violently, he ripped the pouch from his neck, breaking the cord that held it in place. It jingled with the sound of metal on metal as he yanked at the top to open it wide. Hard, furious eyes fixed on them, he reached over the side of his boat and turned it upside down. 'Here are objects,' he cried.

And out they poured, on and on, as if the small bag was a bottomless pit. Torques. Coins. Rings. Chains. Amulets. Pendants. Brooches. Buckles. Bars. Bangles. Rose watched these trinkets sink into the clear water, clinking as they went, sparkling like glitter, like a shoal of iridescent, descending fish. Disappearing into the dark depths.

'*Objects*,' repeated the man, shaking the bag so that the last, small, golden coin slipped out, hitting the water with a tiny splash then swinging down, shining, until they could see it no more.

Then he spat, 'You stand here, gibbering of *objects*, when time has been pulled apart. When something – something *immense* – has been annihilated.

'It has been destroyed!' he shouted. 'Tell me – do you, any of you, know what you have *done*?'

His eyes roved over them. 'I will tell you,' he went on, leaning forward alarmingly, making them all recoil. 'You have destroyed something more important than all the millions of mortal beings in your puny, miserable world!

'You are nothing!' he screamed at them. 'Nothing! You

dolts! How long do you live? Tell me – old man,' whipping his head to fix on Mr Williams, 'You. How long do you have left?'

Mr Williams stood, stunned. But the boatman did not wait for an answer. 'Not long,' he continued, nodding his head. 'Not long now for you, old man. Not long for you all. You may live for, what? Eighty years, ninety – one hundred, if you are lucky?

'There was one dwelt here, one who had lived for millennia. No – more than that. For aeons. One who was a *god*. Was . . .' here his face twisted in agony, 'my master.'

Now tears flowed down his lined, brown cheeks. He sobbed, loudly, a horrible, guttural sound as if he was being strangled – 'Ah–Ah–Ah–Ah–Ah!'

Then he choked out, stabbing at them with a pointed finger, 'One of you. One of you – took his life.'

They stood frozen in place. Watching him in horror.

Dark eyes narrowed to slits, he went on, 'One of you – is a *murderer*. Which one?

'You want to go to the other side? Give me the murderer. That is the price.'

Chapter 37

Rose dared not look at Sal, who stood next to her, hanging her head. From the corner of her eye, she noted that she, like them all, was still as a statue.

No one spoke.

Then, before she knew what she was doing, Rose stepped forward. 'We all killed him,' she announced, daring to meet the boatman's eye.

The little man shot upright in the boat, making her jump backwards in shock. 'Do you take me for a dolt like you?' he hissed at her. 'No. I know that it was one of you. One of you, acting on their own. Give me them.'

'No,' said Rose.

'Then you will all stay here. Stay here – forever.'

Now Rose looked around at her companions. And she met two sets of eyes – Mr Williams's and Ianto's. They nodded, determinedly.

Eddie was frowning hard, watching Sal. Sal was staring at the ground. He sighed. Then he turned to Rose, and nodded.

'Mum?' Rose asked, gently. Slowly, Mum raised her head and, after a pause, she nodded too. At her side, Del whined, faintly, hackles still up.

Still Sal did not look up. Her large body hung as awkwardly as a stringed puppet draped over a chair.

'Er – Aunty?' whispered Rose.

No reaction.

She waited a bit. Still nothing.

OK, then.

'So be it,' Rose announced, to the man. 'We will all stay here.'

The boatman sat down at the prow of his boat, watching her. Then he faced forward and, picking up the paddle, pushed off from the shore. He drew the narrow, wooden boat swiftly through the water towards the horizon, where they could just make out the shimmer of the further shore. He did not turn to look at them again.

And then, shockingly, Sal burst into life.

Before any of them could react she leapt forward, splashing heavily into the water. 'Wait!' she shouted, wading forwards until her feet gave way beneath her and she fell into the deep water beyond the island's shelf. 'I am the murderer!' she screamed, wildly, gasping as she sank up to her neck. 'Take me – let the rest go home.'

Chapter 38

'Aunty Nell! What are you doing? Come back!'

The next moment, Eddie was leaping into the water after her. He splashed headlong into the depths as she swam forward, her air-filled coat ballooning out so she looked like a small, humpbacked whale. Spluttering, spitting water, he made a grab for her leg and yanked her backwards, ducking her head beneath the water as he did so, so that only her coated, humped back could be seen clearly amongst the splashing limbs.

Sal kicked out at him then, her booted foot catching his head. Eddie swore loudly, but kept hold of her other leg, struggling to pull her back. Sal's head came up, soaking hair plastered against her head. 'I am the murderer!' she shouted again, in the direction of the receding boat. 'Take me. Let them go—'

By this stage, Eddie had grappled a hold of her body and now the two of them fell beneath the surface, wrestling madly, the water around them boiling until suddenly, shockingly, they surfaced once more, gripped in each other's arms, gasping for breath – and then they were under again, the water turbulent with their flailing bodies.

'For heaven's sake! They'll drown out there!' shouted Mr Williams, throwing off his coat and wading towards them, shouting, 'Hey!'

But the boatman had heard Sal's call and he'd turned his boat, paddling back towards them. Sal, pushing madly at Eddie's restraining arms, saw him and screamed, 'I am the murderer—' punching out at Eddie and catching his cheek with her elbow, so hard that he cried out, clutching his face; then Sal struck out for open water, kicking at him as he scrambled to catch her legs again. Now she was off, heading determinedly for the wooden boat with strong, even strokes.

Eddie started after her, splashing awkwardly in her wake, but by now she was far ahead. For a few moments he trod water, watching her retreat. And then, defeated, he turned and swam the short distance to shore, where Mr Williams was waiting, knee-deep in water, to haul him out. He was gasping for breath and sobbing with fear and frustration, tears mixing with the water that dripped down his face from his sodden hair.

'What's the matter with her?' he choked. 'She's not a murderer. She can't be! She's not the murderer – is she?' he implored Mr Williams.

Mr Williams did not answer. Instead, he helped Eddie out of his soaking parka and wrapped his own, dry coat about him. Then they all turned to see that Sal had reached the boat – and that her head was bobbing above the surface next to its prow.

The boatman looked down at her. Then he stood up and, taking his paddle in both hands and lifting it high, he held it vertical, blade down, over her head.

Suddenly Sal spun in the water and shouted, 'Eddie!' waving her arms.

Eddie gave a small, agonised cry in reply, breaking away from Mr Williams to run to the water's edge.

'Eddie, forgive me,' she was shouting. 'I'm Sal. I'm not Mam – not your Aunty Nell. I'm Sal. All I ever wanted was for you to come home. So, go home now, Eddie. Go—'

And then the boatman brought the blade of his paddle down – hard, vicious – on to the crown of her head, and Sal disappeared beneath the surface of the water.

Chapter 39

Five miserable people huddled together, silently, in the wooden boat, facing the boatman's hostile back as he paddled towards the strip of land before them. Del, however, moved restlessly from the front to the back of the boat, whining.

'Del!' hissed Mr Williams. 'Come here, girl.'

Del obeyed and sat before him, looking up into his eyes, but she did not stop whining.

She's telling us we've left someone behind, thought Rose.

Because Sal had not surfaced again.

Rose felt as if she'd left a part of herself behind with her. Eddie, dripping wet, held his head in his hands, beneath Mr Williams's protective embrace.

Sal was my aunty . . . thought Rose. And then she began to sob.

Hearing her, Eddie looked up and met her eyes. Then he looked beyond her, to the back of the boat where a pool of water had gathered, shining, on the wooden hull. 'Sal was always a brilliant swimmer,' he said. 'School champion. Did you know that?'

Rose shook her head, miserably. But she could believe it. Sal had swum like a professional.

'School champion,' repeated Eddie, staring, unfocused, at the back of the boat. 'Won every race.'

Eventually, they disembarked on the other side. Without turning his head to look at them, the boatman pushed off from shore and paddled away. Rose looked back at the faraway island, and it was like looking at a distant, dark dream.

Then, *Maybe we should all hold hands?* she thought, but she was too late. A familiar feeling hit her and she wobbled on her feet, falling downwards through herself. She screamed 'Mum!' and desperately reached out to hold on to her, but her fingers closed on air. Surrounded by rushing darkness, she heard a snatch of the tune of the pipe. Then nothing. And suddenly she was breathing in cold air, full of the rich, damp smells of a wood in winter, and her booted feet were in contact with the earth. And so she knew that she was home again.

As her eyes grew accustomed to the sudden darkness she saw a large, grey shape, glinting slightly in dim starlight. The cromlech. She was in the clearing in the middle of the wood. And the others were with her, including Mum. She reached out to grab hold of her hand.

Mr Williams cleared his throat and said, 'Well, well, well. *Dyma ni.* Here we are. I wonder what time it is—?'

His question was interrupted by a sudden, loud crack from the dark sky above. They raised their heads to see a small ball of fire explode, open out with golden rays then drift down in molten drops. That was just the start. Another, then another, then a crowd of them, a host of fireworks from the village beyond the wood, lighting up the sky and exposing the skeletons of naked, winter trees.

Midnight, New Year's Eve.

So, thought Rose, we haven't gone forward in time – or not very far anyway. Is that what the boatman had meant, when he said that time had been pulled apart?

Del had been trembling, cowering against Mr Williams's leg. Now, with an agonised howl, she went shooting off into the trees, a blur of terrified black and white fur.

'Damn fireworks!' exclaimed Mr Williams, running after her, closely followed by Ianto and Eddie. 'Del, *here girl!*'

He soon emerged from the trees, stooping to drag a shivering Del out of the undergrowth by the collar. 'I better get her home,' he said. 'Eddie, bach, you come too. Ianto – take off that gear and get it back to the Canolfan: now, before the policeman wakes up.'

And so they all split up – Ianto, clutching the sword and the helmet beneath his coat and setting off for the village; Mr Williams, Del and Eddie heading up the mountain to his cottage; Mum, shivering with bare feet and no coat, and Rose, still holding her hand, taking the short path home.

And all felt heavy and empty with the loss of Sal.

Chapter 40

Early the next morning, Rose awoke in a dark bedroom with a fast-beating heart. She'd had an awful dream, that she couldn't remember, but its feeling, that something dreadful had happened; was about to happen, stayed with her. Where was she? Then her heart began to slow a little. She was home. She was in her bed, at home.

But where was Mum? The panic returned as she leapt from her bed and rushed to Mum's bedroom. The door was ajar. Rose tiptoed around it and there she was, asleep in the big bed, and Rose hung her head in relief, getting her breath back.

Mum's face was lit up, just a little, by the dim light of the moon through the thin curtains. Rose moved closer then kneeled by the bed, to examine this face, to try to plumb its depths. Mum's skin was pale and there was a little frown between her brows. Her mouth was closed tightly. She looked unhappy, even in sleep. Rose sighed. *I've never really looked at Mum before,* she thought. *Now I am.* How could you know someone so well, and yet, not know them?

It was impossible to look at her properly, really examine her, when she was awake, because she was always moving, her expressions always changing. Now she was still, breathing gently. The thick torque was still about her neck, catching the little light that came through the curtain. The duvet had slipped, exposing Mum's small, white feet. Gently Rose rearranged the duvet so they wouldn't get cold.

Then she padded back to her bedroom, and got into bed again.

The next thing she knew, an insistent, mechanical sound was pulling her cruelly from sleep. It was her phone, lit up on the floor by her bed.

Lifting it, she noticed that dawn light was creeping around the outside of her curtain.

Unknown number.

'That you, Rose?'

'Uh—' Rose choked, her eyes opening wide, sitting bolt upright.

Before she could say a word, Sal's voice continued, 'Listen, I'm in the woods next to your house. Something's happening. You and your mam need to get out here at once.'

At last, Rose found her voice. 'Sal?' she cried. 'Sal!' But the phone was dead already.

Rose leapt from her bed. Throwing jeans and sweatshirt over her pyjamas, she rushed into Mum's room.

'Mum! Get up!' she shouted.

Mum groaned and turned over, so that her face was hidden in the pillow. Rose grabbed her shoulders and shook her. 'Wake up, Mum! Something's happening in the wood. We need to get out there, now.' Mum turned over, lifted her arms to push Rose's hands off then sat up, facing her. '*What?*' she said, wearily.

Rose was tearing open Mum's wardrobe, pulling out clothes. Randomly, she threw Mum a woolly jumper and some sweatpants. 'Put these on.'

But Mum had lain down again, pulled the duvet over her head.

'Mum!'

'Go away,' came a muffled voice. 'I'm not going anywhere. Not going anywhere, any more.'

Rose leapt on to the bed and yanked at her shoulders again, frustration making her brutal, while her mother cried out in protest.

'Shut up, Mum,' she hissed, urgently, 'and listen. It was Sal who told me to go to the wood. Sal phoned me. Just now. Said we had to get out there—'

Now Mum was up – alert, frowning. 'Sal? How—?'

She didn't waste any more time. She dressed, quickly, and soon the two of them were hurrying through the wood to the cromlech's clearing. The sun was lighting the sky through thick clouds in the east, though the wood was still clothed in the cold, dusky shadow of the mountain.

But when they burst through the trees into the clearing they could see well enough.

Rose gasped in horror. Two figures were before them. One, upside down, hanging in the air from the high branch of a tall tree, feet held together at the ankle by a thick rope noose. His arms hung loosely, swinging slightly, a couple of feet off the ground. Shaggy, dark hair hung down from his head.

Next to him, standing upright, a large hunting knife – the kind with a long, shining blade and a jagged ridge along the top – in his hand, was a tall, broad figure, dressed head to toe in camouflage gear, a khaki beret on his head. This man was holding the knife across the throat of the hanging man, and the hanging man was squirming away from it, throwing back his head, swinging alarmingly close to the blade.

The figure of the man with the knife was familiar, but Rose couldn't place him.

Then he turned, saw Rose and her mother at the edge of the clearing, threw back his head and laughed, still holding the knife at the victim's throat.

It was the hunt master.

'I got him!' he shouted, excited. 'I got him.'

Turning back to the hanging man, he stabbed at his midriff, not quite making contact, and the man writhed away in fear, crying out wordlessly in a deep, agonised voice. The hunt master laughed again, delightedly, and spun back to Rose and Mum.

'Saw there was someone here,' he told them. 'Living rough, some kind of tramp. Outsider. Who knows where he's from? Been using the cromlech as a shelter. Then I saw who it was! Look!' He pulled something from a pocket and, despite themselves, Rose and Mum crept closer to see it.

Still holding the knife, the man hurriedly smoothed a crumpled piece of paper on his leg then shoved it, shaking, under their noses. It was the poster, the awful *HAVE YOU SEEN THIS MAN?* poster. With the identikit picture of the antler-man, without his antlers.

Rose found her tongue at last. 'No!' she cried. 'Let him down – it can't be him—' and then the hanging man spun round so they saw his face. Dark, frightened eyes, open wide, stared into Rose's. And she saw that it *was* him. It was the antler-man, without antlers. Without – *power*.

Beside her, Mum screamed, 'Let him down!' and she rushed forwards.

Frowning, the hunt master grabbed at her arm, stopping her. Pulling her back, he held her before him and focused on her. The frown grew, then he opened his eyes wide.

'Wait a minute – you're Cath – Cath Morris! The missing woman! Well – would you credit it? I've got you both! Caught you both, red handed! He been hiding you somewhere, has he?'

Mum looked at him. Then, suddenly, she ducked her head to bite down into his hand, hard. He cried out in surprise and let go as she shouted, 'Cut him down! Let him go!' Then she lunged for the hunt master, grappling with him for the knife.

Stepping back, he held the blade high above her reach, laughing as she punched and kicked at his large body, and said, 'Hey, hey, hey, lady! This is a dangerous man – you should know that.' He put out his hand and grabbed her arm again to hold her away from him as she screamed in protest. 'We're not going to cut him down. Not yet, anyway. Not till we've taught him a lesson.'

Rose, meantime, was digging in her pocket for her phone. But the huntsman had spotted her. 'What you doing?' he yelled, letting go of Mum's arm and stepping towards her.

'Calling the police,' she said, backing away with the phone in her hand.

With a surprising burst of speed the hunt master ran at her, knife outstretched, and snatched the phone from her grip. 'No!' he shouted, red-faced. 'No police here. We know better than them. We know what people like him need.' With this he flung his arm backwards and threw her phone high and far, into the bare trees.

But he'd taken his eye off the ball. Mum was behind him now, yanking up his arm behind his back. He screamed in pain and fury; his hand opened wide and the knife dropped to the ground. 'You ungrateful witch!' he spat, his back arched in agony.

Quick as a flash, Rose sprang on the knife, gripping it tightly by its rubber handle. At the same time, he managed a vicious kick backwards that sent Mum flying and landing with a painful thump on the ground.

Then he advanced on Rose, arms outstretched, eyes narrowed. He was huge. Huge, strong, and seemingly fearless. Rose swallowed, holding the knife out before her, stabbing at him with it and backing off. She didn't know what she was doing, and she knew that he could tell. Now he was smirking, chuckling. Enjoying himself. 'What you doing, girl?' he whispered.

'Get away from me,' said Rose, her voice shaking, lunging at him with the blade.

Then she saw movement behind him. Mum was climbing the hanging man's tree, hauling herself up into its branches. The huntsman saw her focus change, turned his head to follow her gaze and, on pure instinct, Rose stepped forward and swiped at his hand with the knife. She felt flesh tear against the blade, saw blood spurt from his fingers and run, like a trickling tap, to the ground. The huntsman swore and grabbed his injured hand around the wrist, holding it up while Rose bolted, sprinting, bloody knife in hand, past him to the tree.

Here, in a single, split second, she realised she had only one option. And that was to grip the razor-sharp, bloodied knife between her teeth while she used both hands to climb the tree and reach Mum, who was edging along the branch that held the hanging man's rope.

Rose was breathing hard, hauling herself up, her boots skidding against the trunk to find purchase, grazing her cold hands against the rough bark, tasting the steel of the blade and the iron of the hunt master's blood in her mouth.

Soon she was high up in the canopy. At the junction with the branch. Clinging to the trunk with one hand, she took the blade from her mouth and reached out to hand it to Mum, who grabbed the handle, leaned over and, with a swift, slicing action, cut the rope that held the hanging man.

The branch rebounded, but Mum and Rose held on like monkeys, watching from above as the man fell to the ground, cushioning his fall with his hands. Then, awkwardly, he tried to stand, but his legs were still bound together and he stumbled forwards, falling down. At this point, the huntsman, roaring with rage, blood dripping from his injured hand, ran at him.

'Ceri!' screamed Mum and he looked up at her with wide, dark eyes, while behind him Rose saw the barrelling huntsman trip over something, land, sprawling, full out, then try to scramble to his feet again. But, oddly, he stayed put on the ground. 'Get off me!' he yelled, squirming.

And then, from out of the trees came two tall figures, striding forwards, both so alike. Mr Lewis, the policeman, and Ianto, his son. Rose had never, ever been so glad to see them.

'*Beth sy'n bod fan hyn?* What's going on here?' called Mr Lewis, looking about and taking it all in.

The huntsman, with bloodied hand, pinned to the ground; the dark-haired man with the bound ankles; the mother and the daughter up a tree – the mother holding a bloodied knife.

'You two OK up there?' he asked.

Then he said, 'Cath – you want to drop that knife now? Just let it go, bach.'

And she did. She let it go and it sliced, blade first, deep into the damp earth beneath the tree.

Mr Lewis pulled on a blue glove and took a large plastic bag from his pocket, picking up the knife and dropping it in. In the meantime Rose and Mum climbed down the tree, while Ianto helped the bound man undo the rope that held his ankles together.

At last, Ceri stood before Mum. A freed man.

Rose looked at his face, as he stared, wide-eyed, at her mother. It was him. It was Cernunnos, the antler-man. But he was so different. He looked – *ordinary*. He was still tall, and handsome, in a wild kind of way, but his eyes were worried and full of warmth.

'Cath,' he said, in his deep voice. '*Des i 'nôl i ti.* I came back to you.

'Here I am,' he went on, anxiously.

Then he reached out to touch the torque around Mum's neck. Mum's face was shining now, her mouth quivering into a smile. She reached out, in her turn, to touch his cheek. And then they embraced.

'*Dw i fel ti nawr*,' announced Ceri a little more confidently, stepping back and holding Mum's shoulders. 'I'm like you now. I am human. I, too, will die. That was the choice I made. But before I die, I am all yours.

'And I want you to know . . . that you will always be free.'

Mum's eyes sparkled with tears, her gaze holding his dark, earnest eyes.

'Thank you, Ceri,' she whispered.

And then they embraced again.

It was as if they were the only two people in the clearing. The only two people in the world.

It was getting a bit embarrassing, and Rose wasn't sure what they'd do next. She caught Ianto's astonished eyes and they grinned at each other. Then she felt an insane impulse to giggle and she had to look away from him to stop herself. She saw that Mr Lewis was watching Mum and Ceri attentively, with his slightly impersonal gaze. Abruptly, he turned and strode towards the hunt master, who'd been writhing on the ground, yelling in protest, throughout.

'At last!' shouted the hunt master, pointing madly at Ceri as the policeman approached. 'Tegwyn, arrest that man. It's him – the one who abducted the woman – I caught him! Trapped him! Don't let him get away!'

Mr Lewis did not respond. Instead, he reached out a hand and helped the huntsman to his feet. Once upright, the man whipped his head about as if there was something behind him. Then he dusted himself down, brushing wet leaves from his front. Rose was glad to see that his hand had stopped bleeding now.

And then Mr Lewis said, in a cool, calm voice, 'Mr Thomas, you are under arrest. For possession of an offensive weapon, and for intent to inflict grievous bodily harm.'

Chapter 41

Ianto and Rose were alone in the clearing now – after Mr Lewis had escorted a wildly protesting, handcuffed Mr Thomas to his car, and after Mum and Ceri had taken the short path through the woods back to the house.

At last, the sun was peeping over the ridge of the surrounding hills, and Rose lifted her face gratefully to receive a little of its distant, winter warmth. She and Ianto were crouching against one of the cromlech's great upright stones, the heavy granite warming behind them already with the rays of the sun.

'So . . .' said Ianto. '*Daeth dyn y cyrn 'nôl*. The antler-man came back.'

'*Do*,' said Rose. '*Heb gyrn*. Yes. Without his antlers. And you know what's really weird?'

Ianto smiled and shook his head.

'It feels completely normal that him and Mum are together. Already. Even though he's only just appeared. It feels . . .' There was only one word for it – 'right.'

'But,' said Ianto, tentatively, 'isn't he, like, a god? Cernunnos? Is he supposed to be normal?'

'Well,' said Rose, 'he *was* a god, that's for sure. But I think he's happy to be one of us humans now.'

'In our puny, miserable world?'

Rose burst out laughing, remembering the boatman's words. 'That's right. But I'll take our puny, miserable world any time, over Annwn.'

'Me too,' said Ianto. 'I hope I never see that boatman again, or the Hounds of Annwn. But . . . how come the antler-man's alive at all? I thought Sal had murdered him.'

'She did, Ianto! She shot him with a pistol, right in front of me and Mum. It was awful – one of the most awful things I've ever seen.' Rose shivered. 'But Sal was acting on instructions. She had one of those englyns – you know, like mine about the thirty-third owl. And hers told her to kill him, in order to free him and reunite our family.'

Ianto whistled. Then, 'Poor Sal,' he said, shaking his head. 'She was always just trying to do her best. Always just trying to find Eddie.'

'Ianto,' said Rose, grasping his arm. 'I had a call from Sal this morning. It was her. No question, it was her. She told me we needed to get out here. That something was happening and we needed to get out here.'

Ianto stared at her. 'Dad had a call too,' he exclaimed, 'from a woman telling him that a man with a knife was about to attack someone in the wood. Then she hung up, without giving her name.'

'Sal!' exclaimed Rose. 'She phoned you too!'

Then Rose squeezed Ianto's arm in excitement. 'Hey! She called your dad, Ianto. You know what that means? That means she's changed her mind!'

'Huh?'

'She's changed her mind – about the police. Something awful happened to her when she was our age, after Eddie disappeared. She was put in a youth offenders' institution. And ever since then, she hated the police. But now, maybe, she's forgiven them, and she's changing her mind. Maybe, she's changing her mind about other things, too.' This idea filled Rose with hope. 'Ianto!' she said, standing up. 'She's changing her mind! And she's still alive! Somewhere! We just need to find her.'

'That's easy,' grinned Ianto. 'Phone her back.'

Of course! Rose delved into her coat pocket, then began running towards the trees. 'The hunt master threw my phone over here, Ianto. Phone it, will you?'

Soon they heard its familiar tinkle and together they bounded through ferns and undergrowth until they saw it, alive with light and buzzing on the woodland floor.

As they headed back out to the clearing, Rose, hesitantly, dialled the unknown number. Her heart beat fast as she got a ringing tone. And then the tone clicked off, almost immediately. The phone went dead, the lights went out.

'She didn't pick up, Ianto. It cut off,' she cried out.

'Hey, it's OK, Rose,' said Ianto, reaching out to hold her hand as they approached the cromlech again. 'It's OK, you know? If I know Sal, she'll let herself be found when she's ready. She knows where you are, where we are. Sometimes – sometimes people just don't want to be found.'

Rose looked up at his face. How did Ianto get so wise, all of a sudden? And how could anyone not want to be found? Everyone was home again, everyone was found. But not Sal.

Rose's heart ached to include her in the picture. The thought of never seeing her again was unbearable. Almost as unbearable as when she'd thought she was dead.

But – you couldn't force people to do things. If this adventure had taught her anything, it was that. She sniffed and looked down at her feet.

'Hey!' said Ianto again, squeezing her hand. 'Here's something that'll cheer you up. You want to hear the latest?'

Rose swallowed and tried to smile. 'What?' she said.

'Uncle Thomas's carefree, bachelor days are over. It's official. He phoned to tell us last night. Gwenllian is moving in with him, up at the cottage. So you'll be seeing a lot more of her.'

'Oh!' This was wonderful news. 'That's great!' Mr Williams had waited for Gwenllian, for sixty years. Now they were together again. 'He's gathering ye rosebuds, while he may,' she murmured.

'He certainly is,' replied Ianto. 'Plus, they want to adopt Eddie – look after him, till he's ready to decide what to do with himself. Apparently, Eddie's really happy about that too. Look out!'

Wow. This was more good news. Everything seemed to be happening very quickly, but everything . . . felt right – again.

Just right – apart from one, little doubt that niggled at Rose's mind.

How on earth was Sal going to feel about that?

Chapter 42

As it happened, Rose didn't need to wait long to find out.

She slept well that night, excusing herself early in the evening, leaving Mum and Ceri to talk together and to be alone, cosy on the sofa before the fire.

'*Nos da, cariad*,' Mum had called as she left the room. 'Good night, love.'

Mum's Welsh is coming on leaps and bounds, thought Rose, *now that she has no choice but to speak it.*

Then came a deep voice: '*Nos da, cariad.*' Ceri was looking up at her with his dark, gentle eyes. '*Cysga'n dawel.* Sleep peacefully.'

'*Nos da, Mum. Nos da, Ceri,*' she'd replied, heading for her bedroom.

Then she pulled on her pyjamas, got under the duvet and fell asleep almost immediately, and she slept as peacefully, as soundly 'as the boy' or '*fel y boi*'– as Mr Williams would have put it.

The next morning she awoke, late, to the warm, lazy smell of toast and freshly-brewed coffee and . . . frying mushrooms, was it? And to the sound of laughter – Mum's raucous chuckles and Ceri's deep guffaws. Then talk, talk, talk. She couldn't make out what they were talking about, through her closed door.

How do they find so much to say to each other? she wondered, idly. Then she thought, *Well, if Ceri's lived for aeons, perhaps he's telling her his life story.* This idea put a smile on her face, and she saved it up to tell Ianto, later.

Leaning back into her pillows, she thought how lovely it was to be able to stay in bed. It was still the Christmas holidays, after all. No school, for how long? She couldn't work it out – didn't know what day it was. No school today, anyway, and that was the important thing. She didn't have to leap up out of bed, to greet anyone. To make sure Mum was OK. And she knew that a little burden, a burden she'd never realised she carried, had been taken away from her. *Mum is looked after again*, she thought, *I don't have to do it any more.* This revelation was a surprise to her, a shock. Why had she felt like that? Had Mum expected her to look after her? She didn't know. She puzzled over it. Then she sighed and smiled, nestling further under her duvet.

Whatever. Everything felt right.

It felt just right, apart from—

And then her phone rang.

She scrambled to pick it up. 'Rose,' said Sal.

'Sal!' cried Rose. Then she tried to pipe down a bit. She didn't want to scare Sal away. '*Ble ydych chi?* Where are you?' she went on, more calmly.

She heard Sal take a breath in. '*Dw i gartref.* I'm home, bach. I'm home again. Trying to decide what to do with my life. The rest of my life. Now that Eddie's back. Now that Eddie's safe.'

There was a pause. Rose, trying to be very careful, let the

pause be, though she was fairly itching with questions. Then Sal went on, a little nervously, trying to sound casual, 'How is Eddie, anyway?'

'He's fine, Sal. I haven't actually seen him since we got back, but I know he's fine. He's staying up at Mr Williams's, you know. And Gwenllian, Mr Williams's er, girlfriend, is up there too. And Del of course . . .' Rose tailed off.

'Good,' said Sal, gruffly. 'That's good. As long as he's happy.'

'Oh, he is happy,' said Rose. 'Ianto told me yesterday that he's happy.'

There was another pause. And Rose was afraid that she might lose Sal, by telling her that Eddie was happy, without her. So she rushed in with another question.

'Sal,' she said, 'how come you're here? I thought – we all thought – you'd, er, died.'

Silence, on the other end of the phone. Rose, scrambling to keep her, said, 'Oh, sorry, Sal. What I should be saying to you is, I am so, so glad to hear your voice. So, so glad you're alive, that you're not dead. That you're not stuck in Annwn. That you're safe.'

Then Sal chuckled. A new sound. Had she ever heard Sal laugh before? She consulted her memory. No, she had not.

Sal said, 'Ask Eddie how I got here. He'll know.' Then she went on, 'Hey, what happened to Tomo in the end?'

Huh? 'Tomo? You mean, Mr Williams?' asked Rose.

'No, I don't mean Mr Williams. I mean Tomo. The one and only. The sneaking, treacherous, snake in the grass Tomo.'

Rose frowned. 'I don't know, Sal. How would I know? Is he even . . . er, still alive?'

'Oh, he's alive, all right. Alive and kicking. And you *do* know.'

'I – er,' said Rose, racking her brains and coming up with nothing.

'Guy I tripped up,' went on Sal, 'back at the cromlech. Then I sat on him, for good measure. Giving you girls a hand. Mind you, you were doing pretty well by yourselves, I have to say. Nice work with the knife.'

'Wait a minute. You mean, the hunt master? *He*'s Tomo? But – but you weren't there, Sal!'

'Oh, I was there all right, Rose. I was there.'

'But how?'

'Ask Eddie how, Rose. Ask Eddie.'

Silence again. Rose's head was spinning with the idea that Tomo, 1973 Tomo, was the hunt master.

Then she blurted, 'Hey, Sal. I've just realised something. We've been speaking Welsh. When we first met you, me and Mum, you didn't speak Welsh.'

'No, bach, you're right,' Sal replied, softly. 'You got me going again. You, Ianto and Mr Williams. And Eddie, of course. It's part of me, part of my family. I won't let it go again.'

Then she paused, and her voice shook a little as she said, 'I – I hope you and Eddie will come and visit soon.' She cleared her throat. 'I'd love to see you both.'

Then she hung up.

Chapter 43

Next morning, early, Rose climbed the track up to Mr Williams's cottage. The sun was shining brightly already, and the air was clear and cold. A strong wind buffeted her hair as she walked, and she breathed in icy air. She was carrying a large, canvas bag, slung across her shoulder.

Soon she reached the flag on the corner of the track, at the junction where the drive led on to the farmhouse. The wind was holding the material out straight, as if it had been starched, and the fierce red dragon looked magnificent in the sunlight. The edge of the flag rippled just a little, with a ruffling sound, and it was getting frayed, Rose noted. Mr Williams had to buy a new one every couple of years, because the wind up here wore them out.

She turned down the drive. White smoke was puffing from the chimney of the cottage, and the warm smell of burning wood pervaded the cold air.

Del usually ran to greet visitors before anyone else. But not today.

Instead, as she approached the farmyard that was littered with machinery – ancient and new – she heard the sound of metallic banging, coming from the cow shed. Approaching, she stood outside the large, open entrance.

'Mr Williams?'

'*Diawl!*' came a heartfelt, echoing cry from within. Then he appeared in the doorway. In his hands he held a hammer, and he was grasping his left thumb.

'Ah, sorry bach. Sorry for swearing. Just trying to straighten out these pen hurdles, see, ready for lambing, and caught my blasted thumb.'

Rose screwed up her face in sympathy. 'Ow. Sorry, Mr Williams.'

'Well! I feel better now already, seeing your dear little face!' Mr Williams said enthusiastically, hurrying out of the cow shed to stand before her. 'How are you, bach? Mami doing well? What about, er . . .'

'Ceri,' supplied Rose.

'Ceri, is it? What about Ceri, then? He settling in all right?'

'Yes, I think so. He's fine. Everything's fine. Mum's really happy.' Rose smiled, then she said, 'Er, how are you?' It felt strange to be having this formal conversation with Mr Williams.

He grinned, pulled himself up straight then cleared his throat to make an announcement.

'Ahem. Well, don't know if you've heard, but me and Gwenllian are living together now,' he said. 'Getting hitched, as it were, but without actually getting hitched, if you know what I mean. About time, you might say. Only taken us sixty-one years – heh heh heh heh! And well, we've got young Eddie living with us too – that should keep us on our toes and—Well now – here he is!'

Rose heard the approaching buzz of the quad bike and

turned to see Eddie bumping at speed down the track towards them, dodging puddles and the worst of the stones in the rutted lane. Del was riding with him, sitting up on his lap between his outstretched arms, her ears blowing back in the wind, her tongue lolling happily from her mouth.

Eddie came to a stop in the yard in front of them and switched off the engine. As Del jumped neatly down to greet her master, Eddie glanced at Rose. Then he turned to Mr Williams. 'Hey Tomo – just fed the sheep in the bottom field – but one of them's not looking too good. You want me to go and— '

At this point Gwenllian stepped out of the cottage behind them and called, 'Hello Rose fach, hello Eddie. Who wants a cup of tea? Kettle's boiling!'

'Oh, hello Gwenllian,' said Rose. 'Um . . .' she hesitated.

Then Mr Williams said, 'I should think you two have some catching up to do,' looking between her and Eddie. Eddie looked down at the ground for a moment, then he looked up, glanced again at Rose, and nodded.

'Yes,' said Rose, thankfully. 'Yes, we do. I wondered,' and here she turned, awkwardly, to Eddie, 'if you wanted me to show you the top of the mountain?'

For a moment Eddie's eyes were afraid. Then he took a deep breath in. 'Sure,' he said.

'Good boy,' said Mr Williams to Eddie, resting his hand on Del's head, who was sitting at his side. 'I'll see to that ewe. You go with Rose, bach.'

Gwenllian came from the doorway to stand with Mr Williams and Del as Rose and Eddie made their way down the drive to the flag on the corner.

Then, together, they climbed the mountain. As they climbed, the grass gave way to heather, to dead, rusty bracken and to a few bare hawthorns whose berries had all been stripped now by hungry, winter birds.

They did not speak.

Eddie was wearing a brand new padded jacket and trousers. He looked good in them, Rose thought, stealing a glance at him as he strode by her side. His dark, curly hair came down past his ears, and the wind was blowing it about.

Finally, they reached the large, flat stone at the top of the mountain.

Rose turned to him. '*Ti moyn edrych dros yr ymyl?* You want to look over the edge?'

He nodded.

So Rose left her bag on the stone and they both got down on their hands and knees and crawled forward, to the edge where the mountain sheared away, suddenly, breathtakingly, dropping metres and metres to the stones and rocks below.

They lay with their heads over the edge, facing down, the wind blowing their hair about their faces, and Rose's hands gripped the springy turf of the edge. This view always made her a little dizzy.

'You want to go first?' said Eddie, not looking at her; looking down.

Rose had prepared for this. 'No,' she said. 'You go first. Tell me about the staff. Tell me about the englyn.'

Eddie turned on his side, so he was facing her. Then he reached into his coat pocket and pulled out a scrap of parchment, only a couple of inches square, which had been folded in half. Turning to face him, Rose took it gently and opened it, gripping it tightly to stop the wind from blowing it out of her hands. It looked just like the other two, but on it was a different poem. Its title was '*Ei Fab Ieuaf*' – 'His Youngest Son'.

Rose looked at Eddie. He looked back. Then she looked down and read the englyn out loud. And it went something like this, though the original Welsh was much more polished:

> '*I am a stick; I am spell-bound yet free. I serve but the one,*
> *   royal, family;*
> *I am their staff, I bring them together – I am a snob; I will*
> *   serve no other.*
> *I will be split; I will be jailed – Steal me! Cross me! And you*
> *   will be saved.*'

Rose paused for a moment, digesting this. Then she said, 'His Youngest Son,' and she frowned.

'Yeah,' said Eddie, turning back on to his chest to look down the drop again. 'I was confused about that too. I said to Mamgu, when she gave it me, isn't that Tony – isn't Tony the youngest son? But she said, No. She said this englyn was definitely my englyn, and she had another one for Tony. But now . . . I guess . . . I'm younger than Tony.

'Mamgu knew,' said Eddie, sighing, addressing the long, stony drop before his eyes. 'Somehow, she knew.'

Rose said, 'Mamgus always know.' Then she went on, 'So – it belongs to our family, and it only works for us. That's why nothing happened when Mr Williams – or anyone else –

handled it. OK. And it was split – Ianto split it in half in the summer. Then it was jailed – put in the glass case in the Canolfan. Then you stole it.'

'That's right. I stole it,' he said, still looking down. 'And I crossed it. Crossed it as soon as I picked it up, after I'd smashed the case. I crossed it, because I thought it would bring Mam and Dad and Tony and Sal and everyone back. Because the englyn says it will bring the family together.

'Then I realised that crossing the two pieces made me invisible.'

'*Invisible?*' Rose exclaimed, then lots of things, one after the next, quickly fell into place. 'Right – that's how come the policeman said they saw nothing on CCTV, after you'd gone in.'

Eddie frowned. 'What's CCTV?' he asked, turning to face her.

Of course. They probably didn't have CCTV in 1973. 'It's like a little camera they put on buildings, that films things. It recorded you going in, but not going out.'

Eddie whistled and shook his head, looking back down the sheer cliff. His hands gripped the turf at the top, and his knuckles were white. 'This – this future thing,' he said. 'It's hard. I keep seeing things, hearing things, that I don't understand. It's like, like being in a foreign country.'

Then he said, 'Did they see my face?' He sounded afraid, suddenly.

'No. They couldn't make out your face. But Mr Lewis, Ianto's dad – you know, the policeman – found the woolly hat at the scene of the crime. The one with the sheepdog on it, that Mr Williams gave you.'

Now Eddie grinned. 'Oh, yes. Got Tomo into trouble, I did, with that hat.' Then he stopped grinning. 'We gotta get the staff back to the Canolfan,' he went on, 'then hopefully they'll forget about the whole thing.'

'Yes, you do need to give it back,' said Rose, nodding, watching him.

'What?'

'Well, don't you have it on you? Or, at least, half of it?'

'No,' he said. 'No – Sal's got both halves now.'

'Has she?' asked Rose. 'How?' She was losing track. This staff certainly got about.

'Well, remember back in Annwn, when we were all trapped around the tree by those dogs – the Wild Hunt? And they were just about to jump on us? At that moment, Sal pulled out her half of the staff. And I pulled out my half. And we touched them together. Don't ask me why – it was like . . .' Eddie frowned. 'It was like instinct. Like the staff told us to. Anyway, we did. And then Tomo and Ianto and Del appeared, and saved our lives.'

'Wow,' said Rose. 'So it was the staff that brought them to Annwn, not the helmet or the sword – although they came in handy, too.'

'Looks like that,' agreed Eddie. 'And then, then I kind of lost track of the staff,' he went on. 'I could swear I put it back in my parka. But I reckon Sal nicked it.' He grinned again. 'Reckon she nicked it, pick-pocketed it, at that point, and kept hold of it. Always been good at that sort of thing, has Sal. Always been one step ahead. Because later, when she swam out to that mad boatman, when he hit her on the head – or just before he hit her on the head – she must have crossed them, and made herself invisible.'

'Of course,' said Rose, her eyes wide. 'Of course. And then . . .'

'And then, still invisible, she got into the boat too. Not sure when. Maybe when we all got in, on the shore. Or maybe she swam to us, when we were already on the way, and climbed in. I worked it out, when we were in the boat. I worked it out, because I realised I didn't have my half of the staff any more, and I noticed that the back of the boat was weighed down a little bit, and that water was dripping off the bench there, on to the floor. When I saw that, I thought, *Sal's with us. Sal's got the staff, and she's OK.* Course, I couldn't say anything, in case the boatman heard me. Then, when we landed on the other side, I reckon she came with us, back to the wood.

'Now, I'm not sure where she is. Back home, I hope.'

'Eddie – she is home. She phoned me, yesterday. And the day before.'

Eddie whipped his head to look at Rose. 'She did? She's OK?'

'She was fine. She wanted to know if you were all right. And I said you were. And she said she'd love to see us, see us both.'

Eddie turned his head to look down the drop again. He didn't say anything.

Rose's mind was still spinning around the staff. And suddenly, another jigsaw piece fell into place. 'Can we go back to when you stole the staff?' she asked. 'Go back to the hunt. Was it you they were after?'

Eddie screwed his eyes tight shut. Then he opened them and turned on his side again, so he was facing her. 'Yes,' he said. 'I ran through the village square with the crossed staff, invisible, of course, and they were all there – dogs, horses, people in their red uniforms and everything. I thought, I'm fine, no one can see me. And none of the humans could. But . . . but the dogs saw me – or smelled me, or something – and they started barking, then racing towards me. The whole pack, out of control, they were. People were calling to them to heel, to come back, but they took no notice. Chased me up the road. Chased me past your place. Then the horses came too. The whole lot of them, after me. Out of control. Never ran so fast in my life. Never felt so afraid – well, maybe I *have* felt so afraid, actually. But Tomo, and Del, saved me. Stood up to them, in the clearing by the cromlech. Stopped them.'

Then Rose asked, 'Eddie, how did you know to head for Brynafon, on Christmas Eve?'

'Because Mamgu left me a sign. A sign to find the staff.'

He went on, 'When I crept into the back room that night, I saw she'd left a cutting, from a newspaper, on the seld. And a photo – the photo, you know, of me, Tony, Sal and her. So I snatched them up. Then I saw you, on the floor . . . and, well, you know what happened then, and I scarpered. But when I was out of the house, I looked at the newspaper cutting and saw that it was about a Celtic staff, that had been broken in two and was kept in a special centre, a canolfan, in Brynafon. And I knew that this was the staff from the englyn, that I needed to steal. That's why I headed for Brynafon.'

'Eddie,' said Rose, gently. 'It wasn't Mamgu Morris who left the cutting and the photo. It was us – me and Mum.'

Eddie stared at her. 'Right. Of course.' He brought his

hands up to his face, and rubbed at his eyes. Then he hung his head, eyes shut, over the edge.

'OK,' said Rose, and she rolled over so that she was also addressing the drop, rather than him, 'OK.' She had a niggly feeling that there were more things she needed to ask but, for now, she couldn't think of them.

The wind whistled about the mountain, shaking the dead flowers of the heather like tiny rattles. Then Eddie said, 'So,' and drew a deep breath in. 'Your turn now, to talk.'

He shifted on to his side again, to face her. 'I want to know . . .' he said, 'and I don't want to know.'

Rose nodded. She felt exactly the same. But she turned, tearing her gaze from the base of the cliff, and 'Ask me questions,' she said. And she shivered. It was cold up here, but at the same time, it felt like the only place. The only place where they could talk, properly, like this.

'Who are you?' asked Eddie.

'I'm . . . Tony's daughter.'

Eddie stared into her eyes, then he nodded. 'I knew it. I knew it – because you look like him. You look just like him. I thought so the first time I saw your face, back at Mamgu's.'

Rose's heart was beating fast for the next question. The next, inevitable question. She wasn't sure she was strong enough to face it.

But it didn't come.

Instead he said, 'What's in your bag?'

'I'll show you,' said Rose, relieved, and the two of them edged backwards from the cliff edge to stand by the flat stone.

She reached into the bag and pulled out the ripped piece

of the photo – the bit showing Sal, Dad and Mamgu Morris. 'This is yours,' she said, handing it to him. 'Sorry I took it.'

Eddie looked at it. Then, from his own pocket, he pulled the missing scrap, the bit with him on it, and fitted them together. 'This was taken at Easter time,' he said. 'Less than a year ago . . .' Then, as if a sudden pain had hit him, he screwed up his face, doubled up and cried, 'Aah!'

'Eddie!' exclaimed Rose. 'You OK?' Tentatively, she reached out to touch his back.

Eddie cringed away from her, then straightened up again, slowly.

'No,' he said, eyes still closed. 'No. I'm not OK.'

Then he said, 'What else you got in there?'

'This,' replied Rose. And she held out a slim, blue, exercise book.

He snatched it from her, glanced at its cover, then looked up at her. 'How did you find this?'

'It was, er, under your mattress. At your mamgu's. I was up there, trying to find bedding.'

'You read it?'

'Yes.'

He stuffed it, unopened, into his pocket.

Rose swallowed. 'There's one last thing, Eddie, I want you to have.'

Eddie was looking down, down at the surface of the stone. He did not respond.

Then Rose said, 'It doesn't matter, Eddie. It doesn't matter. Shall we just go home, and I can give it you another time—'

'Show it me,' he said, head still down. 'I want to see it.'

So Rose pulled out a thick wad of A4 sheets, held together by an elastic band.

'This is a story I wrote,' she said, nervously. 'It's called *The Thirty-Third Owl*. It's the true story of what happened in the summer, last year. About the adventure that me, Ianto, Mr Williams and Del had. And . . . it'll explain lots of things to you – things about me and Mum, things about Ianto and Mr Williams and Gwenllian, and things about our family – about who our ancestors are – and things about . . . about Dad.' She swallowed, looking at Eddie, trying to meet his eyes. 'About Tony.'

Eddie looked down at the manuscript. The wind riffled the pages in Rose's hands.

'Tony,' he repeated, slowly. Then he crawled to the edge of the mountain. Rose dropped the manuscript on the stone and came with him, her heart beating fast. When both their heads were hanging over the drop once more, he turned to her, and they held each other's gaze.

'Rose,' he said. 'I know – I know that Mam and Dad have gone.' Here he dropped his head again. Closed his eyes. Then he lifted it, sniffed, and continued, 'And Aunty Nell has gone – I know that. I knew it, deep inside, when I went home, and no one was there. Mamgu's gone too. I knew that too. I *know* it too.'

His eyes were searching her face, holding on to her, desperately. 'But little Tony – Tony'll be old now too, of course, like Sal – but not that old.' All in a rush, he said, 'Rose – where is he? How come he's not with your mam? Where is he?'

Rose looked at him. She watched his face, flickering, as

ever, with emotions – hope, despair, fear, bravado. She held all his hopes in her hands. But what could she do? She could not lie to him. Staring at his dark eyes, she saw Dad's eyes in them, and found tears starting from her own.

He was watching her. Trying to read her face. He blinked slowly.

'Eddie, bach . . .' she said, and she reached out to touch his shoulder. A gust of wind blew upwards suddenly, lifting their hair. 'He's gone too,' she said. Tears ran from her eyes, but instead of falling down they slid upwards, into her hair.

'Aah!' Eddie cried out again in pain, screwing his eyes tight, turning from her and shuffling forwards, so that his shoulders, and his arms, were over the cliff edge. Then he went limp, his head hanging down, his arms dangling, fingers loose, over the long drop.

'Eddie – Eddie, don't.' What had she been thinking of, to come up here, and to tell him this, up here? On the edge of the mountain? What had she been thinking of?

Then, 'Little Tony,' came Eddie's voice. She could not see his face, through his hanging-down hair. 'He must— must have been lost without me.'

Rose said, 'He was, Eddie. He was lost without you. He missed you, all his life.' And she knew that this was the deep down, true truth.

Now Eddie was shifting his body, pushing at the turf with his feet to shuffle forward, to lower himself further over the sheer cliff, so that the whole of his chest was over it now, and she could see tears dropping from his eyes and spinning, dizzyingly, downwards.

'Eddie . . .' cried Rose, her mind reeling in panic as she crawled backwards, then grabbed hold of him round his waist, lying on top of him, resting her head on the small of his back, holding him there, weighing him down. She could feel his body trembling beneath his padded jacket.

'Eddie,' she said again, gripping hard, tunnelling with her hands under his body to make sure she gripped him firmly in her arms, 'You're not going anywhere without me.'

And then, loud, sharp – from out of the blue, from very close by – came the magical cry of a ship's whistle.

Two dark heads shot up to see a barcud coch, a magnificent red kite – huge, so close – sail past them, level with their heads, only metres from the edge.

'Aaah!' cried out Rose, in awe.

The kite had already sped past on the wind, wings slightly bent, tail feathers adjusting like a fleet ship's rudder. But its head was turned to them all the way, its fierce, yellow eye fixed on them, and soon it was wheeling about and coming back for another pass, crying out again.

Rose fell backwards now as Eddie scrambled back then raised himself upright, eyes fixed on the bird, following its movements in the air just above their heads.

'What is it?' he exclaimed, turning to her as she clambered to her own feet, retreating from the edge. Then he whipped his head back to watch the bird again, as it balanced on the wind, tail feathers busy, looking down, calling again, with its piercing, musical whistle. Its feathers glowed, the same rusty red as the dead bracken around them. 'It's a— no, it can't be! But I think it is! Rose – look! It's a barcud coch, a red kite! I never seen one before! You know how rare those are?'

'Yes, Eddie,' said Rose, reaching out a hand and, gently, pulling him back with her to the stone. 'It's a barcud coch. Isn't he beautiful?'

Together, they watched it soar away from them – out over the long drop, to circle in the air, level with their heads, over the bog below, in long, lazy loops.

'You know Eddie,' she went on, her voice shaking slightly, 'they're not so rare these days. There were only a few left, and all of them in Cymru – but then, oh, it was in the eighties, I think, eighties or nineties, people started really looking after them properly, protecting them. And then new pairs were introduced in England, and they spread, and now – now there are quite a lot of them. We're so lucky, up here. I see them often. I talk to them too – and sometimes they answer. It's a good news story, Eddie, one of those rare, good news stories, about nature. They almost disappeared, and now they're thriving.

'Thriving. Happy. Look how beautiful he is. A good news story, Eddie . . .'

'A barcud coch,' he whispered, turning to watch as it came schooning back to them, sailing on the wind over the tops of their heads then drifting away, over the valley and the wood below.

Then he grabbed the manuscript of *The Thirty-Third Owl* from the top of the stone and raced away from her, following the path of the red kite down the mountain track, his curly, dark hair streaming in the wind.

Rose watched him as he disappeared from view beyond

the mountain top, then looked up, at the heavy, grey clouds that were blowing in now from the north. The windswept sky was full of that strange, expectant light you get just before it snows. And presently, sure enough, snowflakes began tumbling from the blue-tinged clouds, first one or two, then clouds, drifts of soft, white matter, dancing through the air.

There was much more to say to Eddie; many more questions to ask him. But they all could wait. Lifting her face to the falling snowflakes, she laughed as they fell into her eyes, into her mouth. Then, grabbing the empty bag from the stone, she set off, running, skidding, letting her legs carry her of their own accord down the mountain, following the tracks of the barcud coch and of Eddie, homewards.

One month later:

TRUSTED NEWS SINCE 1869

Western Post

Saturday 3 February
PAPUR CENEDLAETHOL CYMRU

NATIONAL NEWSPAPER OF WALES ◇◇ £1.70

WalesOnline.co.uk

TEENAGER FINDS 'HOLY GRAIL' OF MEDIEVAL WELSH MANUSCRIPTS UNDER SOUTH WALES DRESSER

GARETH WALTERS

A vellum manuscript of huge historical significance entitled *The Book of Erwain* has been discovered hidden under a dresser in a South Wales home. Thought to have been written in about 1050, it is the earliest surviving complete manuscript written in the Welsh language, giving a fascinating glimpse into this medieval period.

The manuscript has an interesting history. Acquired in the 17th century by antiquary Robert Vaughan of Dolgellau for his vast collection, it was stolen shortly afterwards. And though countless collectors and historians have searched for it ever since, it took 13-year-old Rose Morris of Brynafon to find it again – hidden under a dresser in her great grandmother's house. The manuscript, thought to be the work of a single scribe, will now join the Black Book of Carmarthen, the Book of Taliesin and the Red Book of Hergest as one of Wales's most precious handwritten documents, because Rose has donated the book to the National Library of Wales, where it will be housed in their special collection.

> 'Although the supernatural elements of the story are clearly fiction, we are fairly certain that a Princess Erwain really did exist at around this time ...'
>
> Lowri Haf Ellis, Chief Archivist at the National Library

The manuscript tells the story of a Princess Erwain, her abduction to Annwn (the Otherworld) and her return to Wales. Lowri Haf Ellis, Chief Archivist at the National Library, comments 'Although the supernatural elements of the story are clearly fiction, we are fairly certain that a Princess Erwain really did exist at around this time, as there are many references to her in contemporary poetry. She laid claim to a large region of south-west Wales, thought to be centred around the present-day village of Brynafon. After leading a successful campaign to take back the kingdom she established a peaceful, thriving region where poetry and the arts were allowed to flourish.'

It seems that being stored under a dresser has not significantly harmed the manuscript. Lowri comments, 'It's in almost immaculate condition but for one thing – there are three, square holes on the last page. It's hard to speculate what has been removed, or why. Perhaps the missing text will turn up again some day too!'

Though the original manuscript will be kept at the National Library in Aberystwyth, there will be a digital copy for public viewing at the Canolfan y Cromlech in Brynafon.

This canolfan is itself the centre of a mystery. On Boxing Day it was broken into and two pieces of an ancient wooden staff, dated to at least 2,000 BC, were stolen. Ten days later, local police, already baffled by a lack of CCTV evidence, were astonished to find the staff inside a locked safe together with the Canolfan's Celtic sword and helmet. Chief Inspector Tegwyn Lewis commented, 'The whole thing's a bit puzzling, but all's well that ends well, as they say. We've made recommendations to the Canolfan to step up security for these priceless objects.'

> 'The whole thing's a bit puzzling, but all's well that ends well, as they say ...'
>
> Chief Inspector Tegwyn Lewis

See COMMENT page 5: The Historical Importance of the Lost Book of Erwain by Aberystwyth University's Dr Elfed Edwards.